Outstanding Praise for Caleb Carr and His Novels

THE ITALIAN SECRETARY

"A fleet-footed, atmospherically gothic, and often amusing Holmes tale . . . Carr displays a gift for adopting another author's literary techniques." —Amazon.com

"Carr acquits himself with honor . . . the novel captivates." —*Publishers Weekly*

"Fans of *The Alienist* will eagerly read *The Italian Secretary* . . . aficionados of Conan Doyle . . . are apt to be . . . satisfied . . . Carr has always brought a sense of authenticity to the time periods and locales about which he writes. Here, he effectively evokes the dark, dank atmosphere of rain-soaked Scotland. The similarly bleak and dismal palace, with its hidden stairway and 'the blood that never dries,' is a perfect setting for a Holmes tale. . . . Carr is astute and unerring in his portrayal of Holmes and his techniques." —*USA Today*

"[Carr's] canonical characters are briskly brought back to life." —*The New York Times Book Review*

"[Carr] uses his considerable talents as a re-creator of historic period detail to provide an entertaining continuation of the Conan Doyle canon." —*Chicago Tribune*

"[Carr] has crafted a straightforward story." —*Los Angeles Times*

"Caleb Carr gets every possible atom of excitement and intrigue out of the traditional Sherlock Holmes format. Seemingly without effort, Caleb Carr deftly weaves accepted elements from the Sherlock Holmes canon with new suppositions and plotlines, expertly adding new spice to a familiar favorite old stem, and the results are delicious."   —*Times Leader*

"Holmes's intelligence activities . . . ground the novel. Much of the authenticity of *The Italian Secretary* has to do with its author."   —*Newsday* (Long Island/Queens)

"Sherlock Holmes and Dr. Watson live!"
                                        —*Richmond Times-Dispatch*

"Placing these famous characters into Carr's capable hands is a gift to anyone who enjoys mysteries, historical fiction, or just a great read."   —*Library Journal*

"The book is exciting and the plot holds the reader's interest."   —*DarkTales.com*

"Both Sherlockians and fans of Carr's Alienist series will enjoy this re-creation . . . a strong addition to the Holmes oeuvres . . . crisp narration."   —*Audiofile*

"Great setting, intriguing history."   —*Booklist*

THE ALIENIST

"A first-rate tale of crime and punishment that will keep readers guessing until the final pages."
                                        —*Entertainment Weekly*

"A high-spirited, charged-up, and unfailingly smart thriller."   —*Los Angeles Times*

"Gripping, atmospheric . . . intelligent and entertaining."
                                        —*USA Today*

"Caleb Carr's rich period thriller takes us back to the moment in history when the modern idea of the serial killer became available to us . . . [and] tracks the efforts of a team of far-sighted investigators working frantically to solve a string of hideous murders . . . absorbing . . . suspenseful . . . gratifying." —*The Detroit News*

"Engrossing." —*Newsweek*

"Keeps readers turning pages well past their bedtime." —*San Francisco Chronicle*

"A rip-snorter of a plot . . . a fine dark ride." —*The Arizona Daily Star*

"A delicious premise . . . its settings and characterizations are much more sophisticated than the run-of-the-mill thrillers that line the shelves in bookstores." —*Washington Post Book World*

"Great fun." —*Star Tribune* (Minneapolis)

"The method of the hunt and the disparate team of hunters lift the tale beyond the level of a good thriller—way beyond . . . a remarkable combination of historical novel and psychological thriller." —*Buffalo News*

"Mesmerizing." —*Detroit Free Press*

"Remarkable . . . the reader is taken on a whirlwind tour of the Gilded Age metropolis, climbing up tenement stairs, scrambling across rooftops, and witnessing midnight autopsies . . . a breathtaking, finely crafted mystery." —*Richmond Times-Dispatch*

"A fine summer read." —*Atlanta Journal and Constitution*

Also by Caleb Carr

Fiction

Casing the Promised Land
The Alienist
The Angel of Darkness
Killing Time

Nonfiction

America Invulnerable (with James Chace)
The Devil Soldier
The Lessons of Terror

The
ITALIAN
SECRETARY

A Further Adventure of Sherlock Holmes

CALEB CARR

St. Martin's Griffin
New York

Grateful acknowledgment to the Conan Doyle Estate for permission to use the Sherlock Holmes characters created by the late Sir Arthur Conan Doyle.

www.stmartins.com

ISBN 978-0-312-35204-2

First published in the United States by Carroll & Graf

10 9 8 7 6 5 4 3 2

For Hilary Hale

best of friends, finest of editors,
without whom I would never have seen
Holyroodhouse

and for Suki
2001–2005

who always stood watch

The

ITALIAN
SECRETARY

In the interest of accommodating modern readers, the anachronistic spellings of several words used by Dr. John H. Watson have been updated.

Chapter I

The published compendium of the many adventures that I undertook in the company of Mr. Sherlock Holmes contains only a few examples of those occasions on which we entered a variety of service that no loyal subject of this realm may refuse. I refer to cases in which the calls to action were delivered by various government ministries or agents, but in which our true employer was none other than that Great Personage whose name has come to define an age; herself, or her son, who has already displayed some of his mother's capacity for imprinting his name and character upon his era. To be plain, I refer to the Crown, and when I do, it must surely become more apparent why the greater portion of my accounts of such cases has come to rest—perhaps never to be removed or revealed—in the tin dispatch-box that I long ago entrusted to the vaults of Cox's Bank in Charing Cross.

Among this momentous yet largely secret sub-collection, perhaps no one adventure touches on more delicate particulars than that which I have identified as the matter of the Italian Secretary. Whenever I joined Holmes in attempting to solve one of his "problems with a few points of interest," it was an odds-on wager that lives would ultimately hang upon the outcome of our efforts; and during several such endeavours, no less than the continuation in power of one political party or another—or even the physical safety of the realm itself—was also exposed as having been at risk. But at no other time did the actual prestige of the monarchy (to say nothing of the mental peace of the Queen Empress herself) rest so perilously upon the successful conclusion of our exertions as it did during this case. The reasons underlying such a bold claim, I can relate; that those particulars will strike any reader as entirely credible, I can no more than hope. Indeed, they might have seemed, even to me, no more than fevered imaginings, a series of dreams inadequately separated from the waking world, had not Sherlock Holmes been ready with explanations for nearly all of the many twists and developments of the case. *Nearly* all . . .

And because of those few unresolved questions, the matter of the Italian Secretary has always been, for me, a source of recurring doubts, rather than (as has more generally been the case regarding my experiences with Holmes) reassuring conclusions. These doubts, to be sure, have remained largely unspoken, despite their power. For there are recesses of the mind to which no man allows even his closest fellows access; not, that is, unless he wishes to hazard an involuntary sojourn in Bedlam. . . .

∞

Chapter II

A STRANGE MESSAGE, AND A STRANGER TALE

The crisis took place over the course of several
unusually cool and volatile September days, during a year in which the state of both our Empire's
and our Queen's health made it difficult to con-
ceive of either ever declining; yet how close, I now
can see, were the onsets of both those maladies!
Was the nature of the crime we were summoned
to investigate during that late summer a harbinger of those twin twilights? And was the Queen's
subsequent fascination with the matter an indication of some inner awareness of eternity's approach, of a desire to know what awaited her
when finally she cast off the burdens of a long

and predominantly lonely rule and was allowed to follow where her beloved Consort had long since gone? I cannot say; nor may I give any greater clue than I already have as to the precise moment at which this case commenced, so great is my concern that the private history of the monarchy remain untainted by scandal or controversy. (Reliable as its officers have always been, Cox's is ultimately but a bank; and should traitorous or merely thieving hands ever find themselves with entire power over its assets, who can say what use might be made of these secret accounts?)

As to the actual beginning of the affair, it took a form that had become familiar, for me, in those latter days of my association with Holmes. I entered the front door of our Baker Street residence one afternoon to be greeted by sonic evidence that something was (in a literal instance of Holmes's own oft-repeated phrase) "afoot": The house was reverberating to the sound of agitated pacing, coming from the sitting-room on the floor above. It was a staccato, deliberate pounding, interrupted occasionally by another sound, made by a violin but hardly to be called music: the irregular bouncing of a taut bow off the instrument's strings, which produced a noise that might best be likened to a hoarse-voiced, hungry cat. Stepping further inside, I determined at once to summon Mrs. Hudson and see what letter, note, or other communication had arrived that might have produced such obvious signs of cerebral activity in my friend.

I soon ran almost headlong into our landlady, just outside the door of her own rooms. She was glaring up at our sitting-room door whence the cacophony was emanating, looking rather less alarmed than angry, perhaps even a little injured; and although I was by no means surprised that Holmes was the source of her agitation (rather the reverse, in fact), I *was* taken aback when the kindly woman announced that she had no intention of serving tea that day—a restorative that I had been eagerly anticipating during my walk home from a daylong medical symposium.

"I'm sorry, Doctor—but I warned him" was Mrs. Hudson's contained but no less violent declaration. "I stated quite clearly that if he continued in that vein, I would not utter a word to him for the rest of the day, and perhaps not for a few *more* days, much less serve him anything to eat!"

"Why, my dear Mrs. Hudson," I replied, calling on the secret sympathy which existed between the two of us, who had suffered more under the sometimes cruel and always caustic force of

Holmes's mercurial moods than had any other two people in the world. "I would not urge you to spend a minute more in the man's company, if he is indeed in one of his offensive humours— but won't you tell me what particularly he has done to upset you so?"

Tempted to speak at greater length, the proud lady finally said only, "What is laughable to some, Dr. Watson, is not so to all. That is all I will say, for doubtless he will explain the rest himself." Folding her arms, she allowed her spirited eyes to roll upward, indicating that I should go up. I knew well enough to follow the directive, for Mrs. Hudson could be a truly unbending personality—a fact that Holmes and I sometimes bemoaned, but for which we had more often had reason to be immensely grateful.

Taking the stairs to the sitting-room quickly, I formed a mental picture of the disarray that must lie within—for it was Holmes's irregularity of habits and periods of something suspiciously close to slovenliness that most often produced objection from our landlady. I was surprised, then, to find that all was neatness and order when I entered, and to further see my friend's wiry but evidently vigorous and acceptably attired silhouette pacing by the windows that looked out onto

Baker Street. He had his violin beneath his chin, but was, as I suspected, barely aware of what he was doing with it.

"Mrs. Hudson, I really do not know what I can do, beyond offering my apologies!" Holmes called through the doorway as I entered the room. Nodding once at me quickly with an equally brief smile which indicated that he had, indeed, been up to some tormenting mischief, he continued in this vein: "If you can recommend any other rite of contrition, I should be happy to undertake it, so long as it is within the parameters of reason!"

"Dr. Watson, will you please inform Mr. Holmes that he may try all he likes!" The thin but decisive voice rose from below without hesitation. "But he'll have no service from me today—and I know that service is his sole reason for trying to make amends!"

Holmes raised his shoulders at me and indicated the door with another movement of his sharp chin, directing me to close it. "We shall be left to our own devices for tea, I fear, Watson," he said, as soon as I had closed the portal. Laying down his violin and bow and disappearing for a moment into the adjoining chamber, he returned with a large chemical beaker set in a stand, as well as a spirit burner. "And, far more disturbingly, for tobacco—have you any? I've smoked the last of my reserves while considering this remarkable communication"—he picked a sheet of telegraph paper from the table on which he had placed the beaker and burner, waving the message in my direction with one hand as he struck a match with the other—"which arrived not two hours ago. Our landlady, as you have heard, refuses to perform even so simple a service as an errand. . . ."

I laid hold of the document, asking, "Holmes, really, what *have* you done to distress the poor woman to such an extent? I've rarely seen her so angry."

"In a moment," Holmes replied, as he filled the chemical beaker with water from a nearby pitcher. "Give that telegram your full attention, for now." He succeeded in producing a healthy ignition of the spirit wick beneath the beaker, after which he glanced about the place. "I once secreted a packet of biscuits," he mused, on his way to fetching a mahogany tea box and two rather dubious-looking cups and saucers, "against just such an eventuality. But where they might be, or in what condition we might find them, I dare not conjecture. . . ."

From the agitated manner in which he continued to speak and to dart about our various rooms, seeking out such apparently exotic paraphernalia as spoons, one might justly have questioned whether the preparation of his own tea did not present Sherlock Holmes with a greater challenge than most of his scientific and investigative undertakings. But I was by now paying little attention to him, so intriguing was the communication that I held in my hand. When Holmes barked, "Tobacco, Watson!" I did manage to produce a pouch from my pocket, but I then sank into a nearby chair, ever more oblivious to my friend's incessant commentary.

The message had originated in the telegraph office of the Aberdeen railway station, and was composed in such a manner that it would likely have been taken as a mundane or even a nonsensical collection of comments by both the Scots operator who dispatched it and his English counterpart who received it in London:

YOUSE DONE A SPECIAL ONE, AT NO. 8 PALL MALL— "THE SUN BURNS TOO HOT, THE SKY FILLS WITH FAMILIAR EAGLES"—READ MCKAY AND SINCLAIR, COLLECTED WORKS—KEEP MR. WEBLEY CLOSE; HAVE YOUR PALM READ FOR PROTECTION—A PAIR OF BERTHS IS RESERVED ON THE CALEDONIA—MY OLD CROFTER WILL PULL ALONGSIDE AT QUARANTINE.

I could not pretend to make sense of the entire thing, particularly given the increasing distraction of Holmes knocking about the room looking for the mythical biscuits, all the while erupting with complaints at the mildness of my tobacco; but one initial guess seemed worth hazarding:

"Your brother?"

"Bravo, Watson!" said Holmes merrily. "Mycroft's rather heavy-handed concealment of his name may be excused by the message's office of origin—only in Scotland would a reference to an 'old crofter' go unnoticed, and only in a message emanating *from* that country would the reference go unremarked by prying eyes—or listening ears."

"Ears?" I repeated, in confusion.

"Certainly, Watson—surely you recall that British telegraphy lines have been vulnerable to electronic eavesdropping, at the very least since that rather unseemly business concerning our friend Milverton, who numbered such a technique among his methods of collecting information concerning those he intended to blackmail—although we only determined as much *after* you had written your account of the matter." He removed his pipe and stared down his long nose at it. "I don't wonder if you *have* forgotten so important a point, even momentarily, given what must be the appallingly low content of nicotine in this effete tobacco of yours. However"—he set the

stem of the pipe back between his active jaws—
"we shall have to make do, given our predicament. Ah! Our water is boiling!"

As, indeed, it was: boiling and rumbling about
the bulbous base and long stem of the beaker,
producing steam that was lightly and noxiously
tinged by trace amounts of chemical agents.

"Fear not," Holmes said, opening one compartment of the tea box. "The Ceylon component of
this blend should eliminate the effects of my last
experiment quite adequately." The tea was left to
steep in a worn old pot, with a coiled scarf serving as a cosy, while Holmes kept after me about
the telegram. "Well? What else can you divine?"

Trying to focus my thoughts, I said, "It's certainly extraordinary, if it *is* your brother. As I recall, the last time we three were engaged in an
undertaking, you told me that any occasion upon
which he varies his daily triangular route from
his rooms in Pall Mall to his offices in Whitehall
to the Diogenes Club is the equivalent of encountering a tram-car on a country lane—".

"As indeed it is."

"And yet now he writes from Aberdeen? What
can have happened, to make so sedentary a fellow travel so comparatively far?"

"Just so!" Holmes's voice contained a hint of
the same rather evasive quality that I had noted

in it every time we had discussed the subject of his extraordinary brother Mycroft, a senior but anonymous government official to whom even the deepest secrets of state business were known. Although Holmes acknowledged that his kinsman was his superior in mental prowess as well as in years (they were separated by seven), the elder Holmes was nonetheless a pronounced eccentric, whose movements, as I had only just said, rarely exceeded the bounds of a small corner of London and were focused as much on his club as on his shielded but vital occupation. The Diogenes was the favoured meeting place for such men—or rather, I should say, the favoured *gathering* place, for its members did not go there to meet, but to be left alone among one another. It offered the city's true misanthropes refuge from the crush and forced informality of the London throng, and a member could be expelled simply for violating the principal rule of the place— silence—just three times.

Holmes had revealed to me the fact of his brother's existence many years earlier, but had only told me the truth concerning Mycroft's occupation and connections very much later (and then only in stages). Now, as he handed me my cup of murky tea that September afternoon, smiling in a manner that was only partially forthcoming and yet obviously proud, I had the feeling I was in for another surprise.

"You will recall, Watson, that following the conclusion of the last matter in which Mycroft sought our assistance—that business about the Bruce-Partington submarine plans—I returned to Baker Street one day from a trip to Windsor, somewhat immodestly displaying a newly acquired emerald tie-pin. You asked where I had got the thing, and I made some remarks about a gracious lady to whom I had offered a small service."

"Yes—and a rather transparent lie it was, Holmes," I commented. Then I frowned deeply at my cup. "Good God, this tea really is ghastly—and given the manner of its brewing, quite possibly poisonous. . . ."

"Focus your mind, Watson," came Holmes's reply. "The tea may be roughly flavoured, but it will help you, in this regard. Now, then: You rightly suspected that I had received the pin from Windsor's most illustrious resident, and within the halls of its most ancient domicile—correct?"

"Correct."

"But what you did *not* know was that, when I arrived at the Castle, I found Mycroft already there, engaged in conversation with the afore-mentioned lady in an attitude of—*singular informality*. . . ."

I looked up suddenly. "You don't mean to say—"

"Yes, Watson. He was *seated* in the *presence*. In fact, he told me it is a privilege that he has enjoyed *for a number of years*."

I let the extraordinary idea sink into my mind: Throughout her reign, our Queen had required that all public servants—including, indeed especially, her many prime ministers—obey the strictest rules of ceremonial protocol. Foremost among these was the obligation to stand when in her presence, no matter what their age or the terrible pain of their gout or other complaints. Only in recent years had her own increasing age inspired enough sympathy on her part to allow the stiff-legged heads of government a chair, and then only when necessary; and yet now Holmes was telling me that his brother Mycroft, a man who held no ministerial rank, whose main function was to lend his prodigious brain for use as an infallible mortal repository of all official business, and who had been given no title (and but four hundred and fifty pounds a year) in return—*this* man had been allowed to break the most fundamental rule of royal audiences—and, apparently, he had been doing so for years on end.

"It's too fantastic!" I said, momentarily unaware of the bitter sting of Holmes's tea. "Do you believe him?"

Holmes appeared to take the query as a slight. "Do *you* doubt him?"

I shook my head quickly. "No, of course not. It's only the extremity of the notion—"

His momentary cloud passing, Holmes said, "No doubt I should feel the same, Watson—but remember, I have witnessed the scene: Brother mine, sitting and chatting with Her Majesty as if the two were fellow members of a whist club!"

I glanced at the telegram again. "Then—he is in Scotland because—"

"*Now* you begin to concentrate your powers, Watson. Yes, given the time of year and the information I have just related, you can reach only one conclusion—Mycroft has been at Balmoral. . . ."

Once more, I needed to pause and consider the idea. Balmoral Castle, located in the Aberdeenshire Highlands, had been chosen by the Queen and the late Prince Consort as an expression of their mutual and very real love of Scotland: Balmoral was the Queen's most treasured home after Windsor itself, as well as her informal summer residence, and visits from those outside the royal clique were rare. Yet, apparently, Mycroft had not only been invited in, but had been assigned what appeared to be, if the encoded telegram was any indication, an important role in some sort of an investigation. "Should your credulity yet be strained," Holmes continued, doubtless reading the expression on my face, "there are quite specific clues in the communication to confirm it all."

I continued to stare at the telegram. "But why Aberdeen? Surely there are telegraph offices closer to the royal residence."

"Where Mycroft would no doubt be observed going in, and the operators harassed, or worse, upon his departure."

"By whom?"

Holmes pointed a long finger at the telegram. " 'The sun burns too hot, the sky fills with familiar eagles.' " The finger went upward, and Holmes smiled. "A hearty luncheon in Aberdeen, safe from all teetotal eyes at Balmoral, preceded the composition of this message—I would swear to it. Mycroft had certain poetical inclinations as a youth, but it was very fortunately decreed that he should develop his true talents, which were purely intellectual. Yet an unfortunate tendency towards banal verse can still emerge now and again, particularly when he is under the influence of a few glasses of wine and port—or, better still, brandy. If we wade through the phrasing, however, we can see that there has been activity of some intense variety going on in and around the Castle, specifically concerning the summering royal party, and that it has provoked the interest of some of our foreign friends."

By which phrase, I knew, Holmes meant that despicable class of men and women from around the Continent who practice that lowest of all trades, *espionage*. "But who is in the country at present that would dare follow the Queen herself to Scotland—"

"Only the cleverest and worst of the breed, Watson. Mycroft refers to 'eagles'—no testament to personality traits, I suspect, but rather an indication of national symbols. If I am right, we may number German and Russian agents first among our suspects, with the odd Frenchman not far behind. Although I know of no suitable candidate from that country who is currently at work within our borders—the Austrian government shot the French spy LeFevre just last week, and the act has had a most salutary effect on the rest of France's operatives throughout the Continent. But among the other indicated nationalities, there are two or three names we may consider as 'in play.' All that, however, we can and indeed must discuss on the train."

"The train?" I echoed.

"Really, Watson—surely, even after a day of absorbing medical minutiae, you can find the meaning in Mycroft's excessively colourful opening: 'Youse done a special one, at No. 8 Pall Mall'? The slang of the New York Bowery, apparently combined with a London address—one located mere steps from Mycroft's very rooms? Doubtless, we are meant to—"

"Yes!" I felt my own features brighten, despite the still-inescapable stench of the bitter tea, which, as Holmes had predicted, seemed at least to be waking my mind from a long day's mental labour. "'Youse done,'" I said again. "Euston—Euston Station; many of the trains for Scotland leave from it!"

Holmes laid hold of the beaker. "Allow me to pour you another cup, my dear fellow. If a mere homophone can confound you, even momentarily, then you need it. . . ."

My hand rose instinctively to cover the cup, but too late: The steaming, murderous brew was already on its way in, and not worth stopping at the price of a serious burn. "But what does he mean by his next reference: Euston Station—'a special one'?" It was one of those embarrassing moments when the mind answers a question as soon as it is asked. "Never mind, Holmes. I have it. A 'special'—an unscheduled train."

"Which," Holmes agreed with a nod, seeming to take actual and inscrutable delight in another cup of his tea, "since it is unlikely that a Bowery

hoodlum would take an interest in what tran-
spires along Pall Mall—"

" 'Eight Pall Mall'—eight *P.M.!* The special will
leave Euston at eight *P.M.*, and we are meant to be
on it."

"Indeed."

"All right, Holmes: I now believe that, since
you have explained your brother's thwarted boy-
hood aspirations to me, I can apprehend the rest
of his meaning during the course of our train
ride north, without any further assistance."

"Bold words," Holmes mumbled, again frowning at his pipe, or rather at its contents. "I don't
suppose you would care to hazard three days'
supply of tobacco on the outcome?"

"Why only three days?"

"I cannot imagine the project requiring a
greater amount of time to bring off—particularly
if we are to have the services of a special train,
and one that travels under royal imprimatur, at
that. But surely you will reach the same conclusion," he added, with a quick, taunting curl of his
mouth (very much like the one that had, I suspected, set off Mrs. Hudson's fit of pique), "once
you have decoded the entire message. Very well,
then—the point of origin of Mycroft's communication indicates that he is on the move. I suggest
that we use what time we have before our train

departs to assemble a few indispensable items for the trip—not least our trout and salmon rods." I glanced at him, wondering a bit at his tone. "Well, Watson, it would be a shame not to enjoy a little recreation on the royal streams, at the end of our labours."

"Splendid notion," I agreed. "But among those 'few indispensable items' to be packed, I hope you will allow me to include the evident advantages concerning Mycroft's message that you yourself have already exploited."

"Advantages?"

I pointed in the direction of a small collection of newspapers that lay lightly scattered beyond the sofa and atop the Persian carpet. "I assume those are there for a reason, especially as I note several Scottish editions among their number. No doubt you located and purchased them *after* you had received word from your brother. Indeed, I submit that you returned home with them in such anticipation that you neglected to ascertain whether you had an ample supply of tobacco to last you through the evening. When you *did* discover the lack, you were so anxious to delve into the mystery that you did not wish to venture out again, but asked Mrs. Hudson to do so for you—and something in the manner of your request has caused her current mood."

"Ha!" came that sudden, piercing thing that was the closest approximation of joyous laughter that Holmes could produce. "In all, a triumph, Watson—I really must remember what chemicals were last in this beaker, and advertise their combination with Ceylon and pekoe teas as a brain tonic! And so—we pack!"

"We do, indeed," I said, rising as Holmes began to leave the room; but then, as I picked up the newspapers, two articles that Holmes had evidently clipped—one from the Edinburgh *Evening News* of almost two weeks ago, the other from the Glasgow *Herald* of that very day—fluttered from the mass and onto the floor. I picked the pair up, and glanced at their headlines.

The *Evening News* was, typically, more staid in tone, although the subject matter was grim, indeed:

TERRIBLE ACCIDENT AT HOLYROODHOUSE:
Royal Official Falls Beneath Farm Machinery on Palace Grounds

The story beneath the headline told of the horrific fate of Sir Alistair Sinclair, an architect of the historical variety, who had been given the commission of restoring and even redesigning some of the more ancient and dilapidated sections of Holyroodhouse, the official royal residence in Edinburgh (Balmoral being, as said, the informal summer home of the royal family in Scotland). Once an ancient abbey, later a medieval dwelling of Scottish kings, and most famously the preferred home of Mary, Queen of Scots, Holyroodhouse had still later been transformed into a baroque palace by Charles II, following a devastating fire. But during the century between the flight of Bonnie Prince Charlie and the coronation of our own Queen, the palace had fallen onto hard times. In keeping with her genuine passion for Scotland, however, the Queen had soon taken to indulging those Scottish subjects anxious for a glimpse of her by using Holyroodhouse as a convenient stopover lodging on her way to Balmoral. Her Majesty had refurbished the baroque sections of the palace; but the west tower—the last remaining medieval element and, significantly, the only area to survive the fire intact—had not yet received the same care, and Sir Alistair Sinclair had been given the job. The commission had proved a short one, however, for the architect had, according to the newspaper reports, been taking his ease amid some high grass when a new example of steam tractor–drawn groundskeeping equipment had riddled his body with wounds.

"I remember a small item concerning the accident in *The Times*," I said, looking over the *Evening News* version quickly. "But, Holmes—you would not have clipped this if you did not suspect that the official explanation is inadequate. What do you propose?"

By way of answer, Holmes only indicated the other notice I was holding. In it, the Glasgow *Herald* told of a second mishap, displaying the paper's far different journalistic style—and its city's attitude towards its eastern rival:

ANOTHER BLOODY DEATH IN HOLYROODHOUSE!
Dennis McKay, Honest Glasgow Labourer, Found Brutally Slain in Plain View of Royal Apartments!
ARE POLICE DOING ALL THEY CAN?

The rest of the account went on in the same vein, giving very few actual details, save that Dennis McKay had been the foreman brought in by Sir Alistair Sinclair to oversee the workforce that the latter intended soon to assemble. His body had been discovered lying among the ruins of the old abbey in the palace grounds, pierced by an unspecified number of wounds. With that, the *Herald* dispensed with actual reportage, filling the

rest of the space it devoted to the story with resentful inferences that McKay had been done in
by Edinburgh labourers, who were (supposedly)
angry that the foreman intended to bring in most
of his workforce from Glasgow.

"And so you agree with Mycroft that the two
deaths are related?" I ventured.

"*Does* Mycroft believe as much?" Holmes replied.

I tucked the newspaper clippings away and held
up the telegram again. "'McKay and Sinclair,
Collected Works'" was my reply.

Holmes let another sharp laugh go, and then
declared, "At your present inspired rate, Watson,
you'll leave us no entertainment for the train.
Hurry and pack your things!"

"Very well," I said, tucking the rest of the
newspapers—which contained accounts of the
two deaths that had appeared in our own London
press—under my arm. "Oh—but I'll require one
thing more, Holmes." He turned once again, his
manner increasingly impatient; but I was quite
insistent. "I must know what it was that you said
to Mrs. Hudson, so that I can at least *try* to heal
the breach—as I don't suppose *you* intend to."

Holmes made ready to protest, the fever of a
case beginning to exercise its full power over
him. But seeing that I would not move without

an answer, he simply shrugged and sighed. "Very well, Watson, very well." He returned to the window before which I had found him pacing, and I joined him there. We looked outside to see Baker Street calming after the conclusion of a hectic day. "Have you ever wondered, Watson, about that little shop just across and down a few doors from us? The sundries purveyor from the Punjab, I mean."

"A decent enough fellow," I replied. "I've purchased the odd item from him, on occasion."

"Yet our landlady will not."

"True. She says that she cannot understand the man's accent."

"Do *you* find it incomprehensible?"

"No—but then, I have some experience of that part of the world. What *are* you driving at, Holmes?"

"Only that Mrs. Hudson has no more trouble understanding our friend from the subcontinent than do you. Her refusal to patronise the place has another origin altogether. . . ."

"Well?"

"The present owner of the shop has held his lease on the property for some thirty-five years. Before that, it stood vacant for another ten—no British native dared set up shop there, despite the obvious volume of business that is offered by the street's pedestrian traffic."

"But why not? And what has any of it to do with Mrs. Hudson?"

"Mrs. Hudson was a young bride at the time of which I speak, and new to Baker Street. Apparently, that shop and building were then the home and place of business of a pork butcher and his family. The fellow enjoyed a very favourable reputation—that is, until it was generally noticed that his wife and several children had begun to disappear, one by one. To make short work of a rather fascinating tale, there was some talk of a relationship between their disappearances and the particular quality of the butcher's product—until a neighbour heard screaming emanating from the place one night, and the police were summoned. The man was discovered in the basement—which, by then, more closely resembled a graveyard."

"Good heavens! Was he mad?"

Holmes nodded. "The usual mania, in such cases—he believed the world too full of sin for his family, all of whom he loved; and each of whom, in turn, was despatched to the more loving care and perfect realm of the Almighty."

I shook my head, staring out at the busy street.

"Yes—not an uncommon delusion, as you say, for all its wretchedness. But I still don't see any connection to Mrs. Hudson."

"Don't you? Imagine the kind of stories that would have circulated after such a discovery— and their effect on a young woman, a newcomer to the street, who was left alone the greater part of the day. Inevitably, some gossiping acquaintance who lived adjacent to the tragic house began to tell of strange nocturnal noises drifting through her walls: a moaning woman and crying children, as well as the distinct sound of a shovel breaking earth. Still another neighbour, perhaps inspired by a need to outdo her friend, swore that she had seen a young girl in a white nightgown on several evenings, wandering aimlessly and mournfully about the small yard behind the building. The tales multiplied—and to this day, those residents of this part of Baker Street who were present when the crimes were uncovered will not enter that shop."

I felt a reflexive chill enter my bones, despite my best efforts to react rationally. "But, Holmes— why have you never told me this before?"

"It has never come up," Holmes said simply. "But today, when I discovered my lack of tobacco, I did—as you rightly surmised—ask Mrs. Hudson if she would not mind going to the tobacconist's for a fresh supply of shag. She claimed to be too busy to make that particular pilgrimage, and so I enquired if she wouldn't at least step across the way and see what our Punjabi friend had in stock. She protested—and I fear I made a rather ghoulish comment concerning her reasoning, one that she interpreted as entirely sarcastic."

I attempted the most severe tone possible, given the increasingly late hour and our growing need for haste: "You might have shown more respect for her beliefs, Holmes, different though they are from your own." At that, I hurried off to my bedroom, and began hurriedly packing some few items into a Gladstone.

Holmes's distinctly puzzled voice drifted in: "And what makes you think they are so different, Watson?"

"All I mean to say," I elaborated, going into a closet to fetch my rods and tackle, "is that if Mrs. Hudson entertains notions about hauntings and ghosts, why go out of your way—"

"Oh, but I entertain such notions myself, Watson."

I stood quite still for a moment, waiting for the piercing laugh—and was suddenly unnerved when it did not come. "Just what *are* you talking about?" I asked, returning to the sitting-room.

"Precisely that: In a manner different from, but

just as strong as, our landlady's, I give entire credence to the power of ghosts. And I must warn you, Watson, that your own views on this subject will likely be tested before this case is over." And then it was Holmes's turn to disappear and begin packing.

"You're joking, surely," I called out, aware of my own need to believe that he was not serious, and puzzled by its urgency. "We've worked on a score of cases that were supposed to have involved other-worldly forces, and you have never failed to—"

"Ah, but Watson, we've never been called to a place like Holyroodhouse!"

"And why should a royal palace make any difference?"

As Holmes replied, I found myself staring out the window at the shop across the way with far greater dread than I had previously felt, or than seemed warranted by the situation:

"The bodies of two men in the Queen's employ—scheduled to have been involved in reconstructing the oldest portion of the structure, those rooms that were once the private realm of the Scottish Queen—are found dead as a result of an untold number of terrible wounds, before they could even begin their work. Do not the circumstances, the awful coincidences, call something and someone to mind?"

I was about to protest continued ignorance; and then the beginnings of an old, a very old story began to draw in from the furthest corners of my memory, bringing a shudder with them.

"Yes, Watson," Holmes said quietly, joining me at the window. "The Italian secretary . . ." He, too, looked out the window, and spoke the name with a strange fascination: *"Rizzio . . ."*

"But—" My own voice, I noted, had dropped considerably in volume and conviction. "Holmes, that was three centuries ago!"

"And yet it is said that he walks the palace halls still, seeking revenge. . . ."

My body shivered involuntarily again, a reaction that angered me. "Nonsense! And even if true, why in the world should—"

"That is what we must determine, my friend— preferably before we reach our destination." Holmes glanced at the mantel clock. "The time, Watson—we must be away!"

∞

Chapter III

NORTHWARD TO THE SCOTTISH BORDER

Whatever illusions I had entertained about the experience of riding in a special train that had been commissioned by the royal household were dispelled when I saw the beast that awaited us alongside an old, disused platform just outside the main lines and structures of Euston Station. We had only just arrived at our departure point on schedule (wager or no wager, case or no case, Holmes would not think of getting aboard without at least a healthy amount of his own tobacco, prepared by his most trusted supplier, which had meant an indirect route to the station); and even in the near-darkness, or perhaps, indeed, *because* of it, the enormous engine, its lights glaring and its boiler at the steaming, snorting ready, stood in considerable contrast to the small, extremely solitary passenger car that, save for the coal trailer, was the train's only complement: Our journey would sacrifice all luxury for speed, it seemed, an impression that was confirmed when we approached the car and found ourselves faced with a succession of cheerless, plain compartments. Those furthest ahead and behind were occupied by plain-clothed young men who, we were quickly given to understand, were not policemen. Just what they *were*, they did not say—and, knowing that this would present an irresistible and perhaps amusing challenge to Holmes, I did not give voice to my own instinctive impression that each of the men had a distinctly military bearing.

Two of the squad, who appeared to be the leaders, approached us: one a sour-faced fellow with an arching nose that ended in an accusatory point, the other far more appealing and affable.

"Good evening, gentlemen," said the latter. "If you'll just climb aboard, we can get under way. Not a great deal of time for pleasantries, I'm afraid—but may I just say what a great honour it is for us all to have you both aboard?"

"You may, Lieutenant ——?" Holmes inquired leadingly.

The second young man smiled, as the first began to pace uneasily. "An excellent attempt, Mr. Holmes. But I'm afraid we have orders to forgo names, as well as ranks—for the time being."

"And I suppose it would do no good to enquire as to who issued those orders?"

"Not really, sir, no."

"We ought to be under way by now," said the first fellow brusquely.

"Certainly," Holmes said, moving to the middle compartment of the passenger car. "But do remember, young sir, that reticence is not *always* the best guarantee of secrecy."

"Meaning, Mr. Holmes?" said the sour-faced young man, rather indignantly.

"Meaning that, by refusing conversation, you force me to rely on my observational skills," Holmes replied. "Which, I can assure you, are far more developed than my social talents. For example—while you were so conspicuously *not* speaking, I was able to make out the immutable stamp of the army upon your posture; and yet, your frame does not display any signs of rigorous physical exertion, nor your skin of outdoor duty. From which it is no great job to divine that you are either a low-level staff officer or a higher-ranking member of military intelligence. Given our present circumstances, which conclusion

would *you* draw?" The unpleasant fellow looked
eviscerated, and Holmes approached him. "An
amiable conversation can often be the best
method of obfuscation imaginable—as your col-
league from the Royal Navy, here, seems already
to have learned." Rapping the army officer on the
chest lightly with his knuckles, Holmes said, "Do
remember that, won't you?" as he boarded the
train. "And *you,* sir," he added, lowering the compartment window to address the second young
man. "If you wish to succeed in your present career, some determined retraining of your sea gait
would do you no harm!"

The second fellow could not help but laugh
quietly and give both Holmes and myself appre-
ciative looks as he closed the door to our compartment. "Enjoy the trip, gentlemen," he said,
"and do let us know if there is any way in which
we can be of assistance. . . ." He then signalled to
the other men before and behind us, and the
train jerked into forward motion.

Despite the more cheerful officer's demean-
our, a very unpleasant sort of anticipation—the
foreboding that one has when one is not even
sure upon whom one may rely, or why, a sensation that I had experienced quite often in
Afghanistan—began at once to gather around our
mission; and it would develop into a deep sense

of philosophical malaise, even dread, during the trip northward. Holmes and I started out bravely enough, with a return to Mycroft's telegram and an attempt to resolve our wager; but there really was very little left in the thing that could genuinely be called challenging. The mention of "Mr. Webley" was positively blatant (unless one happened to be unacquainted with British firearms); and in making such an obvious reference to the service revolver that he knew me to carry during our most dangerous cases, Mycroft indicated only that he believed our antagonists in the present business to be capable of extreme violence—arguably (given the fates of the two men who were the apparent subjects of the case) a superfluous warning. The somewhat absurd mention of a palm-reading as a means of self-protection *might* have been slightly esoteric, had I not been aware that at least one of Holmes's criminal acquaintances, a certain "Porky" Shinwell Johnson, was in the habit of carrying a devilish, peculiar-looking weapon that was actually called a "Palm-protector": a single-shot pistol that fired a .32 calibre short round, and that fit neatly within the palm of the hand. Its small barrel extended out from between the middle and ring fingers and its firing mechanism was triggered when sufficient pressure was applied by the heel of the hand to a lever. It had originally come to the London underworld by way of the criminal gangs of Chicago, and Shinwell Johnson, knowing of Holmes's interest in exotic weapons, had even presented him with one, after they had co-operated on a particularly difficult matter; but why Mycroft should have specified bringing it to the palace, neither his brother nor I could tell. Holmes, however, had not questioned the directive, although he had entrusted the thing to my care on our departure for Euston.

With our train by now firing like some gigantic rocket through a very black night—for a storm front had rolled in from the North Sea, as if to definitively extinguish any hope that we might not have entered into a sinister affair—we moved on to Mycroft's next reference. "A pair of berths on the Caledonia" seemed, to me, to serve a double purpose: It confirmed, in the unlikely event that we were in any doubt, that our destination was Scotland, while giving our opponent or opponents the impression that we had taken ship for a foreign port. A quick check of *The Times* told us that Mycroft had been careful to make sure that the Cunard steamship *Caledonia* was indeed departing Southampton for New York the very next day; and this offered me a small measure of reassurance, for (as Holmes had already

mentioned) we knew that several truly determined and creative criminal minds correctly
viewed the integrity of England's telegraphy lines
as a fairly minor obstacle to gathering intelligence
on their antagonists; and the idea that some few
among our own enemies might believe us bound
for America met with my sincerest approval.

The first section of the telegraph's final line—
"My old crofter"—Holmes and I had already interpreted; the second part—"will pull alongside
at quarantine"—could, I reasoned, be taken simply
as the completion of the analogy, nothing more
than a statement that Mycroft would meet our
train at "quarantine," in nautical terms a station
just outside a ship's destination (where the condition of vessel, passengers, and crew could be inspected), and in our own case, some point far
enough outside Edinburgh that Mycroft would
have time to acquaint us with the true facts of the
case under scrutiny before we reached the city. In
this way did the matter of the telegram come to
an abrupt end; and under ordinary circumstances,
I should have felt a bit of pride at my own analysis of the thing. But there was a great deal of
track yet to be traversed, on this particular night,
and even at our considerable speed, many hours
would pass before we reached the Scottish border. It seemed unlikely that we would be able to

pass any of the intervening time sleeping, or in any other way avoiding the dark subject that Holmes had so tentatively broached before we'd left Baker Street, which had caused me to feel such mortal dread—to say nothing of doubts concerning my friend's mental integrity.

"It is a hideous story, Watson," Holmes mused, finally happy that he had a great quantity of his own "invigorating" shag at hand. As some of it roasted hot in his pipe, he settled into a detailed analysis of man's savagery to man in the same manner that an ordinary person might face a full plate of hearty food. True, the particular outrage of which he spoke that night had happened over three hundred years ago; but his idiosyncratic code of good and evil made no distinction between a crime committed recently and one that had taken place during another age altogether—if anything, the fact of justice long deferred only made his intellectual wheels grind all the faster.

"Hideous, indeed, but instructive, in at least one sense," Holmes continued, his voice momentarily disdainful. "We have been accustomed, during our own era, to treat the Elizabethan as the age of Shakespeare, Marlowe, and Drake—of high literature and higher patriotism. We forget that it had a particularly unseemly side, that it was a time during which far more Englishmen were burned at the stake than ever played upon the stage; when there were more spies trading in secrets and cutting throats than there were heroes walking the decks of defiant ships. Did not Marlowe himself meet death not as a wise, aged poet, but in the course of duty as a young secret agent, with another spy's dagger driven through his eye-socket?"

"Come now, Holmes," I protested, not without a certain sternness. I had always considered my brilliant friend's political and historical opinions to be rather simplistic (I can still recall the fact that, when we first met, he confessed to never having heard of Thomas Carlyle, much less to having read any of his works), but in the main this presented no cause for argument between us: Simple though his interpretations may have been, they were usually in agreement with my own sentiments. But on occasion he could be what I considered naively cynical about such matters—and any man with a military background feels insults to his nation and its history with his heart, whatever his head may think of the actual facts of the case. "We're talking," I continued, "about Scotland, not *England*."

"We are talking of a particularly revolting crime which, without the backing of powerful Englishmen—indeed, without the implicit cooperation of that supreme shape-shifter, Elizabeth—would never have been so much as attempted. No, Watson—this is one act of bloodshed that we cannot simply file away under 'the sorts of things that happen in Scotland'—although its final form has led many supposed English 'patriots' to so dismiss it."

However much it might have lacked nuance, his point was essentially correct. Indeed, it forced me to realise (less than comfortably, given my previous, rather scolding tone) that I had forgotten most of the details of the infamous murder of David Rizzio, private secretary, music instructor, and confidant to Mary, Queen of Scots. But Holmes was a master, as I have noted, of all such tales, regardless of the time and place of their occurrence; and I quickly found that he was only too ready to overlook the arch reaction of the retired soldier and to reacquaint me with every aspect of the business, as we continued to hurtle along through the Midlands and then the Yorkshire moors—a setting that, given the raging storm outside, could scarcely have been more perfect for the tale.

The year was 1566; the scene of the outrage, of course, Holyroodhouse, or, as it had been more simply known, then, the Palace of Holyrood (a name derived from the most precious relic of the

long-abandoned abbey, an object that its caretak-
ers firmly believed to be a sliver of the True
Cross). As the young Catholic heir to the Scottish
throne, Mary had been taught that she had a
likely and legitimate claim to Elizabeth's English mantle as well: for while the most direct
Tudor line looked to end with the Virgin Queen,
Mary was a young and presumably fertile great-
granddaughter of that dynasty's founder, Henry
VII. She had, therefore, been enlisted as an unwitting pawn in the attempt by France (her
mother's native land) to ring Protestant England
with the armies of True Belief: Besides spending
most of her youth in the French court, rather than
in her father's troubled realm, Mary was ultimately selected to be the bride of the sickly young
French king. When her new husband's complaints
quickly proved mortal, the lovely young widow—
only eighteen years old—discovered that a life
full of noteworthy new opportunities, rather than
one of mournful seclusion, opened up before her.
Continental princes beat a hasty path to her door,
and it was soon apparent that, of all the roads she
herself might take, return to Scotland was by far
the most difficult and dangerous, since that king-
dom had become an officially Protestant domain
during the years she had been away from it.

But Mary had a spirit that, in our own era, would have placed her in that ever-growing class of women we call *adventuresses:* After many months of entertaining this and that princely suitor, as well as sparking the start of what would become a deadly rivalry with her "English cousin" (a rivalry both political and personal, but more the latter than the former, according to many who witnessed it), Mary decided to risk all on a lonely return to her homeland and a solitary reclamation of the Scottish throne.

Much of her native country responded warmly to the courage of her ploy, for it implied great respect for the wishes of her people. The citizens of the capital, in particular, welcomed her—so much so that when she (being used to and indeed loving Continental ways) moved the royal seat from formidable but gloomy Edinburgh Castle to the courtly Palace of Holyrood just outside the westernmost edge of the city, there was no great outcry. Mary surrounded herself with Scots ladies to join those that had accompanied her from abroad, and immediately set herself to studying the Scots dialect (so that she could speak it while receiving the country's nobles), as well as to learning the favourite Scottish pastimes of hunting, archery, music, golf, and dancing. In general she did well at all such pursuits—and she put the capstone to her efforts by making no move to reassert Catholicism as the land's true faith.

"And yet what a shock it must have been, for such a still-young queen, Watson!" Holmes observed. "To come home from almost a lifetime amid the fineries of Europe to a country considered so barbaric by her French in-laws and friends that the very term for being repeatedly run through with a blade was simply *poignarder à l'écossais*—a terrible harbinger of the crime that Mary was to herself witness." Holmes settled further into the comfort of his overcoat as the air that blew in through the compartment's open window grew ever colder. "And a telling point of convergence between that crime of long ago and the more recent evils that we ourselves are on our way to investigate. . . ."

At that, I remembered anew just how Messrs. Sinclair and McKay—those poor, dead men who had been almost forgotten in the creeping timelessness of Holmes's steam-powered ride through some of the less creditable episodes of our history—had met their fates: *poignarder à l'écossais,* "stabbed in the Scottish mode." Was my friend, I wondered silently, really suggesting a connection between those nearly ancient royal intrigues and our current case?

"A rather obvious question fills your face, Watson," Holmes remarked, quite accurately. "But believe me when I say that only time will provide your answer. Allow me, therefore, to finish my tale:

"After four years of successfully navigating the troubled and often frighteningly bloodied waters of Scottish politics, Mary encountered the issue of marriage once again: Her nobles and subjects wished an heir, and they continued to make it clear that they did *not* wish the father of that heir—a child who might, after all, grow to be the ruler of both Scotland *and* England—to be either foreign-born or Catholic. A native, Protestant nobleman was required; and Mary displayed an unfortunate and utter lack of judgement when she suddenly fell in what she believed was love with Henry Stuart, Lord Darnley. In France he was called 'the agreeable nincompoop' (the original French phrase is quite beyond my powers), but Darnley was nevertheless reputed to be as physically beautiful as was Mary—their brief passion seems to have been based on little other than lust. Darnley's stupidity, however, would prove to have longer-lasting effects than his charms: It made her new prince a desirable instrument for those nobles who wished to finally eradicate all Catholic influence on their queen,

beginning with those Papist courtiers, foreign
and Scot, with whom she continued to people her
most intimate circle."

Holmes paused, shaking his head just percep-
tibly. "There were so many ways in which these
men could have achieved the effect they desired,
Watson. . . ." The disdain in Holmes's voice assumed an almost mournful quality. "So many
rational ways, I should say. And the simplest
would likely have been the most effective. Mary
was not a stupid woman, by any means, and had
men of equal intelligence explained to her the nature of those worldly pressures that were at work
in their land—most of all the manner in which
her own marriage and prospective progeny were
now bound up in the question of the English
succession—she could doubtless have understood their point." The sadness gave way to anger,
once more. "But, as always, such beings believed
that a starker explication of so crucial a point
would make it strike home the harder. They determined on an act of coercive and illustrative
violence, a terrorising demonstration of what political power looks and feels like, when it reaches
down to take hold of an individual life. . . .

"Mary's marriage to Darnley was quickly revealed to have been nothing more than an intense but passing infatuation, on both their parts;

and her subsequent disappointment with and coldness towards her husband bred in the dull-witted young man a determination to show his wife that he could be not only a masterful husband but a forceful politician. That Mary was many months pregnant with the result of their brief initial passion perhaps spurred Darnley on, in this regard; certainly, it made his co-conspirators even more anxious to show the queen that, as she now held the future of the realm in her womb, she must cease her dalliances with Catholic courtiers. And there was another factor to consider: So long as she did practise the Roman mass and allow Catholic advisers and ladies-in-waiting into her private chambers, so long did her obnoxiousness to Elizabeth—and to Elizabeth's most cold-blooded councillors, led by the murderous spy-master Walsingham—grow more intense.

"There remained, for Darnley's brave band, only the selection of a victim—and on whom did they fix their collective eye? David Rizzio . . . music instructor, dancing master—as much jester as 'secretary.' Certainly, a creature of more limited and superficial influence could scarcely have been found in the Scottish court. Indeed, his relative insignificance only betrayed the lack of imagination and the viciousness of his detractors—they

would have done as well to murder one of the
queen's spaniels. Oh, he was charming, certainly,
and as deft at dancing as he was playing and
teaching music. And he did enjoy an unusual
degree of informality with the queen, often sup-
ping in her private rooms and entertaining her
ladies there until very late hours. There were ru-
mours, of course, that he was providing more
services than these for the collected women, but
even at the time such talk was revealed to have
been baseless. Far more important, if the truth be
known, was the mere fact that he was Italian,
and as such could be portrayed to the ignorant
and the idiotic as an agent of 'the Bishop of
Rome.'" Holmes nearly spat another column of
smoke out of the window. "Through such profound mental workings are the fates of harmless
fools and empires sealed. . . ."

Suddenly, my friend rose to his full height, his
aspect defiant despite the pitching of the train.
"And yet it is the absurdity of believing Rizzio
anything but a happy reminder of Mary's careless youth on the Continent that endures as the
instructive fact of the affair, Watson, rather than
his murder!" Holmes's anger now burst into its
more active form, and our compartment could
barely contain him, as he renewed the thunder-
ous pacing that he had begun in our rooms in

Baker Street. "Consider the barest facts of physiology: Rizzio was a small man, of surpassing ugliness, by some accounts a hunchback, while Mary was unusually tall and fair, with a personal history of favouring men of a similar type, such as Darnley. Did a woman of such breeding and predilections suddenly abandon her habits of birth and taste, in the blinding glory of this gnomish Italian musician? You will find sensible Englishmen today who yet believe it, who propagate medieval superstitions about the lusty powers of hunchbacks, despite the fact that there is no true evidence that Rizzio was such, or indeed *anything* more than exceptionally entertaining and humorous. No, Watson!"

"My dear Holmes, I do not argue the point—"

"No, I say!" It was clear that, in the absence of the general English public, I would suffice, in Holmes's mind, as its representative. "Murder often relies on calumny for its rationalisation—and never more so than when it occurs among princes and their servants! I ask you only to imagine the scene:

"In the bleakness of a March night in Scotland, Mary—six months into bearing the child who would indeed become not only the Scottish monarch but also that most elusive quantity, a legitimate heir to the crown of England—calls some few of her closest ladies into her private rooms, in the west tower wing of Holyroodhouse. We are speaking—lest you think, Watson, that I have quite lost the thread of our case, as well as my wits—of those same rooms that Sir Alistair Sinclair was asked only weeks ago to rehabilitate: rooms that have remained almost untouched since the night of which I speak. Remember this fact, for if it is not vital, then we may safely return to London and entrust this business to Mycroft and the rather extraordinary collection of young men"—Holmes gestured towards the front and the rear of the train, where those same officers were sequestered—"who are now gathered around us. No, the setting is all-important, for how often have you and I observed that blood exerts a special power over those locations where it is spilt?

"And, into this place in particular, Mary—desirous of music, of entertainment, of laughter—once again naïvely summons the even more naïve Rizzio, who sups with the ladies in the queen's small, intimate dining-chamber, and supplies all that is asked of him: jests, likely ribald and at Darnley's expense, music, played as only an Italian can, and dancing, although the queen herself, *enceinte*, does not take part in the latter. A charming moment, all in all, one that requires only a faithful and understanding husband for its completion, rather than a drunken, ambitious fool. But all too soon—the fool comes. . . .

"He appears, in an obscene irony, via the small privy staircase that connects the queen's rooms with his own, below. At first, the company is bewildered to see him—for he rarely ventures into these rooms, his royal duty having been done half a year ago—but he is greeted with the respect his title commands. But soon, the prince's coarse henchmen come, uninvited and unannounced, through that same amorous passageway, which Darnley has revealed to them. They flatly and roughly inform the queen that they intend to cleanse her private chamber of the man they call a Roman bawd acting above his station. Mary, a true queen, is at first less alarmed than angered; but then the husband makes no protest. He shows guilt all over his face, and his drunken mouth is incapable even of proclaiming its own treachery. Soon, more rough country nobles appear, and they try to lay hands on Rizzio, who, like the pet he is, seeks the safety of his mistress's skirts, clinging to them for what he now suspects—too late!—must be dear life. Defiantly, Mary demands to know what these men intend—and they tell her plainly, for a second time, that they will purify her chambers of the supposedly lascivious plotter at her feet.

"The mighty hands of the lords are finally laid upon Rizzio—Mary intervenes—and as the degenerate Darnley, potent in every way save that which matters, stands fearfully by, his henchmen produce pistols. Intending to coerce Rizzio, they hold the weapons first to the pregnant womb of the queen herself, causing her to believe that her own life and that of the precious child are in fact at risk; but then, over Mary's protests, as well as the fearful shrieks of her ladies, Rizzio is dragged through her bedchamber and into the stairway, screaming pathetically for his life: *'Justizia! Justizia! Sauvez ma vie, Madame!'* But Mary cannot save him. In the main stairway of the tower, the brave Scots nobles produce long, hefty daggers and stab the small man a fantastic number of times: by some accounts as many as sixty, by no accounts less than fifty-five. Fifty-five to sixty! How much of that small frame could actually have been left intact? How much—"

"Holmes—" I ventured to interrupt.

"How much might we today, on encountering such injuries, be tempted to think some modern *machine* had inflicted them—?"

Suddenly, both Holmes and I were hurled

against the forward wall of the compartment; and a screeching noise—one that I would almost have taken for the cries of the long-dead Scottish Queen, so engrossed in Holmes's tale had I become—cut through the stormy night with an awesome, deafening power. The train was clearly in some sort of trouble, and the screaming of the halted steel wheels against the rails, along with the blasting whistle of the engine, indicated that the trouble was serious. We had just had time to right ourselves, the mighty vehicle sending showers of sparks up from the track as far back as our car and beyond, when a second, even more ominous noise roared out from somewhere in the darkness around us:

It was the unmistakable sound of an explosion, and not the variety that might have accompanied some malfunction of the steam engine.

"A shell-burst, Watson?" Holmes cried out to me.

"I think not!" said I. "The report was too dull for artillery!"

Holmes rushed to a window to scrutinise the scene ahead. "A *bomb*, then—yes, there! Near the rails!"

"Can you see if the tracks are damaged?" I asked, rushing over and straining to get my head and upper body out of the window next to Holmes's.

"No, they do not appear to be—however—"

At that both Holmes and I turned at the sight of a rushing shadow that was moving quickly towards our car; but before either of us could acknowledge it in words, the shadow had leapt up onto the compartment step and, with stunningly strong arms, pushed us back so quickly and unexpectedly that we both lost our footing.

I found myself on the compartment floor; Holmes managed to swing himself into a seat, avoiding the same fate.

"Stay inside, I beg of you!" said the young man who Holmes had identified as a naval officer prior to our departure from London. A few sailor's oaths followed this outburst, after which the formerly calm, pleasant-voiced fellow produced a naval service revolver and slammed our windows closed. We heard shouting voices and the crunch of heavy boots running along the gravel beneath the rails—

Then, just as we were beginning to collect ourselves, several shots rang out.

Producing my own service revolver quickly, I determined to make for the door again, indignant that I should have been given orders about my own safety, and that of my noteworthy friend, by this pup of an officer who did not even belong to a combat arm of his service. "Why, the very idea," I murmured, cocking the hammer of my revolver. " 'Intelligence,' indeed . . . !"

I had already grasped the latch of the compartment door, when Holmes seized hold of my arm, crying, "Watson—look out!" and pulled me back. He had seen what I could not: yet another young man, this one even more agitated than the last, with an expression on his pale face that was fanaticism itself. This last effect was dramatically heightened by a fiery red beard, unkempt hair of a similar length and colour, and, most fearsome of all, a long, terrible scar that made a tangled mess of his right cheek and obscured his right eye hideously. The fellow's powerful arm and sharp elbow were more than a match for the compartment door's window, and in a burst it shattered inward, driving Holmes and me away from the flying glass.

"We know why ye've come!" declared the young madman in a thick brogue; and even as he did, I detected the ominous smell of burning black powder. "But we'll nae let ye muhrder more Scots patriots! Have a taste of what ye gave Denny McKay!"

Before either Holmes or I could react, the young man had disappeared from the window—not, however, without depositing something inside the compartment:

Looking down, both my friend and I saw the ominous form of a small homemade bomb.

What appeared to be a moderate-sized tin had been stuffed to overflowing with a granular explosive that was compacted by something that looked and smelled all too much like pyroxylin, or "gun-cotton," the highly explosive and inflammable wadding used in modern artillery. The lid, which was wired on tight, had been punctured in the centre, and a homemade fuse was stuffed into the hole.

I heard Holmes issue a short sound that, even for him, was a rather abominable approximation of laughter. "A tobacco tin!" he declared; and then he turned to me. "A *bomb* in a tin of tobacco—there is a double irony in that, don't you think, Watson?"

"No, I do not, Holmes!" I cried, resisting an impulse to seize my friend and shake some sense into him. "That fuse is burning!"

Chapter IV

FROM OUT OF THE MIST

Holmes shrugged, almost casually, and approached the deadly device. "Burning it may be, Watson—but these Scots nationalists could learn a few things from their Irish cousins. . . ."

Reaching down with what seemed to me suicidal daring, Holmes simply pulled the fuse from the tin, dropped it on the floor, and rubbed it out with his boot. Looking at my thunderstruck features, his face filled with disappointment. "Really, Watson—surely you detected the aroma of slow-burning black powder."

I felt a sudden pang of embarrassment. "Why— yes. Now that you mention it."

"We had, at the very least, ten to fifteen seconds in which to devise a solution."

I concealed my service revolver back beneath my jacket, regarding my friend with an odd mixture of admiration and anger. "I apologise if I was overly alarmed, Holmes, but—"

"Please, old friend," he answered quickly, holding up a hand. "After all—who knows how I should have reacted in your place on the North-West Frontier, facing a wave of onrushing Afghan fighters with their Jezail rifles?"

It was a very decent concession; but before I could acknowledge it, we both heard the sound of rapidly approaching footsteps, again moving along the gravel of the railway line: likely our escort. Holmes gripped my arm securely, pocketed the deadly tobacco tin, and murmured, "It would perhaps be best if we did *not* reveal all the details of what we have seen, Watson—these men have clearly not told us all, about either our mission or theirs; why should we show them any greater courtesy?"

I nodded once, and then the face of the young naval officer appeared again at our now-vacant window frame.

"Ah!" he noised. "So the fellow was here, as well, was he?"

"*Someone* was," I lied quickly. "We had little chance to see him, however—he shattered the glass, but could do nothing else before your approach."

The young officer nodded, still holding his pistol aloft. "That's lucky," he said with a grin, his affability returning; then he seemed to catch wind of something. "Hello—what's that smell?" he said, eyeing the pair of us with increased scrutiny.

"That is my fault, I'm afraid," Holmes answered, seeing that I had exhausted my capacity for extemporaneous fabrication. "The excitement made me rather anxious to smoke, but the bursting window unsteadied my hand. I ignited an entire box of matches"—he held up his unlit pipe—"to no effect."

The officer's eyes narrowed. "*You*, Mr. Holmes?"

"With age, we all lose some measure of our steadiness under fire." Holmes gave the man a friendly nod. "With luck, you will never experience as much yourself."

The young officer, evidently satisfied, smiled again and stepped back from the door. "Would you care to take another compartment, gentlemen?" He indicated the window frame. "The temperature is dropping rather quickly, I'm afraid, and the rain shows no sign of relenting."

"An excellent suggestion," answered Holmes.
Then he held out an arm to the door. "Watson?
You would not like to add ague to the list of the
evening's entertainments, I trust. . . ."

I wondered why Holmes was so insistent about
my leaving the compartment first, but I did not
wonder for long: When I had fetched my bag and
my rod case from the overhead rack and then
moved to the doorway, I observed him using the
cover of my body to swiftly reach down and scoop
up the remains of the burnt fuse of the bomb.

"Certainly not," said I, lingering in the opening
to allow my friend a moment to complete his work.
"No damage to the rails, I trust?" I asked the officer.

"No, Doctor—the member of their group who
was responsible for hurling the bomb did so far
too soon, and it fell well short."

"One wonders why they did not simply *plant*
the thing."

"No doubt you've encountered these types before, Doctor," said the young man dismissively.
"More conviction than spine or knowledge."

I perceived an opening: "Indeed? You know
who they were, then?"

The man's smile—as evasive as it was charming, I now recognised—flashed once more. "I

would really rather leave such discussions for the rendezvous, Doctor. If you don't mind."

I eyed him with friendly scrutiny. "The 'rendezvous'?"

"Yes. It's fortunate, really—a few minutes more, and we should have been at a full stop and much more vulnerable."

I saw that Holmes was now ready, and said, "Well, confident in the knowledge that you also intend to explain nothing about *that* cryptic remark, let's indeed move. One compartment back, I think, eh, Holmes? I've no desire to be any closer to another such performance."

"My precise sentiments, Watson," Holmes said, joining me with his own bags at last.

Watching us take up our new accommodations, the young officer called out, "We'll be under way in a moment—but, as I say, it won't be long before we stop again, though for a reason that will, I trust, be far more welcome!"

With that, the fellow disappeared forwards at a run. The shouting voices around us—no one of their statements fully distinguishable—indicated failure to locate the lunatic whose wild features were now impressed quite vividly on my mind. We locked ourselves into the compartment, and in mere moments we were moving again.

"Imagine it, Holmes!" I said. "Not the least word of explanation from that fellow about this ominous business!"

"No," said Holmes, taking both the unexploded bomb and the fuse remnants from his pockets and laying them atop a handkerchief he had spread out on a vacant seat. "But does that really surprise you, Watson? We still have no precise idea of who they are—and now this business of a 'rendezvous'!"

"Absurd" was all I could think to say, as I joined my friend in examining the device that had been meant, it seemed, to kill us. "Are there any clues to our *attackers'* identities, at least, in that thing?"

Holmes did not appear hopeful. "A brand of tobacco common to southeastern Scotland—inexpensive, with a grotesque flavour."

"Holmes, I was more interested in—"

"But a double irony, all the same, Watson—our investigation begins with a discussion of tobacco, and just as we turn to reviewing the tale of the Scottish Queen and her opponents, what appears to have been a Highland fanatic drops this device. . . ."

"'Appears to have been'?" I said in amazement. "If that is the appearance, I should not like to encounter a genuine example."

"Nor should I. . . ." Holmes's voice trailed off

as he continued to examine the bomb, carefully disassembling it. "Pyroxylin—gun-cotton," he said, pulling some of it free. "No doubt you noticed it?"

"Indeed" was my reply. "I encountered the stuff in Afghanistan, when we began using the first Armstrong guns. Had the creator of this package known his business, he would have realised that gun-cotton can be even more destructive than black powder. Given the proportions, had the fuse been of an appropriate length to explode this bomb when he threw it, he would likely have been killed as well."

Holmes inhaled the distinct aroma produced by the nitric and sulphuric acids in which ordinary cotton gunnery wadding had been soaked to create the additional propulsive power of pyroxylin.

"Indeed, Watson," he said at length, "and that incongruity is noteworthy. It is quite . . ." Holmes fell to silent examination again.

"Holmes?" enquired I. "What made you say that a bomb is ironic, given that we were discussing the Scottish Queen and her enemies?"

"Hmm? Ah—yes. Why, the moment in the tale that we had reached, Watson. Do you not recall the fate of the Scottish Queen's cowardly husband, Darnley? Within months of the birth of the child she was carrying on the night of Rizzio's murder—the child James, who would be the Sixth of Scotland and the First of England—Mary became deeply enamoured of—"

"The Earl of Bothwell, yes," I said, recalling the story at last. "A man of great physical strength and unshakable loyalty, or so the story goes."

"So, indeed. And less than a year after the prince's birth, the house in which Darnley was staying—for he had been cast out of Mary's palace—was destroyed by a massive explosion. Darnley himself escaped at the last moment—only to be found strangled just outside the wreckage."

I sat back, somewhat overcome at the mounting level of violence that seemed to be closing in on us as we continued shooting through the storm and the night into an ever less hospitable climate. "Furious stabbings . . . bombs . . . Holmes, what in Heaven's name are we entering into?"

Holmes glanced up and out of the window. "Scotland, I should say. . . ."

"Yes, yes, but—" I made a concerted effort to get hold of my nerves by returning to rational thought. "I should like to bring you back to one central notion, Holmes."

"Indeed?"

"Well," I began, realising that the speed of our train had once again diminished; but the process was at least gradual this time. "It's only that—and I say this with no disrespect for your outrage over Rizzio's murder, which was truly a ghastly crime—but you seem peculiarly focused on the coincidence of location and wounds, between that crime and the deaths of Sinclair and McKay. Yet these *are* matters of sheer coincidence, and nothing more, surely. Unless . . ." I stopped, not knowing how to precisely frame my next statement, much less give voice to the doubts that underlay it.

Holmes seemed to take little note of my discomfort, saying, "I despise coincidences, Watson—never more so than in matters of murder."

"How well do I know it."

"Then it would seem imperative that you finish the statement you have begun with 'Unless. . . .' "

"Very well." I bested all anxieties with a forceful rush: "I was simply going to say, *unless* you truly do believe that there is some—some *spiritual* connection between the murder of Rizzio and the cases we are on our way to investigate."

Holmes stared at me, a bit blankly. "I should have thought it plainly apparent that I *do* consider such a 'spiritual connection' to lie at the very *heart* of these matters, Watson."

"But, Holmes, you surely are not—you *cannot*

be saying that you believe a—a *ghost* to be at work here? Some vengeful wraith that is haunting Holyroodhouse?"

Holmes's features began to widen with a smile that, had it broadened any further, would have turned my discomfort to the beginnings of a far deeper alarm. He opened his seemingly amused mouth as if to speak—but at that precise instant, the train began to decelerate more deliberately: Moving to our compartment's door and opening its window, I could see nothing in the vicinity that resembled even a house, much less a station, and Holmes—who joined me after carefully wrapping and again concealing the bomb elements—had no better luck. We therefore ignored the instructions of our young "hosts" by opening the compartment door, unfolding the small set of steps beneath it, and descending to the ground. This vantage point afforded us a good look at yet another alarming scene.

The various intelligence men were again out and scouring the areas along both sides of the tracks, weapons at the ready and doing little to support the naval officer's earlier contention that this was some sort of scheduled stop. Amid a thick mist made even more impenetrable by the enormous amounts of steam being expelled by our engine through what appeared to be every hole and seam in its iron skin, the men went about their search in an even more frantic manner (or so it seemed to me) than they had exhibited during the attack. The only conclusion I could draw was that we were now facing a threat greater than nationalists armed with bombs—and all too soon I saw something that indicated that their anxiety might be justified.

"Look there, Holmes!" I cried.

A scant thirty yards in front of the engine, we could both discern a glowing red light, some six or seven feet from the ground and seeming, through the fog and mist, to blink like the eye of some mythical beast.

"One would expect," Holmes mused evenly, "to find a dragon in *Wales*, rather than Scotland. . . ."

It soon became apparent that the light was moving towards us, although at no hurried pace; and before long, it became equally obvious that our "dragon's eye" was, in fact, a signalman's lantern fitted with a brilliant red lens. As a human figure became discernible beneath the lantern, the intelligence men called to one another and descended on the exceptionally tall, heavyset newcomer, who wore a long cloak and a homburg and steadied himself with a very fine walking stick. But it was obvious that this fellow was no enemy, for the barrels of the young men's pistols all turned skyward as they approached him and their manners turned quite deferential. A few seconds more, and the man was within a dozen feet of us, his face plainly visible in the lantern's glow:

It was Mycroft Holmes, who had never appeared to me so utterly out of his element. He stood, exhaling great, condensed clouds as he listened to the young men tell him what I assumed to have been the tale of our attack; then he issued instructions to the collected officers, in a firm but not entirely familiar manner, and they obeyed him by immediately dashing off again, in every conceivable direction. He then approached our car, all the while puffing and heaving and trying to catch his breath.

Holmes leapt nimbly onto the steps beneath our compartment, then slipped one arm through the open window and swung to and fro with the door. "Well, brother!" he called out. "You appear to have become the high panjandrum of some Eastern cult, complete with acolytes and bloodthirsty rituals! Which of your rites is so arcane that it must take place under the cover of a stormy night in the middle of—I shall not hazard a guess as to our precise location. I should have put us at just over the Scottish border, but my attention has been diverted during the last hour!"

"Do remove yourself from the doorway, Sherlock," Mycroft replied wearily, his broad face
never more florid, but his extraordinary grey eyes
never more full of purpose. As his brother obeyed
the order by retreating into the car, Mycroft
added: "There is much to speak of, and if I do not
sit down quickly I fear I may collapse into use-
lessness." With no little effort, I assisted the elder
Holmes up and into the car; and as I did, he
glanced back at me and offered the peculiar expression that was as close to kindness and appreciation as either of the Holmes brothers ever
came. "I am grateful that you have been able to
come along, Doctor." I followed Mycroft into
the car and seated myself opposite him and next
to Holmes, as the intelligence men readied our
compartment doorway for departure. "I may assume, then," Mycroft continued, "that neither of
you was in any way injured during the earlier
episode?"

"You may—*if* you care to engage in such men-
tally debilitating habits as assumption, Mycroft.
You really might have included some warning
about lunatic bombers in your message, you
know."

The elder Holmes's features filled with enormous embarrassment. "I apologise for this un-
foreseen development, Sherlock—and to you,

especially, Dr. Watson. I simply did not believe that the matter would turn so deadly so quickly."

"Which implies, however, that you believed it would turn deadly *eventually*," replied Holmes.

"Of course," said Mycroft simply. "I should have thought that my message indicated as much." He seemed momentarily surprised. "I trust that the communication did not pose an insurmountable problem?"

"Not at all, sir," said I, aware that our circumstances had caused me to regard this man— whose company I had shared on several other dangerous cases—with an involuntarily heightened respect.

"Don't allow Watson to humbug you, Mycroft," Holmes replied to his brother's query. "*He* at least found your message a most diverting exercise!"

Mycroft regarded his brother with a look of indulgent irritation and said, "How deftly you insult us both, Sherlock." He then glanced at me. "He was a peevish boy, Doctor, ever on the lookout to build himself up by running others down—a habit he has maintained through adulthood."

Just then, the face of the naval officer appeared at the window. He opened the door enough to insert his head. "All clear, Mr. Holmes," he said to Mycroft. "Nothing and no one about, except a few sheep."

"Excellent," Mycroft answered, again with a peculiar blend of authority and awkwardness. "If you will, then, assemble the others on board and let's be on our way—I should like to be within the precincts of the palace before full daylight."

"Yes, sir." With that the young man was off again; as were we, within seconds.

"They're enthusiastic fellows, but they have an irritating habit of mistaking keenness for efficiency," Mycroft said, as we rumbled back up to full speed. "This business of not using names, for example—it all smacks rather too much of the Continental variety of espionage. Alas, Sherlock . . ." The lamentation seemed genuine, if ever so slightly theatrical. "I envy you. There will always be a place in the world for the consulting detective—but the solitary intelligencer? A threatened breed! After all, if you two, having been asked into this business, cannot be trusted with the very *names* of our cohorts, who can be?"

"So these creatures are *not* yours, Mycroft?" asked Holmes.

His brother shook his head. "You know my methods, Sherlock, as well as I know yours. I labour alone, drawing only those who are already involved or who are for some reason necessary into each endeavour. It is the sole manner in which even a moderate amount of security can be obtained. As for these"—he raised an enormous, gloved hand and indicated the front and then the rear of the train—"they are members of the intelligence arms of the army and navy. But come, Sherlock, you have determined as much already, I'm certain of that."

Holmes inclined his head ever so slightly to acknowledge the correct presumption. "Are they seconded to you, then?"

"They are—and they are not. Until we have resolved the matter, and despite my strong protest, they are ordered to assist—but I have the distinct impression that 'assist,' in this case, includes 'monitor.' Under ordinary circumstances, I should never have permitted such shadowy men the opportunity to observe my methods, or yours—but these are far from ordinary circumstances, as you have already seen."

Holmes nodded once more, saying, "And by 'ordinary circumstances,' in this case, you mean a routine pair of deaths, even a routine pair of murders, involving two royal employees." When Mycroft only cleared his throat uncomfortably in response, Holmes pressed him. "Come now, brother. It is apparent that such a collection as is aboard this train would not be assembled merely to investigate two deaths, just as you yourself have said—nor would a band of Scottish nationalists—or what we were clearly meant to *believe* were Scottish nationalists—have attempted to destroy us in so patently inexpert a manner!" To his brother's puzzled expression, Holmes offered a quick summary of the incident concerning the second bomb, as well as his reasons for having withheld the details of the matter from the intelligence officers, an attitude of instinctive suspicion that Mycroft, we now knew, not only understood but shared. Then Holmes pressed: "And so, perhaps you will tell us, Mycroft. What is it that *actually* brings us all together?"

"I shall tell all I can—but pay close heed, Sherlock. You, too, Dr. Watson." Mycroft produced a hefty flask, filled to brimming with what I would soon find was an excellent brandy. "There is much you need to know, and I believe we just have time for me to reveal all, before we reach Holyroodhouse. . . ."

Chapter V

"You have no doubt made Dr. Watson aware of the extent of my relationship with Her Majesty by now, Sherlock," Mycroft Holmes began. "In fact, I suspect you made him aware of as much even before you left Baker Street."

"An elementary deduction, brother, and unworthy of mention," replied Holmes. "Of course I would have *had* to do so, in order to convince him that your rather melodramatic message did indeed relate to an urgent case."

"Just so." Mycroft trained his penetrating grey eyes and masterful brow—which, like all the other noble features of his face, seemed so very out of place atop his huge, rather corpulent body—on me. "And you, Doctor—*have* you been convinced of as much?"

Before answering Mycroft's question, I glanced uncertainly at Holmes, whose attitude toward the possibility of an other-worldly explanation of the Holyroodhouse murders had, prior to his brother's arrival, become a source of some concern to me. "Well, sir," I replied at length, "of course one does not experience an attempted train bombing *without* becoming convinced that one has fallen into *some* extraordinary business. But as to the matter of an 'urgent case'—I fear my answer must necessarily depend upon which case we are discussing." From the furthest corner of my eye, I thought I detected a shaking movement of Holmes's head and even a patronising smile on his face, although my actual gaze remained fixed upon Mycroft.

"Why, the murders of Sinclair and McKay, of course," replied the elder Holmes simply; and then an expression of comprehension quickly replaced the close scrutiny that had been in his face. "Ah. I perceive that Sherlock has been at work upon you, with fanciful notions concerning the history of Holyroodhouse."

"My dear Mycroft, I do not allow 'fancy' to enter my analyses. I have merely given Watson the background necessary to a full understanding of *any* murder that concerns the palace."

"Indeed? And is it your habit to number local legends among the background points of *every* case you undertake, Sherlock?"

"We have had to weigh the merits of such tales more often than you might think, brother." Holmes sat back in his seat, once more settling into the upturned collar of his coat with an immense air of self-satisfaction. "And when the circumstances of some current crime match those of a legendary one so exactly, it is my experience that the legend is in some way involved."

Mycroft lifted just one of his authoritative brows sceptically. "I hope I have not made an error in enlisting your help, Sherlock—I assure you, this matter shall require as great a seriousness of purpose as you can muster."

Before the conversation degenerated into further fraternal bickering, I thought it best to intervene: "There is one point of fact upon which I remain unclear, gentlemen, and should appreciate clarification." Both men turned to me. "You have each referred to this case as involving *two* murders—yet every newspaper account describes Sir Alistair Sinclair's demise as an accident."

Mycroft Holmes cleared his throat in the uncomfortable manner that was habitual with him during moments of uneasiness, as it is with many similarly phlegmatic characters. "That was *my* doing, I fear, Dr. Watson. And in explaining why I so deceived the press, I can"—he sent another admonishing look his brother's way—"*at last* get to the real business at hand. You read that Sir Alistair fell asleep in some tall grass, and was there run down by an automatic farming implement—correct?"

"Indeed, sir."

"A necessary invention, I fear," said Mycroft.

"Ah!" noised Holmes, smiling and shifting forward in his seat, the better to hear and be heard above the din of the hurtling train. "Now we do *indeed* get at the heart of the thing!"

"Yes, Sherlock." Mycroft, too, seemed quite prepared to let their momentary verbal feud pass. "You have rightly surmised that my own presence in this infernally wild and climatically unpredictable country indicates that something far more serious than a mere pair of murders has taken place. And 'pair of murders' they were, Doctor, for Sir Alistair's body—not long dead, but dead, all the same—was quite deliberately *placed* beneath that piece of farm machinery."

"This interests me particularly, Mycroft," said Holmes. "What was the machine, and what made you select it?"

I was entirely taken aback, and stared in shock at Mycroft. "You, sir!"

"Of course 'him,' Watson," said Holmes impatiently. "He is here, and he has said that the story concerning the accident was a fabrication. Your mind ought to make the immediate connection that it was Mycroft—with the aid of these temporary minions, or of some others that we have yet to meet—who placed the body beneath the machinery, in order to throw the local police completely off the scent."

The statement was riddled with so many extraordinary assumptions that I could only blurt out, "But why? Why should you wish the authorities *not* to know what had happened, if the man was murdered? And why so deliberately extend the deception to the press and the public, by way of the police?"

"Because we needed to deceive the press and the public even *more* than we did the police, Doctor," said Mycroft. "But allow the facts of the matter to explain it—such is almost always the most efficient use of energy. And do take some brandy: These are not easy things of which to speak. Or hear . . ." After first availing himself of its contents, Mycroft Holmes passed his large, leather-skinned flask to me. I took a stiff draft, Holmes refused the same, and then his brother's account began.

"I do not suppose that even you, Sherlock, can know the precise number of times that attempts have been made on the life of Her Majesty during her reign."

Holmes paused, looking up and out the compartment window, as though he had overlooked something; and watching him, I, too, suddenly realised that in fact we had *both* overlooked something quite crucial: a phrase in Mycroft's wire, one that we had passed over almost blithely in order to attend to what we had considered the second and more important half of the statement. Holmes turned to me as he spoke it softly: " 'The sun burns *too* hot. . . .' "

" 'The sky fills with familiar eagles,' " I replied, repeating the section of the phrase that we had already interpreted; but now, with this new subject of the Queen's safety broached, it seemed obvious that the "sun" burning "too hot" implied that Her Majesty was actually *attracting* the "familiar eagles."

Holmes turned to his brother. "I know that there have been several such attempts, at the very least," he said.

"There have in fact been nine," replied Mycroft.

"So many!" said I, in renewed astonishment. "Is it possible?"

"We are fortunate that there have not been more," answered Mycroft. "That is my own opinion, as well as the royal family's. You see, they are a peculiar collection of crimes: All were perpetrated by quite young men—mere youths, really. All used pistols as their weapons of choice; yet in every case save the first and the penultimate, the pistols were charged but loaded only with wadded newsprint."

Holmes's every muscle seemed to grow tense at these words—but he made no move. "That was not mentioned in the accounts given to the newspapers," he said quietly.

Mycroft shook his massive head slowly. "No, Sherlock. It was not."

Holmes's strangely still demeanor at that instant might have confused me, years earlier; but I could now calculate that it was one of his eerie calms, which would shortly be followed by the intellectual and verbal approximation of a breaking tempest. Mycroft seemed also to be anticipating something along these lines: We were both surprised, therefore, when our companion said only, "I suppose that all of them received the punishment of the few that I remember: 'not guilty by reason of insanity,' with either a term in a lunatic asylum or transportation to the colonies as the condition."

Mycroft Holmes nodded. "Again, much to the displeasure of the royal household, particularly when the Prince Consort was still alive. It was only through Albert's influence, following the first incident, that brandishing a deadly weapon in the Queen's direction—regardless of whether that weapon was loaded or did any harm—was made a crime; and even at that, such behaviour was declared only a misdemeanour. The Prince also came close to having that first offender declared sane and convicted of high treason; but the youth had not actually *fired* his pistol—a young Eton lad had subdued him, before he was able to—and so that harsher judgement was perforce set aside, despite the seriousness of the matter. An additional punishment of multiple public canings was eventually added to transportation to the colonies for even those offenders judged mad, to be exercised at the discretion of the jury. But the simple fact was that, because the young men all *appeared* to be so deranged, no decent English jury could ever be made to bring the full force of the law down upon their heads."

The cloudburst was late, but it did arrive: "This really is too much!" Holmes declared, dismissing some invisible judge or jury with a wave of his hand. "Was a firearms expert *never* consulted?"

"Well done, Sherlock," replied his brother. "The essence of the matter, economically stated. Alas, however, no. No such expert was ever called to testify, remarkable as the fact seems."

"But that is an error of a rather unbelievable magnitude," said I—for the "essence of the matter" had not escaped me, either. How many times had I treated wounds inflicted when cap-and-ball weapons were charged with powder, then the powder packed with a bit of wadding—and finally the user, considering the weapon no more than a toy or an instrument of fright, went on to play some prank that resulted in an injury, occasionally a serious one. Indeed, when a full charge of wadded powder is fired from near enough, it can create heat sufficient to inflict serious burns, along with a concussive force that can make a weapon out of air alone. Add any stoutly packed, apparently innocent material—even newsprint— in place of the usual projectile, and one would certainly be in a position to inflict a grim and even fatal wound, particularly if the victim was already weakened by youth, infirmity, or age; and provided, again, that one fired from a close enough distance, as all of these would-be regicides had at least tried to manage. From Jezail ri-

fles in Afghanistan to antiques kept in some of
the great country houses of England—education
concerning the many ways in which firearms can
be deadly has perpetually been among the rarest
forms of human knowledge.

"Most of the youths did not *seem* to understand firearms well enough to know that they
were placing Her Majesty's life in any danger,"
said Mycroft. "Their apparent goal was nothing
more than a sort of perverse notoriety; yet there
were a few among the mix who were not thus afflicted, who seemed quite aware of the seriousness of their actions, but who at the same time
knew with certainty that the police and the press
would consider their weapons 'unloaded.' And,
of course, the juries they faced—never having
been told any other interpretation—arrived at the
same verdict again and again: not guilty by reason of insanity, with a recommendation against
caning and in favour of either hospitalisation
or transportation. And it is here that the matter
takes on a feature of additional interest."

"Indeed, Mycroft," Holmes said. "I believe that
I divine your next statement as clearly as I would
see this train, were I standing miles ahead of it
and upon a flat track." Mycroft Holmes again
looked momentarily annoyed, but Holmes smiled
quickly and moved to mollify him: "How fortunate

that we are on the same side in this matter, brother!" For all their occasional rivalries over petty matters, the two Holmes brothers were as generous in acknowledging each other's achievements in important concerns as any two closely related geniuses could ever, I suspect, be.

"Well, I shouldn't mind being brought out of the dark, sir," I said to Mycroft. But it was Holmes who replied.

"If I am not mistaken, Watson, Mycroft is about to announce that at least one of the would-be assassins, after embarking on his transportation, never reached his port of destination."

Mycroft Holmes nodded slowly. "Yes, Sherlock. I am."

"And yet your presence here," Holmes went on, "as well as our own, indicates that you have been able, perhaps after a period of some time, to discover just where he *did* debark?"

"You are correct again," replied Mycroft. "The youth in question, the worst of the lot, was also the last of them: The incident occurred only six months ago, and we were able to keep it from becoming public knowledge because of the circumstances. It occurred, you see—and I realise that you must find this shocking—within the grounds of Buckingham Palace."

I accepted Mycroft Holmes's flask, which I noticed had grown considerably less weighty since his tale had begun. "But what explanation can there be for such a failure of her own body-guards?"

Mycroft shrugged. "The Queen herself is the explanation, Doctor. For it is the great personal irony of her reign that, although she has survived more attempts on her person than any other oc-cupant of the throne in memory—and perhaps since Elizabeth—she has systematically disman-tled nearly every organisation put in place over a span of generations to guard the royal person. In this, as in all things, she prefers to rely on a few trusted servants: Scots gillies, for the most part, little more than gamekeepers, though some of them have been valiant and exceptional men. The public has learned only a few of their names— John Brown was, of course, the most famous among them—which is just as well, for if it were widely known how vulnerable she truly is. . . . I myself have been persuaded by both the War De-partment and the Admiralty to allow some few men to be detailed to the job of royal security during this crisis, but they are able to fulfill it only because I have insisted that their presence, to say nothing of their names, should be un-known to Her Majesty—and indeed to all others, as you yourselves have experienced.

"The caution is more than an indulgence in elementary secrecy: If the Queen were to discover that these men were about, or were to learn even of such systems of ad hoc intelligence and protection as have been mustered in the last several weeks, she would certainly put a stop to it all. She considers such activities quite beneath the dignity of the British state. And, while I agree with her, as I am sure you both do, a crisis is indeed a crisis, and principles must occasionally be—*temporarily adjusted.* Then, too, the Queen is, as she reminds me during every one of my audiences, related—either by blood or by marriage—to nearly every royal family on the Continent, and communicates with them all regularly. Were any plot to assassinate her that involved more than simply a deluded youth ever put into place, she insists that she would know of it beforehand. I mean no fundamental disrespect, Sherlock, but your presence here, along with Dr. Watson's and that of the intelligence officers, is an indication of how reliable I consider that contention."

Holmes nodded, taking it all in and finally saying, in that somewhat muted, measured tone that in his case passed for tact, "One is tempted to ask, Mycroft, whence the authority and the imperative for these activities *has* come, if not from Her Majesty . . . ?"

Mycroft nodded, as if he had expected the query. "From the next greatest power in the land, and the steadiest head to hold his office since Melbourne."

"Lord Salisbury?" I asked. "The Prime Minister himself?"

"Indeed, Doctor. Although I bend one of our club's rules slightly in revealing as much, I may say that he was himself once a member of the Diogenes, before his great notoriety forced him to resign. You may know of his recreational habits of solitary scientific experimentation—these were much admired at the club. He and I grew acquainted during that time. He summoned me several weeks ago, to inform me of what he had in mind and to request that I coordinate my own efforts with those of the various and anonymous men that he intended to put into place, as well as take overall charge of the operation. The Prince of Wales was with him—apparently he knows and approves of all. Well, faced with such men and such a request—what could I say?"

"Truly," I replied. "And what can we?"

Even Holmes seemed satisfied, at that: He nodded, and smiled once more. "And so, brother— reveal your tale! What *of* this last attacker?"

"His name"—Mycroft drew closer to us, as if there might be prying ears concealed inside the very walls of the compartment—"was Alec Morton, a lad of but twenty. I had hoped that he might not be connected to any larger plots, in which case his identity would be unimportant. But, although I continue to consider him a largely unwitting pawn *within* any such plot, it is no longer possible to rule the plot itself out. For, you see, early in the course of his transportation to South Africa, Morton slipped his guards with the help of certain foreign agents. He left his ship, we assume in the company of said agents, and subsequently disappeared—in the port of Bremen. . . ."

A silent and seemingly long interval followed, before I almost whispered, "The Germans? But surely you don't believe that *they* have been trying to do away with Her Majesty for so many years?"

"Not for 'so many' years, Doctor," said Mycroft. "But so far as the last several years are concerned . . . I cannot state the matter with any certainty. For most of Her Majesty's reign we have been blissfully able to maintain an amiable rivalry, rather than enmity, with Prussia and the various other German states that Chancellor Bismarck incorporated into their Empire. The Queen herself counts as many Germans among her ancestors as Englishmen, a connection that has been made even tighter, as I have mentioned, by those of her children and grandchildren who hold key positions in the German as well as the larger Continental aristocracy. It is not without cause that our monarch is known as 'the grandmother of Europe.'"

"Is not the current German Emperor himself her grandchild?" I asked; but when I looked at both of my companions, I found that, although each had nodded in the affirmative, neither seemed very much relieved by the fact.

"Yes, Her Majesty holds that dubious honour, Doctor," said Mycroft, "and has generally used it to our nation's advantage. This is a queen, after all, who was not too proud, as an ageing widow, to be tutored in statecraft by Disraeli himself, as well as by Bismarck, and to come away ready to follow that wise Prussian's policy for keeping Britain and Germany on good terms—this, despite the fact that she personally loathed the man, every bit as much as she loved Disraeli. As things turned out, however, she had cause to regret the retirement and eventual death of the 'Iron Chancellor'—for, despite her firm belief that she can control the grandchild who now holds uncontested power in the German Empire, facts have often demonstrated that his behaviour lies quite outside the control of *any* fellow human, whether indulgent grandmother, talented statesman—or qualified mental specialist. . . ."

The subject of the Kaiser's mental instability caused Sherlock Holmes to sigh disdainfully. "Would that you overstated the case, Mycroft. But are you now telling us this Alec Morton was in the employ of so deranged a ruler? The Kaiser might well attempt to thus cut the grandmotherly apron-string which, inadequate as it may be, serves as the sole brake on his behaviour."

"The matter is not so blissfully simple," answered Mycroft. "If it were, we should have only to present to Her Majesty our evidence, and within days, Germany would be as isolated and pariah a nation as one could imagine—the Kaiser's friends the Turks might still do business with him, but no one else would dare. No, what I have to tell you is far more confusing, and worrying: We have been unable to turn up any evidence of just who Morton's German friends are. We cannot say with any certainty that he has not acted, and does not continue to act, at the behest of the Kaiser or someone connected with the German imperial circle—nor can we say absolutely that his orders *do* come from that quarter."

Holmes turned round, a rare look of surprise

upon his face as he inquired, "But surely there is more that you *do* know? Why else gather us together in this extraordinary manner?"

Mycroft arched his brows, shifting in his seat uneasily. "Morton comes from a family of skilled labourers—plasterers, in the main—in Glasgow. About eighteen months ago, he began to turn up at the German consulate in that city—we have had discussions with its staff, about which both Her Majesty and the German embassy have been made aware. Morton wished to know what steps he would have had to take in order to make a prolonged journey to Bremen to visit a sickly *grandmother*. There being only one difficulty, as our own consular office in that city has now confirmed."

"Morton *has* no German grandmother?" I hazarded.

"Precisely, Doctor. No German relations of any variety. Yet the Germans themselves, although they must have been aware of this fact, chose not to alert us to the man's misrepresentations."

"Did he visit Germany prior to the attempt on Her Majesty's life?" Holmes enquired.

"If he did, we cannot prove as much. But in the months *since* that attempt, we have learned certain seemingly unconnected yet interesting facts.

About Morton's family, for instance: Various of its members, including his own father and brother, have at one time or another worked as plasterers on labouring teams that were led by none other than Dennis McKay—the man found murdered at Holyroodhouse yesterday. Nor is that all: McKay was known by the police to have been a secret but important official of the Scots Nationalist Party."

" 'Have a taste of what ye gave Denny McKay,' " Holmes said, in an excellent approximation of our assailant's brogue.

"How's that?" Mycroft asked in reply; but he quickly caught his brother's reference. "Ah—a statement from one of the men who attacked the train?" Holmes nodded, and Mycroft declared: "So they *were* nationalists."

"Or," remarked Holmes, "better than average impostors."

Mycroft glanced at his brother. "Would there be any reason that you can think of for such a performance, Sherlock?"

I could see from Holmes's face that he was not without ideas; but he merely shook his head and said, "Mere speculations, brother—and we have enough of those as it is."

"We do indeed. Now, then, gentlemen—I trust you begin to see the true scope of what you have entered into—and why I felt the need to contact you in the manner I did."

"Indeed, sir," said I. "This looks less and less like a murder investigation and more and more like—well, one hardly knows what to call it!"

"One knows," said Holmes quietly. "But one does not like to say. Mycroft—I must put this delicately, but—I should not like to think that *we*, Dr. Watson and I, are to become pawns in some elaborate intrigue—that our talents may be exploited in the cause of ensuring that the public never learns the larger truth of all this?"

The question surprised me: not because it had not crossed my own mind, but only because of the implication that Holmes's own brother would use him in such a way. And yet Mycroft seemed not at all put out—quite the contrary, in fact. "I understand your sentiment, Sherlock," he said simply. "And, were I in your position, I should likely share it. You are on your way into what may be the most recent—to say nothing of the most elaborate—of many plots against our monarch, which is unfolding in a land that has known little other *than* such plots, throughout its history. Intrigue it may well be, but this I promise you—I shall not knowingly allow either of you to become a part of matters that would compromise your integrity." The elder brother offered the younger a fleeting smile. "Your very *unique* sense of integrity. . . ."

Holmes gave his brother a searching look, not yet returning the expression of fraternal friendship. "And your capacity as intimate adviser to Her Majesty . . . ?"

Sinking deeper into his seat, Mycroft suddenly appeared rather discouraged. "There are those in this country today—some of the lesser among them are on this train with us—who believe that, in order to guard our Queen and our country, we must adopt the methods of our rivals and enemies, just as we once did throughout the Empire; that we must be ready to lie, not only to antagonistic tribal leaders in Africa or Asia, nor simply to mendacious Continental agents and powers, but also to our own comrades, if they are not ruthless or zealous enough in pursuing our joint interests. But our reigning monarch has risked her life to demonstrate that this need not be so; to show that the British Empire can behave in a manner that breaks with the vicious traditions of spy rings, secret services, plots, and murders that were established and maintained by royal houses from the Plantagenets to the Stuarts. It may be folly for the queen to think such change possible—but, as I have said, I happen to agree with her. It is for this reason that I have spent my life in the service that I have; and while I may sometimes find it necessary to work in temporary concert with such nameless characters as you have already met, I should greatly prefer it"—again he drew close, unreasonably (it seemed to me) afraid that we might somehow be overheard—"if we three could resolve this matter, to Her Majesty's great satisfaction and the frustration of these agents. Let us, in short, think of them as a sort of 'insurance'—for if we *cannot* frustrate this threat to the Crown, it must nevertheless *be* frustrated. But if we were to manage it first—the Queen herself should regard it with no little satisfaction, as indeed she does your many past services."

But still Holmes kept the same sceptical gaze trained on his brother. "What of your careful exclusion of the police?"

"This is neither a matter for the local authorities nor one for Scotland Yard," replied Mycroft. "You yourself know how unsafe truly sensitive information can be, in their hands. They will pursue their own parochial murder investigations—it is for us to take any other steps that may prove necessary."

A seemingly interminable pause followed; and then, at last, Holmes said, "You have made your case, brother. And I think I can speak for Watson, as well as myself, when I say that you have made it persuasively."

"Indeed you have, sir," said I. "Most honourably."

As Mycroft lowered his head in appreciation of these remarks, Holmes pressed him: "But I fear that there are some few questions that, in my own capacity as the detective you have summoned to consult in these deaths, I must yet ask. To begin with—was Sir Alistair Sinclair *also* something other than what he seemed?"

"Not that I have been able to determine," answered Mycroft certainly. "An architect employed by the Scottish branch of the Office of Royal Works, and a man who specialised in the restoration of historically important structures—particularly late medieval structures. An excellent personal reputation, as well—Sir Alistair's only questionable mark seems to have been his association with McKay, for it creates, among other things, a conduit by way of which he could have known of Alec Morton. But all such ideas are sheer speculation; the truth is, it was perfectly appropriate for a man of Sir Alistair's expertise to have been hired for the work at Holyroodhouse. The Scottish Queen's private chambers are all that survive of the pre-baroque palace, yet they have scarcely been touched since that doomed woman made her final trip to—come now, Sherlock, why do you and Dr. Watson suddenly exchange such meaningful glances?"

Holmes and I—who had, it is true, been exchanging quick looks of recognition—snapped our two heads round. "Ah!" declared Mycroft. "I perceive that indeed you *were* talking of legends and folklore before my arrival!"

"Mycroft, you grow unreasonably suspicious with age and your occupation," Holmes declared, innocently as well as defiantly, his teeth again clenching the stem of his pipe. Then he pulled the thing from his mouth and pointed it at Mycroft. "I stare and I smile only because I can at last *see* how your own unprecedented position within the government has evolved! Rather than send numerous and often unreliable agents abroad to perform arcane tasks, Her Majesty determined to collect her intelligence from one reliable channel, from a man who, like her Scots gillies, she has long known that she can trust absolutely. Your singular talent for making the arcane comprehensible, so amply displayed during this ride with us, has provided her with the regular reports she requires, on this as on so many other occasions— hence the extraordinary informality of your relationship with that august personage!"

It was an example of what theatrical illusionists

call "misdirection" and it succeeded admirably: Despite the ruddiness of Mycroft's skin, I could detect a sudden blush coursing through his features. "You must not assume that the relationship is *too* informal, Sherlock," said he, his voice helplessly proud, "on the basis of a lone meeting that you witnessed only because you entered Her Majesty's receiving room at Windsor unannounced. But on the whole, yes, in matters of intelligence, I have been privileged enough to provide the Queen with what she has both desired and required: a practical counter to the calls that are issued from time to time by various ministries for the return of the old secret service."

"But, Mr. Holmes," I said to Mycroft, "in order for Her Majesty and yourself to actually do away with the old order of intelligence, it seems to me that you should have to *systematise* your approach. What if, God forbid, you yourself should meet with some misfortune? The engine of state would be grieviously, perhaps irreparably, crippled."

"All the more reason for him never to leave his little corner of London, Watson!" Holmes laughed. "And for us to protect him, here in this wild country he speaks of. His arrangements are, you see, perfect—Mycroft's prejudices of habit are reborn as pillars of state security! Do forgive me if I jest, brother. It is only the shock of it—as well as the perfection, as I have said! And why not? It is personal inclination and habit that determines how each of us serves, after all, or *fails* to do so. Look at Watson—the quintessential man of bravery and compassion. These qualities marked him for the frontiers of the Empire, and although a Jezail bullet may have sent him home from those faraway posts, he never fails to venture out with us, revolver in hand, to provide both the force and the succour of which neither you nor I, Mycroft, is capable."

"Thank you, Holmes," I said, trying to contain a feeling of perhaps inordinate self-satisfaction— and having quite forgotten all thoughts of *misdirection.* "That was rather decent of you."

"Not at all, Watson—the simple truth. I, on the other hand, lacking those martial instincts that would make me of use on the outermost lines of imperial defence, perform what tasks I can for the sake of society amid that cesspool we call a capital city, and against the diseases that afflict the organs, rather than the skin, of the state. Why, then, Mycroft, should not the very sedentary habits that nurture *your* refined mental processes, that permit your mind to function with the delicacy by which it is characterised, not be acknowledged for their value to the realm?"

Mycroft placed one hand upon his thigh, then inclined his enormous bulk forward, his grey eyes narrowing slightly as he did: Had Holmes overplayed his role of flatterer? "Forgive me, Sherlock," Mycroft said, "and you, too, Doctor—but I became so accustomed, in our youths, to that streak of sarcasm which my brother often tried to pass off as wit, that I sometimes fail to appreciate his meaning, in adulthood. Certainly those were fine sentiments, and finely expressed." Leaning ever further forward, into a position that was at once confidential and, given his size, slightly menacing, he lifted one finger and narrowed his eyes still further: Obviously he had divined Holmes's game, but did not consider the matter worthy of argument, having more important points to make. "And whether those words were spoken truly or in an attempt to cajole me," he went on, "let me assure you that we shall need to call on every quality, every strength that you have listed, in this matter—upon my soul, I believe it probable. German imperialists may well be behind Morton, and in league with the Scots nationalists, all in an elaborate effort to upset the balance that has kept the central components of our realm together for so very long, and which has also kept the European powers at peace for most of our Queen's reign—for the Kaiser would gladly welcome war, if it meant the ascendancy of his realm and Britain's *Götterdämmerung.*"

"Certainly, nothing could achieve such disastrous ends with greater economy of effort and speed than, God forbid, the harming or actual murder of Her Majesty," I declared, my mood deeply blackened by the turn the conversation had taken.

Holmes, for his part, said nothing to all this (a fact that rather surprised me), while Mycroft nodded, drank one last time from his flask, and then placed it back into the pocket of his cloak. "Indeed," he declared. "And if such characters would not hesitate to threaten Her Majesty, only imagine how quickly *our* three lives would be snuffed out, should we be perceived as in the way. Which brings us to the final piece of information that you will wish to take into account in any theory you may formulate concerning the matter, gentlemen:

"On the days on which both Sinclair's and McKay's deaths took place, Her Majesty was scheduled to pass the night in Edinburgh—at Holyroodhouse itself. And, after attending to a personal matter that is unconnected to our work, she was to review Sinclair's initial plans for the Scottish Queen's old rooms—as well as his choices for a foreman and staff."

Holmes's face had become considerably more excited by this news, but he maintained an air of silent and extreme self-control as Mycroft continued.

"Well, Sherlock? *This* is the crossing point of all these disparate paths and elements, is it not? A seeming set of coincidences—coincidences, those phenomena which, like you, I despise and disclaim, particularly in matters of murder. What says the consulting detective to *that?*"

I am forced to concede that I did not at all discern how this seemingly small matter of royal scheduling could connect to such momentous matters as we had been discussing; but when I looked at Holmes, he was nodding as if he had expected nothing else. He smoked in a measured manner, then rose and took a few steps up and down the compartment. "Just this, brother," he finally announced. "Which tooth, precisely, did Her Majesty have extracted yesterday?"

Chapter VI

HOLYROODHOUSE

Our train did not, thankfully, deposit us on the rainswept outskirts of Edinburgh (a distinct possibility, I had thought, given the apparently overwhelming need for secrecy), but neither did it take us into the convenient (but very public) sheds of Waverley Station at the city's centre. Rather, we ultimately came to a stop within the quieter Prince's Street Station, close by the massive rock formation atop which sat the ancient and ominous silhouette of Edinburgh Castle. Outside the station, we were quickly hurried into a waiting brougham by several of those same nameless, "keen" young men who had been on the train, while the two young fellows from naval and military intelligence, who by now seemed old acquaintances, if not friends, leapt onto the rear of the carriage and perched there as we sped off and away, down side streets in the early dawn mist of the hushed Scottish capital.

That the rain had finally ended was an encouraging fact which I scarcely noticed; for Edinburgh, more than any other city of my acquaintance, is a metropolis of stone—stone buildings built atop stony ground—and even in bright sunshine, it never quite escapes a somewhat solemn and even dour feeling. Given what we had been through on our ride north, however, it did not seem that we could have concluded our journey in any other sort of place or, indeed, in any other mood; and I tried to appreciate, as we sped along in the brougham, that my melancholy feeling was largely a result of recent experience, rather than locale. But mental concentration of this variety requires a certain level of quietude—something that, when in the company of the two Holmes brothers, was rarely in the offing.

Conversation within the vehicle—like that within our train compartment during the last part of our journey—no longer centred on great events and developments in the world, but on how it had been possible for Holmes to determine that the Queen Empress had lately been so troubled by a tooth-ache that she had undergone an extraction just a day before we had heard from Mycroft, as well as on the question of whether or not these facts were of any importance to our work. For his part, Mycroft declared that his brother must have had some prior knowledge of the matter; to which Holmes replied that, while it would likely not have been difficult *for* him to gain such knowledge, being as the entire staff of Balmoral Castle must have been aware of the trip, he had never so much as tried. To Mycroft's continued demands that he explain his correct reading of the situation (the word "guess" was of course never hazarded), Holmes at length explained that the Queen was famous for never leaving the grounds of Balmoral during her yearly holiday, unless affairs of state or some personal emergency demanded that she do so. No official state journeys had been reported publicly; whereas, if there had been a *medical* issue of some kind, any specialist in the world would have (and occasionally had) been brought to her. But the one physical complaint that no one, not even the most powerful among us, can properly attend to without journeying into the dreaded chair of the practitioner is a persistent and painful tooth-ache. That there had been two visits separated by

a comparatively brief time indicated that the dentist in question had prescribed extracting the
troublesome tooth. The first occasion on which he
had declared as much, the Queen had likely refused, preferring to trust to time's curative powers; but the choice had not been a sound one, and
the second visit, caused by sharply increased discomfort, had been for the purpose of having the
wretched offender out.

That Mycroft had been so careful not to name
the specific reason for Her Majesty's presence at
Holyroodhouse on the nights of the murders had
only made Holmes more certain that the matter
was a personal one. There were likely few details
that so meticulous a mind as Mycroft's would
have deemed unimportant to our work, the true
and complete nature of which was, after all, as
yet unknown; and, while intimate aspects of Her
Majesty's health *might* be included in that small
category, they would have to have been of a trivial nature—yet what *trivial* problem could have
brought her on so annoying a pilgrimage, in the
middle of her favourite holiday? In addition,
the loss of teeth, for someone of the Queen's advanced years and high station, might rightly be
considered a potential source of mockery, were it
to become known to the press and public. For all
these reasons, Mycroft had concealed it—and in

so doing, he had unwittingly helped his brother to discover it.

But Holmes did more than simply note the fact of the tooth extraction: He went on to declare, as we wound around the slowly waking heart of Edinburgh and entered one particularly narrow street which would eventually lead to the western edge of the great royal park that surrounded Holyroodhouse, that the fact that the Queen had visited a dentist was of great importance.

"The entire domestic staff at Balmoral," Holmes declared, his concern very evident, "must have quickly discovered not only that the trip was being made, but for what reason—there are few systems of intelligence so effective as the serving staff of an important house. I therefore put it to you, brother, that any analysis of a plot to take her life which either includes or explains the murders of Sinclair and McKay as well—"

"But Holmes," I interrupted, "*can* we so quickly assume that those two murders are even related to each other, much less to a threat against the Queen?"

"Such deadly lightning rarely, if ever, strikes twice in such quick succession, and in precisely the same manner and location, Watson," Holmes replied. "I admire the thoroughness of your scepticism, but this is one basic fact that we may treat as given. And such being the case, Mycroft, we cannot proceed to connect those murders to a plot against the Queen without viewing the entire domestic staff of Balmoral, as well as the dentist himself, as quite possibly involved in the matter."

"The dentist, I will grant you," Mycroft replied (rather testily, it seemed to me), "but the staff at the castle? Impossible. They are all trusted servants, persons devoted to Her Majesty who have vindicated the trust they hold through years of faithful service in a household that, I do not think I need tell either of you, has not been the easiest in which to serve, particularly since the Prince Consort's death."

"My dear Mycroft, you argue *my* point, rather than your own," Holmes volleyed quickly. "Long years of patient service, in certain types of persons, are the fastest route to resentment, rather than loyalty—and this is never more so than when the family being served is royalty. Those who hold their positions 'by the grace of God' are not raised to view their desires as *ever* being unreasonable or capricious; and the rewards of betrayal, in such situations, can be astronomically higher than the usual pilfering of household funds that takes place in the home of, shall we say, some high-handed solicitor."

Mycroft was about to fire back; but he paused, put a gloved finger gently to his pursed lips, and considered the matter, finally nodding slowly. "I do not like your insinuations, Sherlock," he said at length. "But I am not so foolish as to believe them without merit. I presume, then, that you desire a list of all persons who are currently employed at Balmoral?"

Holmes nodded, pulling, to my surprise, a fountain pen and a small notebook from the inner pocket of his jacket. "And I assume that you can provide it to me?"

"Of course," his brother answered.

"From *memory*?" I asked, speaking before I had fully considered the wisdom of it.

"My brother has consigned the secrets of our empire to the grey matter within his skull, Watson," replied Holmes. "I very much doubt that the staff of Balmoral will present any great difficulty. . . ."

And it did not. In fact, although eventually extending into dozens and even scores of names, all that the roster of employees at the Highland castle ever seemed to inspire in the elder Holmes brother was an enormous sense of tedium during its recitation, despite the fact that he accomplished the task even before we had left the urban confines of Edinburgh. This boredom did turn to obvious distaste when, at the conclusion of the exercise, Mycroft finally included the name of the Queen's dentist in the city; but this indignation was nothing to the outright annoyance and even anger that was sparked when his brother conceded—rather quickly and routinely—the probable correctness of Mycroft's arguments *against* the involvement of any royal employees in the recent bloody doings at Holyroodhouse.

"Sherlock!" Mycroft fairly thundered. "Do you think that we have such an abundance of time on our hands that we may fritter it away compiling meaningless lists?"

"Not 'meaningless' at all, Mycroft," Holmes replied, tearing the sheets of paper from his notebook and handing them to his brother. "In fact, it will serve a most useful purpose." He leaned closer to his brother and urged me to do likewise, and then spoke in a conspiratorial tone: "I have asked for this list, and spun my arguments, only so that we will have some plausible business for our 'insurance' agents"—he indicated the rear of the carriage, where the two intelligence officers were riding—"to attend to, while we pursue other, far more likely options. The investigation of the Balmoral staff and the dentist is a task that *must* be completed, Mycroft—it is simply not, I am convinced, the best use of *our* time. We have more primary, and certainly more promising, threads to spin out."

Mycroft fixed a deeply scrutinising stare, crowned by one of his arched brows, upon his brother. "I warn you, Sherlock," he said. "Do not mistake the nature of the situation into which you have entered. Whatever the appearance of these young officers, and however much you may *think* this a routine matter of murder, where state affairs are concerned, human life—even *yours*—loses a considerable percentage of its usual value."

"And do you imagine, Mycroft," said Holmes, his own indignation rising quietly, "that the same cannot be said of the dangers faced when battling the great criminal minds of our time?"

I decided to intervene by diverting rather than wading into the course of their argument. "I understand your concerns, sir," I said to Mycroft, "for your brother is not always the most adroit of men in matters of political complexity." Before Holmes could protest, I added, "But I believe his point here is well taken: I have seen him adopt this diversionary tactic with local police officers and Scotland Yard many times. And, while I will admit that it gives me some pause to consider employing it with regard to officers who—and I know this from my own years of service—are capable of causing enormous difficulties even for

senior military commanders, much less secret investigators such as ourselves, I believe that we
may rely upon the essential soundness of the approach."

"Perverse though it may be?" Mycroft said to
me, drawing back.

"Yes, sir. Perverse though it may be."

Whether or not Mycroft Holmes had been
thoroughly or only temporarily satisfied by his
brother's and my own arguments, I did not
know—nor did time allow me to ascertain as
much; for by now we had passed out of the city
proper and through the elaborate southwestern
gate of the great royal park that surrounded
Holyroodhouse. Looking out the window of the
brougham at the lovely grounds through which
we passed, I could see ahead the first rays of direct sunlight creeping over the gigantic, sloping
hillside known as Arthur's Seat—which was, in
fact, no hill at all, but another of Edinburgh's
massive, pre-historic stone formations, its surface
disguised by a thin layer of soil and grass. The
name matched the deceptiveness of the spot's appearance: The place was unconnected to the legendary king of the same name, but its title was
another example of the Scots' seemingly endless
desire to relate themselves to all persons and developments of romance and importance in the

British Isles. (Indeed, to hear the tales told in the pubs of Edinburgh and Glasgow, as well as their country counterparts, there is little of value in the entire history of the British Empire that does not hinge in some way on the participation of some Scottish laird, regiment, or man of genius—a claim that, to be fair, is not as outlandish as many Englishmen would have the world believe.)

As dawn moved quickly on towards morning, we kept up a quick pace around the curving drive along the western edge of Holyrood Park. Mycroft began to tell us just who we should meet during our stay at the palace—for, he was clear in saying, we *would* be staying at the palace itself, both as a mark of appreciation from Her Majesty and to keep gossip within the comparatively small city to a minimum, once the rumour that Sherlock Holmes had arrived to investigate the already-celebrated deaths was released into the city through the same system that had made common knowledge of the royal tooth extraction: household gossip. Few members of the palace's staff, said Mycroft, had exhibited behaviour that could, in his opinion, be fairly called suspicious, since the time of the first murder; but those few would have to be investigated, along with any others that we ultimately deemed worthy of attention.

From this and other directives, I was given the impression that Holmes and I would not only be guests at Holyroodhouse, but that we would have virtual run of the place—a thought that almost redeemed the train journey we had endured, to my way of thinking. But not, apparently, to Holmes's: He listened soberly as his brother rattled off the names and essential character traits of palace staff members, engraving each upon his cortex and clearly exercising his own talent for the mental organisation and systematisation of disparate information, which if it was not as powerful as Mycroft's, was nevertheless extraordinary.

And yet, as I listened to the siblings go through this rigorous mental exercise, a question began to form in my mind, one that grew steadily more pointed as we continued along the drive to the palace: Why was Holmes taking such an interest in stories concerning the servants of Holyroodhouse, when he had so readily dismissed the notion of any of the staff at Balmoral being involved in any plot against Her Majesty? The obvious answer was, of course, that Holyroodhouse had been where the crimes had taken place (or at least, it was where the bodies had been discovered). But the fact remained that, in an average year, the Queen spent no more than a few nights at the Edinburgh palace: hardly enough time for members of the household staff to develop murderous fixations, whereas the servants of Balmoral endured many weeks' worth of royal whims every year. And the trip from Aberdeenshire to the capital would not have been a difficult one for any young, fit malcontent—thus, I conjectured, the two sets of staff members must surely be considered as, at the very least, equally worthy or undeserving of suspicion; but not, apparently, to Holmes.

The puzzle had no answer that I could see, and that was not a fact calculated to ease my anxieties about Holmes's behaviour. The same doubts and questions about his state of mind that had first troubled me at Baker Street and gone on to be deepened by his often-inexplicable talk and behaviour on the train had been displaced, for a time, by conversation with the eminently reasonable Mycroft; but here in the carriage, in the midst of Holmes's uncharacteristically inconsistent analyses of the possible roles played by royal servants in the murders, they made their presence felt again, and were indeed worsened by the fact that I felt unable to put them to Holmes in the presence of his brother, out of consideration for my friend's reputation as a rational thinker.

But did he *truly* believe that all normal investigative procedures were to be discarded, because

the disembodied spirit of a man horribly butch-
ered three centuries earlier had played a key part
in the murders of Sinclair and McKay? He had
said he believed there to be a "spiritual" connection between the various dark deeds—had he actually meant to assert that the recent deaths were
the work of some bloodthirsty, vengeful *ghost*?

Such queries were bizarre enough; yet new
considerations of the same stripe soon arose. By
the time we reached the point along the lightly
wooded park drive at which the palace of Holyrood first became visible, Mycroft had drawn us
into a conversation that was perhaps even more
macabre than anything I had yet heard:

"The royal prerogative," he announced in a
businesslike, sombre tone, "can be made to over-
rule all questions of local authority and proce-
dure in these cases, so long as it is does not give
the appearance of actually obstructing justice.
Such being the case, I have asked for and received permission to keep the body of McKay on
the premises of the palace until you both have
had a chance to study it. There is an old ice
chamber in one of the cellars, and I have had it
stored there. In all important respects, it may be
taken as representative of the condition of Sir
Alistair's remains, as well. The wounds are nearly
identical—certainly, just as grievous and mortal.

Indeed, there seems to me only one important difference, overall, between the two crimes: Sir Alistair's body was originally found, by a chambermaid, in the room where he had been staying—guest chambers in one of the newer sections of the palace, 'newer,' of course, merely connoting those wings built in the seventeenth century. The remains of Dennis McKay, however, were discovered on the lawns behind the palace and among the old abbey ruins. Though in plain view from the Queen's bedchamber, it was far from any windows or doors, and there is no question of its having been thrown there from within the building—even had the killers ejected it from the upper dormers of the servants' quarters, it would have fallen well short of its actual position. Thus it stands to reason that it was placed there during the night, perhaps with the intention of provoking in Her Majesty a severe—indeed, at her age, a perhaps fatal—shock, should she have glimpsed it before any of the staff discovered the thing in the morning." Mycroft leaned in close, once more assuming his most confidential manner: "And it is for this reason, Sherlock, that I believe some one or more members of the staff to have been involved. For all gates to the royal park are chained and locked at sunset, when Her Majesty is in residence, and the inner fence of the palace's immediate grounds—ten feet of wrought and spear-tipped iron, as you can see from here—is watched carefully throughout the night."

"Who keeps the keys to the inner fence's gates?" asked Holmes.

"There are three sets of keys—one is kept by Lord Francis Hamilton, the resident member of the family that has been charged, for better than two centuries, with the stewardship of the palace. The old duke keeps to their far more expansive and luxurious manor outside town, and appears only when the Queen summons him. The butler, Hackett, has one of the remaining sets of keys, as does the park gillie, Robert, who is another of Her Majesty's favourites. It is he who selects the most trustworthy men to—ah!" Mycroft suddenly abandoned all discussion of bodies, killings, and keys, as we entered the palace forecourt and he became aware of someone moving across the yellow-white gravel towards our carriage. "Here is Lord Francis, to greet us. . . ."

The Hamilton clan (Lord Francis was the third son of the current duke) had first been entrusted with the care of Holyroodhouse by the ill-fated Charles I, son of the same James—the Sixth of Scotland and First of England—who had once been the precious child that lay hidden within the

womb of Queen Mary as she watched her faithful servant David Rizzio dragged from her side
to be murdered. That Charles I had met the same
end as his grandmother Mary (beheaded following a long struggle, Mary's against an English
queen, Charles's against an English parliament)
was a coincidence that had never occurred to me,
before the moment that we stepped from the
brougham and I had my first detailed look at the
edifice of Holyroodhouse. The fact that it occurred
to me at all at such a time may strike some as in-
congruous: Why think of severed heads when
getting your first close look at a lovely royal residence, one made all the more appealing by the
contrast between its grand style and its intimate
scope?

I can only confess, in my own defence, that the
baroque opulence that was the "new" palace
(those wings executed by Charles's son, the Second of the same name) proved powerless against
my anxiety, for no greater or lesser reason than
that I became overwhelmed by a strange pull,
one that I soon realised was being exercised upon
my spirit by the pitted fifteenth-century turrets
of the palace's western tower: the wing in which
the unfortunate Rizzio had been shredded by
noblemen's daggers, and which was now the only

part of Holyroodhouse that seemed utterly devoid of life, light, or activity.

"I see you know your history, Dr. Watson,"
said the fair-haired, clean-shaven Lord Francis,
in a pleasant, indeed a sympathetic, tone. He had
caught me staring to my left, at the heavily shut-
tered windows of the infamous turrets. "The west
tower," the fellow went on, in mock but good-
natured apprehension. "Queen Mary's chambers!
It's interesting, is it not, that when her great-
grandson rebuilt the rest of the palace, he tried to
balance the façade by creating an identical tower
on the eastern end—and yet *its* turrets have none
of the same sinister effect."

"You refer to the effect of bloodshed, Lord
Francis," Holmes declared; and it seemed to me
that his tone was rather deliberately provocative.
"As Dr. Watson can tell you, it marks a structure
for all time."

"As do repeated waves of conquering armies,
Mr. Holmes," Lord Francis replied gamely, looking Holmes full in the eye as he did so and making me instantly like the fellow. "Most of those
'marks' of which you speak were the result of
Roundhead musket-balls—for Cromwell himself was only one of your countrymen whom we
have entertained, over the centuries." Perhaps
worried that he might be alienating the famous

detective, Lord Francis quickly assumed a rather more serious and conciliatory air. "And yet, yours is an interesting thought, Mr. Holmes; interesting, and doubtless true—for the rest of the palace, as you shall see, is quite free of the oppressive atmosphere of the west tower."

Holmes looked at the man quizzically, then glanced at Mycroft. "But surely I have heard that the old tower is closed to outsiders, my lord? And has been these three centuries?"

Lord Francis laughed off Holmes's probing remark. "Oh, you shall not be outsiders here, Mr. Holmes! Her Majesty will not have it, and I certainly have no desire to contest with her, on that score—there is so very much I wish to discuss with you!"

Mycroft Holmes—seeming as disconcerted as was I by his brother's renewed interest in the murderous events that had made the west tower famous, and desirous of restoring a businesslike tone to the conversation—rushed in to say, "Lord Francis will forgive your rather *too* quickly delving into an unfortunate episode in the history of his home, Sherlock, I am sure. And now—shall we go in and give these gentlemen some sustenance, my lord? And then, some rest— they have had rather an exhausting journey, I fear."

"But of course you are correct," said our host. "Do forgive me—Andrew! Hackett!"

From just outside the Doric revival entryway to the palace and its central courtyard appeared two strapping men, one about twenty, the other in his middle years, though no less powerful for it. A strong similarity of features suggested an immediate family relationship, a suggestion soon confirmed by Lord Francis: The young footman called Andrew was indeed the son of the older man, Hackett, who (as Mycroft had mentioned in the carriage) was the palace's butler. Because of what Lord Francis referred to as "the recent misfortunes," however, most of the rest of the palace's staff had apparently been given temporary leave, and a "skeleton crew" was all that would be available to serve us—a fact that I found not only bizarre but unacceptable, and about which I assumed Holmes would lodge an extreme objection: He might be able to argue the irrelevance of the Balmoral staff, but he had already and rightly concerned himself with the staff at the murder scene itself. And yet, not for the first time that morning, his reaction was at shocking variance with what I would have expected: In fact, when Mycroft Holmes was forced to point out the potential difficulties involved in allowing so many possible witnesses (he did not say "and accomplices," although the words certainly hung on the air) to have left the scene of two hideous crimes, Holmes immediately rushed in to assure a rather contrite Lord Francis that he was certain no serious harm had been done.

"I assume you have kept your most trusted staff here with you?" Holmes asked, rather more pleasantly than I would have thought possible, or even necessary, at that instant.

"Yes, Mr. Holmes," answered Lord Francis, embarrassed. "The most senior staff, only—but I assure you, if you find that you require anyone to be recalled—"

Again Holmes assured him that he was sure such measures would not be necessary—and as he did so he looked to me, clearly requesting agreement. I played the role, stating that Lord Francis's minimal staff would be more than adequate to meet our needs, and that Holmes and I were grateful for whatever hospitality he, to say nothing of Her Majesty, might be gracious enough to extend during the term of our work.

But the rather petulant, even resentful attitudes of both Hackett and his footman son as they took our meagre baggage made me wonder if such hospitality would indeed be forthcoming, and whether or not gratitude would be the ultimate feeling we would take away from our stay.

An examination of Hackett's features deepened
this impression: They were weathered, rugged,
and altogether unsympathetic, while the hair
was longer than would have been expected for a
man in such a position; the black beard, meanwhile, was kept close-cropped, and did much to
augment a rather ominous impression. But the
feature that most gave one pause was Hackett's
left eye, which was in fact no eye at all, but a glass
approximation of the same. This alone might not
have been cause for alarm, despite the four very
pronounced scars that ran away from the socket,
one below and three above; but the eye had apparently been poorly fitted, for when Hackett
scowled to excess, the pressure of his descending
brow often dislodged the glass sphere, which the
butler invariably snatched with his hand before it
reached the ground. At such moments, the badly
mauled flesh and exposed bone of the socket itself were revealed: a truly ghastly sight.

The first time this occurred, Hackett was just
bending over to retrieve my rod case, which his
son had dropped. Being quite close by, I was able
to observe the deft manner in which the butler
plucked the falling eye from the air, quickly re-
inserted it, and then stood, all without drawing
attention to himself. On seeing that I alone had
witnessed the process, Hackett darkened consid-

erably, and he said, quietly but with the bitterness peculiar to certain strains of Celtic blood:

"Your pardon, sir—I hope the gentleman was no' *repulsed*."

It might have seemed an extraordinarily odd comment, had it not matched the general impression of the fellow that I had already formed. As our little procession moved to the palace entryway, I brought up the rear, now wholly uneasy: I could see no beauty at all around me, and noticed, rather, how much mist the rain had left behind, how very foreboding it made the landscape, and even how blackened by coal dust the large and rather beautifully designed fountain in the front courtyard had become. Small wonder, then, that, by the time I was about to enter the palace, I was forcing my head and eyes not to turn left, to prevent my taking one last look at the windows of the moribund west tower: I had very nearly become convinced that if I did, I would see there some other-worldly face, silently but desperately pleading for assistance, for salvation, for justice. . . .

And yet, how my mood was transformed by the world into which I next stepped!

The palace's square central court, and the cloister that encircled it, had Charles II's cheerful (if sometimes excessive) hedonism in their every inch, helped along, that morning, by a sudden burst of Scottish sunlight: crisp in its tones, warming in its unobstructed plentitude. Lord Francis Hamilton kept up a steady monologue concerning the building of the palace's baroque wings, and after a few minutes I even began to make sense of some of it, and to think that our stay in this place might prove a not altogether unpleasant experience, after all. We quickly entered the Great Stair, with its massively figured plasterwork ceiling, stone balusters, and charming Italian frescoes, the latter purchased for their present home some forty years earlier by the late Prince Consort—our Queen's beloved Albert himself. By the time we were approaching the relatively small but elegant dining-room on the main floor, my spirits had, thankfully, been quite lifted: an effect only compounded when we entered the room to find that a hearty Scots breakfast had been laid on for us by Hackett's wife, a woman whose temperament was nothing like her husband's, although she nonetheless exhibited the sort of nervous strain that living with such a man almost invariably imparts. This last manifested itself, chiefly, in a rather too quick tendency towards loud and unwarranted laughter; but the woman cut a healthy figure, and despite her highly-strung air I found myself responding to her rather desperate attempts at conversation readily, being as I was myself starving for the company and conversation of someone who was not preoccupied with death.

But the conclusion of breakfast also brought the end of these pleasantries, such as they were: for, much as Mycroft Holmes kindly recognised my own need for rest (his brother, he knew, had no such requirement), he made it plain that we must venture into the palace cellars before further refreshing ourselves. Apparently he was expected to return to Balmoral and personally report to the Queen on our arrival and our initial impressions. Such being the case, we rose from the table, stomachs (or *my* stomach, at any rate) glowing with the warmth of hot oatmeal, fresh eggs, puddings black and white, warmed tomatoes, fine-ground haggis, Yorkshire and Lowland tea blends, as well as a dozen other early morning delights that had changed very little since Queen Mary's time; and, behind the gloomy, powerful figure of Hackett, who dangled a great iron ring of keys from one hand (while he held the other, or so it seemed to me, at the ready, in the event that his glass eye should again attempt liberation from the distasteful duty of serving in his unpleasant face), we prepared to return to the Great Stair, there to descend back into the world of violent death.

"I shall allow Hackett to guide you, gentlemen, if you do not mind," Lord Francis said as we reached the Great Stair. "There is, as you may expect, much business to be attended to, with all this unpleasantness, and my father is quite anxious that I, as the presumably dissipated third son, should prove myself worthy by attending to it." A good-natured laugh followed this statement, again making me admire the fellow for taking the difficulties of his position so lightly. As he turned to leave us, however, his face became rather more serious.

"Oh—but I must ask one thing—" Lord Francis's face screwed up with embarrassment and discomfort. "I *do* realise that we have asked for your help, and that you have every right to feel personally secure, but—well, this *is* a royal residence. And, Doctor, I could not help but notice that rather menacing service revolver that you carry beneath your jacket—I fear that bearing arms within the palace is quite forbidden."

Amid mutual protestations—of regret and understanding from myself, of further mortification from our host—I relinquished my Webley revolver to him; and, after assuring me that I should have it back upon departure, he disappeared down the hall towards the royal apartments. It was not until the rest of us were in the Great Stair, led by the disconcerting sound of Hackett's ancient ring of keys, that Holmes murmured to me:

"A pity to lose Mr. Webley, eh, Watson? But we may still read our palms for protection. . . ." Suddenly remembering the gangster's device that was resting snugly in my pocket, I thought for an instant of turning around and running to catch Lord Francis, in order to surrender it, too; but Mycroft Holmes stopped me.

"Now, now, Doctor," he said. "After all, I'm sure that if the Metropolitan Police do not recognise the device as a legitimate firearm, then the royal family can have no objection to your retaining it on your person. . . ." He gave me a significant look, and said, in an even lower voice, "at *all* times. . . ."

Chapter VII

POIGNARDER À L'ÉCOSSAIS

Dennis McKay's body had indeed been placed in what Mycroft Holmes had referred to as "an old ice chamber in one of the cellars"; what I had not counted on was how very relative the term "old" might be. Hackett informed us that the walls of the chilly space had originally been chiselled out of bare, naturally occurring stone that, over the centuries, had been patched with everything from bricks to granite blocks, all of which were held in place by great, crumbling dollops of concrete. Underground springs (although it was difficult to say just how far "underground" we were, given the several irregular and unconnected staircases we had been forced to navigate to reach the spot) ran down the bare stone in a few spots, the icy liquid disappearing into the earthen floor of the chamber. My uneasiness at being in this latter-day catacomb—likely once a dungeon— along with the additional drop in body temperature that accompanied a stomach full of hot food, no doubt made the place seem colder than it was, as did the arrival, within minutes of our own, of a quartet of our friends from the train journey. But the great clouds of mist that emerged from all of our mouths and nostrils told me that my impression of significant chilliness was not simply a reflection of my mood.

On a great block of what I at first took to be stone, but which was in fact ice, lay the shrouded remains of the unfortunate McKay. The near-bloodless bed-sheet used to wrap him after the discovery of the body mercifully obscured the depth and severity of his wounds, which we would discover only after we had uncovered the body—a task that would require no little assistance, so tightly was the bed-sheet wound about it.

"Mr. Holmes," said I to Mycroft, "perhaps some of your men could hold the body up, so that I can loosen the covering . . . ?"

"Of course, Doctor." Mycroft Holmes needed

only to glance at the various members of military
and naval intelligence who stood in the shadowy
corners of the room (the pair we had met earlier
were not present) in order for them to snap to it.
The fellows took the body by its shoulders and
feet and lifted it from the block of ice in an almost effortless manner: These clearly were not
men to underestimate in a tight spot. As McKay's
midsection cleared the ice, I began to uncoil the
close-spun linen wrapping—

And then I took note of something: something
about the manner in which McKay's body was
drooping above the ice, suspended between the
powerful grips of the young officers. At first I felt
it necessary to make a more concerted effort to
focus my eyes, believing the sight to be nothing
more than the cumulative effects of Mycroft
Holmes's brandy, a lack of sleep, and the afore-
mentioned rush of blood away from my brain
and to my stomach. But a second look revealed
the same curious, indeed stunning, image—
although nothing drove home its reality as much
as a quick glance at my old friend.

Holmes had retreated into his own shadowy
corner of the room before the men lifted the body,
in order to put a match to a cigarette; and, by the
glow of the small ember before his mouth, I could
see that his piercing eyes had been so electrified

by the sight of McKay's suspended body that they seemed to have transcended mere man-made current, and to have entered a state of natural phosphorescence, like some eerie deep-sea creature. Both alarm and excitement filled his features, the latter making itself apparent in a smile that was more than the usual wry curl of his mouth: It was the delight of beholding some aspect of a crime that was altogether different, altogether *new*. Nor did I wonder at his feeling so:

From shoulder to toe, McKay's body was utterly flaccid. In saying this, I do not mean to imply the usual limpness of post-rigor death; no, the lack of any sort of structural integrity in his body—even the arms and legs, which either hung or drooped in so sickeningly slack a manner that his clothing might have been stuffed with meal, rather than flesh and bone—implied things about his death that went quite beyond even the terrible facts that we already knew, and beyond even the contorted expression of agony that dominated what must once have been his handsome Scots features.

I hurried to get the body free of the sheet, and then the four officers lowered his form back onto the ice carefully. (Certainly, none of the four was a veteran of the battlefield, I now realised—for had they been, they would have recognised the extreme irregularity of what both Holmes and I had noted in such amazement.) Once the pitiful remains were back on that frozen surface, I made a great show of inspecting its two- or three-score puncture wounds—some ragged, some star-patterned, still others clean at the point of entry, but all hideous in their depth, their violence, and the amount of internal damage they had caused—as I waited for Holmes to speak.

He did—and quickly. "Brother," he called out, with painfully enforced nonchalance, "I wonder if your men might not be better used patrolling the grounds around the palace. Being as so many members of the staff have been released, and given that it now seems entirely possible that our antagonists possess"—Holmes looked directly at Hackett, who I now noticed was taking rather too much interest in our business—"a key or keys to various of the palace locks."

Mycroft detected the ploy immediately, and dispatched the officers on the errand Holmes had suggested; Hackett, however, showed no inclination to leave of his own accord. "We must not keep you, either, Hackett," said Mycroft. "Once these gentlemen begin an examination, there can be no telling how long it might take, and you must have many duties devolving upon your shoulders, just now."

"Aye," said Hackett in a low rumble. "But it's no trouble, sir—"

"No, no," said Mycroft quickly. "I insist, Hackett. We shall tell you when the body is ready to be transported to the police."

Hackett finally did leave the room; but before I could give voice to any of my extraordinary thoughts, Holmes had dashed to the doorway, opened it a crack, and assured himself that the butler was actually leaving the area. Given this interval, I returned to my ad hoc post-mortem, quickly examining not the wounds to, but the frame of, McKay's body, and just as quickly finding what I was looking for.

"It's incredible," I whispered.

This brought Holmes to my side. "Then it's true, Watson?"

"*What* is true?" questioned Mycroft. "Sherlock, now that I have performed this little charade, would you mind—"

"It's McKay, sir," said I. "His skeletal structure—you saw how the body drooped when the men lifted it?"

"Yes," Mycroft answered. "But I thought that was natural—"

"Natural for an earthworm, brother!" said Holmes. "Or some other invertebrate. Most uncharacteristic for a man, however. . . ."

Mycroft became impatient. "No riddles, now—what *do* you two mean?"

"The body," I said. "There is scarcely a bone in it, and none of any structural importance, that has not been broken in at *least* one place. Some, indeed, have been utterly shattered. And yet, look here, sir—" I pulled one eerily formless arm free of its sleeve. "Notice the lack of bruising—here and here, where the fractures are compounded. That indicates—"

"That McKay was already dead when the bones were broken," Holmes finished for me.

Mycroft's face became a picture of alarmed confusion. "But—the stabbing wounds. They cannot help but have been fatal."

"Certainly," answered Holmes.

"Then why?" Mycroft asked in amazement. "It cannot have been torture, if the man was dead—"

"No. Nevertheless—a day or so after he died—something happened. Some terrible event, capable of simultaneously smashing dozens of bones in the same instant."

"How can you say that it was 'a day or so' after his death?" Mycroft's voice retained an element of involuntary disbelief.

"Watson?"

"The number of breaks, Mr. Holmes, along with the lack of blood on the bed-sheet," said I.

"Had the body not yet entered rigor mortis, it *would* have been flexible enough for the injuries to have occurred together, but blood would have seeped onto the sheet."

"Perhaps they wrapped the body in the thing later?"

"No, sir—look here, where this compound fracture corresponds to a tear in not only his clothing but the linen as well. He was wrapped in the sheet after the blood had ceased to flow, but before the rest of the damage was done— had the body still been in rigor, its own rigidity would have prevented such a plethora of ob- scure fractures. For it to have regained the flex- ibility to allow all this to happen at once . . . at least twenty-four hours."

Mycroft Holmes was not a man who often looked baffled, but this was one such occasion. "But what could possibly . . . ?" he asked slowly. "What could possibly manage such damage, and so speedily? And *why*, in Heaven's name? The man had already been killed, by no less than— what would you say, Dr. Watson? Some fifty wounds?"

"At the very least, sir," I replied. "But as to how it all took place. . . . The puncture wounds are, of course, simple enough to explain—several long and fairly stout blades—note the variation among

the types of skin punctures—although why so
many more thrusts than necessary, I cannot tell
you. For the rest—not even the imaginary farming
implement that you used to explain Sir Alistair's
death, I suspect, could have achieved it."

"Incidentally, Mycroft," said Holmes, "what
was that 'implement'?"

"I'm dashed if I know," Mycroft replied. "Some
sort of aerating device, or so Robert, the gillie,
informed me. The ground beneath the greenery
on much of the palace grounds is nearly as hard
as rock—characteristically so, for the environs of
this city. It must be aerated regularly, to maintain
the health of the grass."

"The ruse was not a bad one, sir," said I, "in-so-
far as the obvious aspects of such wounds are
concerned. It's a pity that suspicions and fears
had been so roused by all the other coincidental
aspects of the two crimes that you were prevented
from using it again."

"That is not the pressing issue now, I fear, Doctor," Mycroft replied. "We must be able to explain
the actual cause of this new and extraordinary
fact, if we are to go on to explain the crime. Have
you no theories at all?"

I puzzled with the question. "What is remarkable is that we find no marks on the skin to sug-

gest an implement—even on a corpse, the head
of a hammer should leave some imprint, or the
wood of a cudgel some splintering or abrasion;
and yet—nothing. I *have* seen some such damage
to the skeletal structure in my career—but only
as the result, for example, of the concussive power
of an artillery burst. A fall, too, might explain
it—but the *height* involved. . . . It is simply incredible. A building several times the height of this
palace would not provide enough velocity to
achieve—*this*. . . ."

Holmes had begun to pace about the cool,
dark chamber, a solitary stream of smoke trail-
ing behind him. After a few minutes he murmured several words, and both Mycroft and I
listened closely—but he seemed only to be repeating what I had said:

"Artillery . . . height . . ." A moment more, and
then he suddenly spun round. "And the wounds,
Watson—what of those?"

I sighed once in admitted discouragement,
and looked down at McKay's now-exposed neck
and chest. "Certainly, the stabbing was terrible—
lacking a dozen men's involvement, it could not
have been quick."

The wisp of Holmes's smoke had grown into
steadily larger clouds. "And yet the fractures, it

seems, *must* have been so. . . ." He turned, and pointed what remained of the cigarette at Mycroft and myself. "That is significant—for it opens entire new fields of possibility. . . ."

Mycroft Holmes studied his brother with great concern. "Sherlock—I am not easy, in this. The purpose behind your involvement—both of you— was to bring the business to a speedier and a quieter ending, not to make it more complex. How am I meant to report all this at Balmoral? The Queen is anxious enough."

"You must *not* report it," Holmes replied simply. "Not unless you wish this issue to involve us all for far longer than it need do. We have been given one additional question to answer, along with the rest. That is all—you cannot afford to view it any other way, brother. Make your report, and make it optimistically—and above all, tell none of those 'keen young men' that surround you about any of it. If I understand this business correctly, Watson and I shall need a free hand here in Edinburgh tonight. Keep the attention of everyone else focused on Balmoral—in fact, you would do us no small service if you took Lord Francis with you. Return tomorrow evening—we shall doubtless need you by then—along with the young lord."

Mycroft studied his brother sceptically. "You

really believe that the matter can be resolved so quickly, Sherlock? Even with this new riddle?"

"It is remarkable, gentlemen," answered Holmes, "how often clues are mistaken for riddles—and vice versa. Yes, Mycroft, so long as you and Dr. Watson are willing to entertain *any* solution, then we can resolve it speedily. After all, we must remember the first rule of investigation—"

"Yes, yes," Mycroft interrupted impatiently. " 'The impossible, the improbable, and the true'— we are hardly likely to have forgotten it." His enormous frame seeming to become ever more of a burden to him, Mycoft began to move towards the door. "Very well, then—if you say that it can be done, then I must believe you. I have enough to take care of, as it is. I shall collect those young men, and make for Balmoral. As to Lord Francis—I shall do my best, invoking the call of royal service. But be warned, Sherlock—I have promised the police that they will be able to release McKay's body to his family today. We have detained it long enough."

"Indeed we have," Holmes answered. "They may come now, for all that it matters."

Opening the door into the dark hallway, Mycroft Holmes summoned Hackett with a single, authoritative bark that drained his energies still further. "I will be back tomorrow evening, then,

gentlemen—and I will expect progress. Hackett!"
he snapped again. "Ah, there you are." As the
shadowy figure of the butler became visible in
the doorway, I could see Mycroft's eyes narrow.
"Rather close at hand, Hackett, were you not?"

"Nay, sir," replied Hackett—a trifle uneasily, it
seemed to me. "But I know these old stairs well
enough, by now—"

"I've no doubt of it," Mycroft said quickly, still
dubious about the butler's behaviour, but un-
prepared to pursue the matter at that moment.
"Now, then—have a carriage brought round.
Mrs. Hackett has turned down these men's beds?"

"Aye, sir, and warmed them," came the response.

"Good." Then, to us, Mycroft added: "Several
hours' rest, both of you—no more, no less. You
shall need to be at the top of your form."

As his brother departed, Holmes returned to
the block of ice. Studying the body upon it, he finally shook his head and roused himself. "Come,
Watson—do let's cover this poor devil again."

Taking up the bed-sheet, I spread it out over the
corpse; and for the first time, I allowed myself to
more closely study McKay's bruised, tormented
features. "A truly terrible end," I said. "And yet he
did not have the appearance of a sinister man."

"Nor was he one—on that I would stake the whole of my reputation," replied Holmes.

It seemed somehow incredible. "But he appears, at the very least, to have led a double existence. And manner of death often tells us as much about a man as do appearances, Holmes."

"Indeed. But if you are reading evil into these wounds, rather than into those who inflicted them, I fear your imagination exceeds your judgment. Remember—*poignarder à l'écossais:* 'stabbed in the Scottish mode.' Not 'executed,' but 'stabbed'—the onus is, as it should be, entirely on the perpetrator of the deed." Holmes glanced up and down the shrouded corpse. "In the unlikely event that there was only one. . . . However—let us get up to our rooms, Watson. You must be exhausted." For his part, Holmes looked as though he had slept a full night through during the time we had been below-ground: an effect that was not unusual when he came into contact with concrete evidence relating to a crime.

"I am indeed," I replied as we made for the first of the cramped, darkened stairways. "And relieved, as well."

"Relieved?"

"Yes. I haven't heard you speak of ghosts and legends since we arrived."

Holmes laughed once. "A temporary respite, I assure you, Watson! For the time being, we have more than enough *facts* to consider—but rest assured, we shall return to other-worldly characters soon enough. Or perhaps it is *they* who will find their way to us. . . ."

∞

Chapter VIII

THE MYSTERY OF THE WEST TOWER

I cannot say that I was altogether surprised to discover, when I awoke later that day in one of the palace's charming, oak-panelled bedrooms, that the sun was near setting. Mycroft's admonition that we not waste too much time with sleep would, I knew, be ignored by his brother, who would choose to get no rest at all, while allowing me to get perhaps more than I should. The decision, I confess, was a wise one, for if I was slightly confused as to the precise time of day and just where I was, upon rising, my mind was not otherwise impaired: Certainly, it was alert enough that I could take fully in my stride the sight of

Holmes perched in the sill of one of the room's tall windows, dressed just as I had left him, and still smoking as he looked out over the lovely, haunting ruins of the old abbey.

"Holmes," said I, swinging my feet out of the enormous, canopied bed and onto the floor. "What's the time?"

"The time," he replied cheerfully, still gazing outside, "is less important than the hour. . . ."

"Are you attempting humour, or mere obtuseness?"

"Come now, Watson—you mustn't discourage my efforts to be lighthearted! I was merely referring to the fact that it will be dark soon. And with the dark shall come"—his voice became theatrical as he turned to me—"those things that *love* the dark. . . ."

I was in no mood for such badinage. "With the dark shall come dinner, I hope," I said, standing. "I'm rather famished."

"I assumed as much," Holmes said. "I had Mrs. Hackett bring you a plate of sandwiches—there—along with a pot of strong tea."

"That was good of you," I said, hurrying to my little repast.

"I thought it best that you not eat *too* heavily," Holmes said, joining me, but only for a cup of the tea. "We may see or hear things tonight that you will find singularly unsettling. Indeed, I have already heard some of them myself."

"As I suspected, then, you've had no sleep. And where have your restless wanderings taken you? Out from under Hackett's watchful eye, I hope." As I took my first bite of a princely mix of roast beef, watercress, and French mustard of some kind, I felt a momentary pang of regret. "I did not intend for that remark to sound as callous as it did. But—"

"Yes, it's quite a sight, that eye, isn't it?" Holmes replied. "Did you note the scarring? Quite distinctive."

"Is it? I noted the marks, but I can't say it struck any particular chord in my memory."

"No? Well—perhaps I am mistaken. Hurry along, Watson, eat! You don't want to miss her, after all."

"Miss who?" I said, as I tried to get into my clothing and finish the last of the roast beef sandwiches.

"Why, the mournful ghost in the west tower! You didn't think Holyroodhouse would disappoint you—not after you've come all this distance!"

I was aware, as I finished dressing, eating, and making myself presentable, that Holmes was of course joking, *must* of course *be* joking; and yet . . . I was still without a satisfactory answer to the question I had asked on the train—was it hours or days ago?—concerning his personal opinion as to the existence of a malevolent spirit in Holyroodhouse, one that was responsible for the terrible things that we had heard of and, now, seen. Just the same, some such being would reconcile the apparent contradictions and impossibilities that had been on display in McKay's corpse; and I cannot in all candour say that I had entirely ruled some such ghoulish explanation out of my mind. Just the same, Holmes's persistent harping on the matter—whether because he himself believed it or because he realised the effect that it was creating in my spirits—was now becoming a distinct annoyance. I determined that I would give him a last chance with his "spirit in the west tower": If such proved to be some grotesque joke at my expense, of the variety that I supposed had so angered Mrs. Hudson the day before, I would have words with him, and sharp words, at that.

It was not until we had descended a relatively small flight of stairs in the eastern side of the building, turned a corner, and were walking through the spacious and impressive Grand Gallery on the northern side of the main floor of the palace, among portraits of English and Scottish

monarchs both real and (in the Scottish case) legendary, that it occurred to me to ask myself:

And if he is not joking? What shall you do then?

Without thinking terribly much more about
it—for the idea that Holmes might be quite serious about a "mournful ghost in the west tower"
was now more than ever a thought I found too
disconcerting and disorienting to be long
countenanced—I came to a stop before the palace's portrait of Mary, Queen of Scots.

"The indifferent work of a Frenchman," Holmes
said quietly, as he came to a stop next to me.
"One sees little to justify the many stories of her
beauty in it. It has, however, the advantage of
having been a life study; there is a rather more
attractive rendering of her in the next room, but it
was painted a full two centuries after her death."

"And yet, Holmes," I replied, studying the portrait carefully, "how much do we really know of
the things that constituted beauty then? Certainly, she has grace, and delicacy; and if the skin
is so pale as to seem deathly, and the forehead far
too high, well—such were fashions then, and
may have been exaggerated. Who knows but that
the great images of beauty produced by our own
age will not be considered grotesque oddities in
centuries to come?"

"There you have me, Watson," Holmes said,

moving on. "As we have often discussed, feminine beauty and feminine charms are *your* areas
of expertise, and never has that knowledge been
of greater use to us, I suspect, than it will be this
night. . . ."

He had reached the end of the Gallery, and
stood by a thick, heavily moulded door leading
into what seemed a distinctly private area of
some kind—certainly, it was a portal scarcely
used, and quite apart in style from the rest of the
palace. "Beyond this door lie those apartments
originally designated for Charles II's queen,"
Holmes explained, in a hushed voice. "Which are
within the medieval west tower. Charles's wife
quickly abandoned them, however—ostensibly
because of the availability of better accommodations in other wings; but in reality, suspects butler Hackett, because they lie directly below Queen
Mary's infamous rooms."

"It seems that you and 'butler Hackett' have
struck up quite a fast friendship during the hours
I was asleep."

"Oh, I should not say that," Holmes replied,
pushing the thick, heavy door before us gently,
so that it made little sound upon opening. "But I
would say that he has confirmed my prejudice
against trusting too much to initial appearances. Once Lord Francis was safely away and it

became clear that we were not agents of the Hamilton clan, Hackett was quite a changed man. Nor is it difficult to see or say why. Incidentally—did you not find your warmed bed marvellously inviting?"

I had grown so used to my friend's conversational rhythms, over the years, to his leaps from important information to mundane comments, that I did not even answer the question; nor was I at all surprised when he proceeded rather gingerly through the doorway, at that moment, without further explanation and into a sort of lobby outside what had once been, he informed me, the "new" queen's antechamber. As we crept on, steadily and silently, I noted, in the turret corner opposite the door through which we had come, the entrance to a stone spiral stairway. If this was indeed the floor below Queen Mary's old apartments, then these must have been the infamous steps down which the Protestant Scots nobles had hurled the murdered body of David Rizzio: small wonder that later queens had decided against lodging in such close proximity to the scene of the infamous killing. The antechamber, like all the rooms on this floor of the tower (including a large bedchamber, off to our left), was much as I had expected to find it, with panelled floors and ceilings, each section of the latter featuring

handsomely carved and painted coats-of-arms.
Nonetheless, time, neglect, and Nature had done
their work, particularly on the tapestries that yet
hung from many of the walls: complex weavings
that must have dated to before even Mary's time,
and that would no doubt have been worth a considerable sum, had not insects and rodents been
allowed to go about their destructive business for
generations on end. The windows were shut-
tered, and heavily draped, as well, with ancient
silks: more food for the vermin to feast on at their
leisure. In the process they had created holes of
varying size, and where these openings corre-
sponded to cracks in the shutters, the last rays of
the nearly vanished sun did what they could to
cheer these long cheerless chambers—

It was just as these melancholy observations
were registering upon my senses that I began to
hear the sound: As Holmes had said, it seemed
to be a woman weeping, sometimes mournfully,
occasionally fearfully and even desperately: a
sound such as would have chilled the most hardened of souls.

"Holmes!" I whispered urgently, no little un-
steadiness in my voice; but he had anticipated the
reaction, and was holding his hands aloft like
some successful conjurer.

"Did I not promise her?" he said, also in a whisper. "Actually, I came to you as soon as I heard it—I knew that you would want to share in the moment of discovery."

"My thanks for your consideration," I said, feeling suddenly quite cold and allowing the sensation to register in my voice.

"Come now, Watson—take heart! Only listen a little more, and then tell me what is wrong with the sound."

I did as instructed, and then noted something unexpected: the sound was emanating from the adjacent bedchamber—not from the stairway or the rooms upstairs.

"In heaven's name, Holmes," I declared. "Why, this is no ghost, it is some poor creature in distress—perhaps desperately so, from the sound of it!"

"Indeed it is—and that is precisely why I went to fetch you." Holmes moved toward the bedchamber door. "There is someone in there, I believe, who is in great trouble—Hackett would tell me no details, but he let slip several hints that led me this far. I might have entered, myself—but as I have said and we have long acknowledged, the weaker sex are *your* area of expertise—and if I am right, you shall need *great* expertise, to keep this woman from bolting."

"Bolting? But surely we bar her way."

"Perhaps, Watson—but I think not. I have reconnoitered already—there is no *apparent* stair by which she may try to run, save that behind us. Palace lore, however—related to me by Hackett— says that the *secret* stair by which Queen Mary was known to move between floors, and which her husband revealed to the men who murdered Rizzio, still exists. It was supposed, by all in the palace, to have been sealed after that crime, but Hackett says that he knows of at least one aged servant who swears that the stairs remain pass- able, behind quite secret mechanical panels. If this woman has taken refuge here and avoided detection, she must know of the existence of those stairs and be using them to escape detection. And so, it would seem that we cannot *physically* pre- vent this creature's escape. Can you devise some other method?"

"You know, Holmes," I answered, perhaps a bit curtly, "there really are moments when you make the simplest of propositions quite complex. I sug- gest that you remain here—at least for the first few minutes."

"Ah!" Holmes replied, as I approached the door to the bedchamber. "You will rely on charm alone, then?"

"My dear fellow," said I. "I happen to be a doctor. . . ."

More afraid of humiliation than of the supposed "ghost," I quickly passed through the bedchamber door—

And as soon as I did, the sound of the weeping
ceased. The near-blackness in the room—relieved
only by the very few holes in the draperies—
caused my eyes some few moments' disorienta-
tion; but I was relatively certain that the opening
and closing of any "secret" doorway must at least
be somewhat visible, or, even more probably (given
its age), audible; and I was proved right when a few
quick footsteps were followed by what sounded
like an ancient mechanism turning, and then the
gentle scratch of wood moving against wood.

"Please!" I said; and I cannot pretend that
there was not a slightly fearful quality to the en-
treaty, for, my brave protests to Holmes notwith-
standing, some irrational part of my own spirit
had been roused by the wailing, the darkness,
and the sounds of furtive movements. "Do not
be alarmed," I went on, steadying my voice. "I
am a friend, sent by friends, and I am a doctor. I
am not an agent either of the royal family's or of
the Duke's—you have my word upon it. I know
that you may flee, without the possibility of my
following—but I do not know why. What misfortune keeps you in this dead place? And what
may I do to assist you?"

A few discouragingly silent seconds passed; and then I heard the same mechanism grinding, along with the same noise of wood sliding, and finally a sound that was anything but ghostly: a small sniffle, followed by the most delicate of coughs. And yet, if the truth be known, it was only when I heard the accompanying voice— small, tremulous, but unmistakably human— that my own breathing resumed its normal rate.

"You—are a doctor?" The voice was much less mature than the weeping had sounded: I should have guessed that it belonged to a young Scots woman of no more than seventeen or eighteen years, probably from somewhere in the west.

"I am."

"And do you carry med'cines wi' you?"

"I can certainly obtain some, if you are ill— will you light a candle, and let me see what is wrong?"

"Aye—but what is wrong with me, ye canna' see." She struck a match. "No' yet. . . ."

My eyes squinted in the comparative glare of a single flaring candlestick; but as they adjusted, I beheld a face and figure that stood in great contrast to the portraits in the gallery without the tower. Straight, sandy-brown hair; skin that, although the face was momentarily paled by fear, was revealed by the neck, the upper chest, and the forearms to be of a healthy colour; fetching green eyes marred by hours of weeping; and thin, trembling lips; all these characterised a girl who, while extremely pretty, was somehow less engaging in her features than her movements, which had a quality of animation even when she was trying to remain still. Above all, there was a sense of enormous susceptibility about her, although her body appeared neither ill nor weak (indeed, she had the hardy frame of a household maid, for all her momentary tremulousness); and the cause of this nervous fragility was soon revealed as anything but obscure.

"Well," she said, embarrassed by the glow of the candle she had lit, "now you've seen me— who has sent you, if no' the master?"

"I—well, I suppose no one has, really. My friend heard you crying—"

"Friend?" she repeated fearfully, making a move to blow out the candle and hide behind the heavy, filthy drapes. "I thought you said tha'—"

"Now, now, there's no need for that," said I, hurrying to her and preventing her from extinguishing the candle. "We are neither here to reveal your hiding place to others nor have we any desire to see you put out."

"Then—what *do* you want wi' me?" A momentary look of relieved anticipation passed over her features. "Did *he* send you? Am I to go to him now? He promised me, aye, he did, he promised me—!"

"Who has promised you what, precisely?"

But she had begun to weep again, and I could get no answer to the question. "These med'cines of yours," she finally said. "Oh, Doctor—do you no' count poisons among them?"

"Poisons?" I echoed, startled. "My dear young lady, why should you wish for poison?"

"Why does any 'dear young lady' like myself wish for poison? I am lost!"

"Hush, now, I implore you." I guided her to an ancient bed with four thick, richly carved posts that was the focus of the dreary, dusty old room. "Let us begin with beginnings. My name is John Watson. I have come up from London with my friend, Mr. Sherlock Holmes—"

"Mr. Holmes?" she cried, leaping to her feet again: It really was almost impossible to keep her still. "The detective from London? You came wi' *him*? Oh, but I shall be found out now, I shall be—"

"You shall be nothing of the sort," said I. "Neither Mr. Holmes nor I has any reason to wish you harm or embarrassment—but I do warn you, all this talk of poison must stop." I managed to get her seated again, and, having drawn some conclusions from her few sensible statements, I put them to her: "So—you are hiding here, waiting for word from someone. A young man."

"No' so young, Doctor," she sniffed. "The devil is no' a boy. . . ."

"All right, then. There is a man, and you are waiting here for him. You have not left the palace with the rest of the staff—although, as young as you are, you were likely told *to* leave." She nodded once, and I proceeded. "Have you no home to go to? No family?"

She covered her face with a soiled apron that must have been serving the same purpose for hours, if not days, on end. "No family tha' will have me! No' as I am!"

I nodded once. "I understand. But he—the man who put you in this predicament—he has said he will return for you."

"Days ago! They told me to wait here, in this awful place, and he said he would come! I'm no' so foolish as that—I know why this tower's closed, I know who walks these halls! He will again tonight—and if I'm forced to hear it even once more, Doctor, the sound o' that step and that voice, I shall go mad! I canna' hear it again—it calls to me, it knows I'm here, and it will have me!"

Finally exhausted by terror and loneliness, the

poor wretch buried her face in my shoulder, and I put a hand to her head. "Quiet, now, you must quiet yourself—whatever happens, from this point on, you shall not be alone in it, I promise you. Do you understand me, Miss—there, now, you see, you have not yet even told me your name."

She came away from my shoulder, once more wiping at her eyes and nose. "Alison," she said through more sniffling. "Alison Mackenzie."

"And a very proper Scots name it is," I replied with a smile.

"But no' a proper Scots girl to go with it!" she declared. "He shall no' marry me, I begin to see it—no, and I shall be left here, to listen to that terrible spirit, and to go mad, or be murdered, or both—oh, Doctor, can ye no' have mercy, and end my terrible troubles for me?"

From out of the gloom surrounding the doorway came Holmes's voice. "I fear your Scottish magistrates would show the Doctor little mercy, were he to agree to your plan, Miss Mackenzie. . . ."

Alison Mackenzie bolted up once again, to spy my friend standing across the room. I could see that he was trying his very hardest to appear sympathetic and even kind; but these were always uncertain efforts with Holmes, and Miss

Mackenzie's wits, already strained, could offer him no trust at first glance.

"But he is right, nevertheless," Holmes went on, pointing to me. "We have no cause to wish you harm of any kind, and every reason to help you."

"Why?" the girl demanded sternly. "Why should either of you help me—a stranger who's alone in a forbidden place?"

"Perhaps because we, too, are strangers here," Holmes said, his voice now full of a much more genuine sort of emotion. "And we are more than familiar with forbidden places. . . ."

Miss Mackenzie gave that a few seconds' consideration, her features still hard; but soon she relented, a change signaled by a return to her apparently inexhaustible capacity for weeping. "But you can leave this place, when you will—I never can, save if he comes for me, and I see now that he will no'—he will no' come, no' ever, and I shall be left to go mad at the sound of that step, and that voice. . . ."

It was the work of more than an hour to get the girl truly calmed and composed. Holmes left us to order more sandwiches and a little whisky from Hackett, confiding to me that the butler knew full well where we were and what we were doing (a statement that I initially found almost

shocking, but that I would soon come to understand). Once she had something in her stomach
other than her own tears, and once the whisky
had reached her nervous system and produced
the desired effect, Miss Mackenzie began to tell
us her tale.

Born, indeed, on a small crofter's farm in the
loch country on the other side of Scotland, she had
come to serve at Holyroodhouse only in the past
year, when her aunt—who, it happened, was
Hackett's kindly but very nervous wife—had
recommended her for the position. Almost as soon
as she had arrived, Miss Mackenzie had predict-
ably become the recipient of the attentions of
every young man in the house, whether staff,
resident, or guest; but, unlike so many unfortu-
nates in similar positions, she had been pro-
tected, not only by Hackett, but by her cousin
Andrew, and finally by a third benefactor: the
park gillie, Robert Sadler, the man Mycroft
Holmes had mentioned as being a particular
royal favourite, and a seemingly decent soul who
had taken rather a brotherly interest in the sus-
ceptible girl. Thus, it had not been this Robert
who had been the instrument of her ruin.

"Ye canna' blame Master Rob, gentlemen,"
Miss Mackenzie told us, as the hour approached
eight o'clock and she—having perhaps indulged

in one or two ounces more of the whisky than one in her emotional state could successfully manage— began to grow what could fairly be called philosophical, for such a girl. "I have a gran' in Glasgow, and she tells me—if she's told me once, she's told me nigh on ten thoo'sand times—'you can pick your friends, Allie,' she says, 'but you canna' pick your fam'ly.' " A forlorn sigh followed this colourful homily. "Master Rob can no' help having such a brother. . . ."

Holmes—who had done his very best to be patient, while I coaxed the girl into a state of calm that, if it was not entirely relaxed, was at least conversational—now spun round, hurling the stub end of his cigarette into the tall, handsomely carved granite fireplace that filled the wall of the room opposite the bed. "Such a brother, Miss Mackenzie? Such a brother *as* . . . ?"

Miss Mackenzie sighed heavily, lying atop the ancient bedspread and cradling her heavy head in her hands. "As himself, Mr. Holmes. . . . As William. Willie, to me, but 'Likely Will,' to most. I ne'er could see the reason for such a name, though. Not till it was too late. . . ."

"So. . . ." And with that small judgement, Holmes began his infernal pacing again, that peculiarly insistent form of his usual nervous habit that had been born with this case, and had been my first indication, when I had returned to Baker Street scarcely more than twenty-four hours ago, that something particularly deep in his soul had been roiled by these goings-on. " 'Likely Will,' " he repeated, smiling as he did. "It's an unusual epithet, Watson, you must admit. I half expected 'Black Will,' or some such—"

"He's no need to declare it so openly, Mr. Holmes," interjected Miss Mackenzie, and quite firmly. "For the blackness will out of him, sooner—or later. Aye—they all said so, e'en Master Rob. But I would no' listen. I knew him better than all o' them, you see. . . . And now, look what's become o' me. Ruined by that same blackness. No—he's no need to declare it, at all. . . ."

"Indeed," Holmes pronounced, his moment of amusement gone and the faintest air of contrition in his voice. "I am quite sure. And what is his trade, this Likely Will Sadler of yours, Miss Mackenzie?"

She let her head drop fully to the dusty bed. " 'Twas his trade that first drew me in!" she called, and then, anticipating our confusion, she rose to explain. "They call him 'armourer,' up to the castle, but he does more than that—he repairs all their old, useless things."

"At Edinburgh Castle?" I asked.

"Aye," answered she, "but he works at the palace, too—that was how we met. He'd come here to deliver a suit of armour that he'd dandied up—and had he been wearing it himself, I could no' have been more taken with the sight of 'im! All strength and tall walking, and a smile as would make the moon sink back below the hill-sides, out o' shame . . . that was Likely Will Sadler. . . . One day I finally asked Master Rob about the name, and I dunna think he wished to tell me, for he could see the look in my eye. In truth, I think he even meant to warn me, in a way. 'Likely,' he says to me, 'because what e'er Will sets himself at, he'll likely do. Or *have*.' And Will did set himself at me, oh, how he did. . . . He knew girls like he knew those old machines o' his: I felt a princess, in this palace, for all my scrubbing and hauling. . . . But in the end—'twas all to my everlasting shame and damnation. . . ."

The girl was quite beyond sobbing, at last—and yet I felt myself wishing that she could cry again, for this new form of sadness was not one for which Holmes or I or anyone else could offer any palliative, save the cold comfort of platitudes about other women who had lived through such things, and learned to raise their child, with or without the faithless men who had fathered them. . . . But how much can talk of that kind mean to a poor young girl whose life seems, to her, to have ended before it has really begun?

It was Holmes, oddly enough, who managed the only statement that went near to mollifying her: "We shall not insult you, Miss Mackenzie, by telling you that your life will be easy, in the months to come. But you are not damned—not yet." He went to the bed and crouched down, in order to be able to look the girl in the eye. "And if you can find it in you to help the Doctor and myself, you will also find, and I pledge this to you, that your damnation need *never* take place. You are right to believe that this Likely Will of yours has no intention of returning to take you away to what most would call a 'respectable life'—indeed, you have already realised, have you not, that he has planned on your being discovered by your aunt and uncle in this tower, and returned by them to your home in disgrace." Silent tears drifted down the poor child's exhausted face, as she bravely nodded assent to Holmes's supposition. "Good—then you know him truly, and will not protest that he is better than we suppose. This marks you already as a superior member of your sex."

Miss Mackenzie's aspect changed, at that: Surprise and hope were awakened by Holmes's words. "Does it, Mr. Holmes?"

"Indeed. But you have another shock to bear, and it may be harder. Will you try?" Still heartened by Holmes's estimation of her, the girl nodded again. "The man who has taken so much from you has taken even more from others—and he will doubtless try to take the same dreadful measure from you, when he finds that you are still here."

"Holmes!" I interjected. Seeing the look of dumbstruck confusion and fear on Miss Mackenzie's face, I pulled my friend aside. "How can you say this so directly to a girl in so fragile a state?"

"You are wrong, Watson," he answered firmly. "This girl is not the simple serving wench of Holyroodhouse that this Will Sadler has taken her for—this is a daughter of the Scottish earth, with more Bannockburn than Culloden in her soul!" He returned to Miss Mackenzie, drawing her up by her shoulders until she sat upon the bed. "She has managed these days alone in this rotting, haunted wing of the palace—and she shall yet manage more! Am I right, Miss Mackenzie?"

The girl's cheeks had become flushed with colour as Holmes spoke, and she had just opened her mouth to give voice to assent—

When, from the floor above, came a sound:

the slow, hesitant step of booted feet against the
wooden floor. With a ponderous quality that,
under the circumstances, seemed doleful, the step
advanced a few paces, and stopped; advanced,
and then stopped; never at regular intervals, and
never moving in an intelligible direction or pattern. In addition, as if the step were not enough,
it was soon joined by another chilling noise: a
human voice, a man's voice, and one that slowly,
ever so slowly and mournfully, hummed a tune—
an air at once familiar and utterly alien.

Miss Mackenzie instantly covered her mouth,
and all the newly found colour drained away from
her face. " 'Tis him!" she whispered desperately.

"Him?" said Holmes, eyeing the panelled ceiling. "Sadler?"

"No!" the girl wept. *"Him!"* She glanced at us
both, horror in her every feature. "The poor man
they murdered here, all those years ago! He has
ne'er left, can ye no' see?" She looked at the ceiling once more. *"The Italian gentleman*—'tis his
spirit, come for revenge. . . ."

∞

Chapter IX

My hand went quickly to the pocket in which I had been keeping the Palm-protector obtained from Shinwell Johnson (as well as a store of a dozen rounds of ammunition that were carefully wrapped in a handkerchief). The move was an instinctive one, of course—what good, after all, would a firearm be against a spirit?—but it steeled my nerve, nonetheless.

" 'The Italian gentleman'?" whispered I. "Holmes, can she really mean—"

"Indeed," Holmes answered, listening carefully to the step and the humming voice above. "David Rizzio."

"Aye!" Miss Mackenzie breathed. "So he called him, right enough!"

"Then Sadler told you the legend," said Holmes.

"And showed me!" the girl answered. "It is no' a legend, Mr. Holmes—I've seen the blood that never dries!"

I turned to Holmes. "What on earth . . . ?"

"Yes—Hackett told me of it, Watson. And showed me this." From his pocket, Holmes produced a crudely printed pamphlet, one that I perused as the footsteps above continued to tap out their eerily distorted units of time.

The headline of the pamphlet declared,

"ALL THE DARK AND SECRET LOCALES OF EDINBURGH, REVEALED!"

The few pages of the thing described many spots where those willing to first part with an unnamed (but obviously considerable) amount of money and then venture out into the depths of a Scottish night might encounter "EVIDENCE OF THE WORLD BEYOND!" And the featured attraction among this roster was clearly a visit to the royal Palace of Holyrood, in particular the scene of "the most ghastly murder in Scottish history, one so terrible that its victim yet visits the spot where he died every night, renewing the pool of blood that he shed there and searching for some unsuspecting Scotsman—or woman!—upon whom he may vent the rage he still feels against the nation that used him so cruelly, and that has, for centuries on end, left him unavenged!"

I studied the patently nonsensical but (loath though I was to admit it) effective document for several minutes. "But—where does one obtain this? Who conducts these 'tours'? Some member of the staff, surely. But should Her Majesty discover it—"

"Should Her Majesty discover it, the entire staff of the palace would likely be replaced," Holmes said. "For who among them could she ever truly trust again? How could they not *all* know that such a breach of confidence had been committed, *has* been committed, not once or twice, but on almost a nightly basis?"

"Aye," said Miss Mackenzie. "True enough, sir—and that is the very reason why no' a soul will speak of it, though all who work here do, as you say, know of it."

"And do all know *who* conducts these illegal visits?" I asked, still trying to keep my thought processes logical and coherent, despite the noises that drifted down relentlessly from above us.

The girl shook her head quickly. "They're told

from the start to no' be curious. And they all obey the order—for there's none as wish to lose their position." She looked up fearfully. "And none as wish to have the spirit come for them. I obeyed the rule, for as long as—oh, had I but known! But he made such a game of it, sir—only one of his many lies. He said that he could show it to me, and I would be safe in his company! But now—now I see. . . ."

"That he used it to keep you in his power," Holmes completed for the girl. "He said that he would show you the spot, 'the blood that never dries'—he made an adventure of it, recognising your nature, and then said that if you ever betrayed him. . . ."

The poor wretch trembled so fearfully at that instant that I rushed to her and placed an arm around her shoulders, as she whispered, "Aye! That if I betrayed what I knew, the Italian gentleman would come for me—and now he has! But I did no' betray him, Mr. Holmes, upon my life, I never did! Why, then? Why does this poor, unfortunate spirit torment me—"

As near to hysteria as she had grown, the girl was struck dumb when yet another sound joined the ongoing footsteps and occasional humming from the floor above. It was a male speaking voice, one tinged by an accent that called simply:

"Signorina . . . signorina . . . it is almost time. . . . "

Scarcely able to breathe now, much less speak, Miss Mackenzie clutched at the lapel of my jacket fearfully, and pressed herself hard against me.

"You need have no fear," I whispered to her, tightening my grip on her shoulders. "Spirit or man, he shall not harm you, I swear it."

I looked to Holmes, expecting him to second my pledge—and was surprised to find him instead smiling again: Neither for the first nor for the last time did I wonder about the strange amusement that my friend seemed almost determined to take from the entire subject of spirits. Recognising that I did not share his reaction, Holmes moved swiftly to the great fireplace, indicating the chimney; and then I realised his point. As the seemingly spectral voice returned to the humming of that same elusive tune, at once recognisable and unknown, I realised that the sound was not, in fact, emanating from all around us, but simply travelling down the chimney, to be projected onto the room as a whole by the enormous firebox behind the granite surround and mantel of the fireplace.

"This is a cruel trick, indeed," said I, my hand again reaching for the Palm-protector, "and he shall pay for it, by God!"

I looked up, and was about to call out the worst

threat that I could summon, when Holmes urgently murmured: "No, Watson! Not yet! This fellow counts himself clever—but like so many of
the kind, he is too clever by half." Listening to
the sound of the humming, Holmes seemed to be
waiting for something: He was anticipating the
return of the footsteps, and waiting for that sound
to pass back over us, and into the area above
the antechamber. Only when it had faded altogether, in the direction of the newer wings of the
palace, did Holmes speak again.

"One would not expect such an audible step,
from such an ethereal being—and the tune!"

"Yes, what *of* the tune?" I asked, as I encour-
aged Miss Mackenzie to take a little more of the
whisky.

"You did not recognise it?"

"It was in keeping with the voice, I believe—
vaguely Italian—and there were moments when
I thought that I might know it. But ultimately, I
could not place the thing."

" '*Vaguely* Italian'?" Holmes replied, quite dubiously. "Watson, there really are times when I
despair for your musical education. But never
mind—it is but a distraction. Our solution is at
hand, now, but we must move swiftly!"

I had persuaded Miss Mackenzie to release my
lapel, and to resume her seat upon the bed. She

clutched the little silver whisky cup I had given her as tightly as if it were life itself, and, though I knew that she must be near drunkenness, I poured her still a bit more of the stuff.

"Miss Mackenzie," Holmes said to her. "You have said that this man, this Likely Will Sadler, frequents 'the pub'—which of this city's many establishments would that be?"

"The Fife—Fife and Drum," she blurted out at last. "Off Johnston Terrace—just below the castle."

"A soldiers' pub, then?" Holmes asked.

"Aye," the girl said. "The men from the garrison, he's friendly with most of them—by way of his work there. He repairs the old weapons—even some of the old cannon."

Holmes stood and turned to me, clearly perturbed. "A complication, Watson. No doubt these soldiers are Sadler's drinking companions, and they will protect him, in his lair. We must be careful how we move. . . ." He looked up at the ceiling. "So he works on the old cannon? Quite a talented fellow, I should say." Crouching again before the girl, Holmes put a final series of questions to her: "Miss Mackenzie—do you understand that it was not a spirit that you heard just now, but a man?" The girl tried to indicate assent, but the movement was no more than an anxious quiver of her head. "And do you believe as much?"

"I—am trying, Mr. Holmes. You canna' ask for anything save my best. . . ."

"Well said, young lady—well said. This child of yours may have no father, when he comes, but he shall have a mother to more than make up the lack!" Miss Mackenzie even smiled a little at that. "Now, then—the first of your trials. Clearly, you are no longer safe here—you must go down to the kitchens, to your aunt and uncle and your cousin. They will—"

The green Scots eyes popped wide open. "To the—no, Mr. Holmes, I canna' do it! I canna' go below stairs again! My uncle, he shall have the hide from off my—"

"He will have no such thing," Holmes answered. "For we shall go with you, and make certain that they understand what bravery you have shown, and how you have helped us in our efforts to break the grip that fear has so long held upon this palace. I believe, from my conversations with your uncle, that he will accept you, once he knows that you have chosen to actively oppose Sadler—and we both know why he shall, do we not?"

Giving the matter a moment's thought, Miss Mackenzie reluctantly nodded.

"Aye, sir. He's reason enough to hate Will, 'tis true. But—what makes you think you will not suffer the same awful fate that Uncle Gavin—Mr. Hackett—did? Can you no' simply go to the police—"

"Unfortunately, this matter requires the greatest secrecy—and so it is left to us. But fear not, we shall have help, come tomorrow night—not just Dr. Watson and myself, but others of our acquaintance, who are more knowledgeable and reliable than any policemen we might ask for. And no doubt your uncle and cousin will lend their aid, as well." Holmes rose. "Only say that you will stand with us, thereby making it all the more necessary that Will Sadler return here, and I promise you some measure of redemption."

He waited several long seconds for his reply; and when the girl's assent came, it was in the form of the smallest inclination of her head. "Well done, Miss Mackenzie—well done. And now, come—" Holmes turned, to begin the procession out; but then he checked his step, seeming to recall something. "Oh, and incidentally—you have been, I presume, to Likely Will's workshop?"

"Aye, sir. Many a time."

"Is that where he keeps the bird?"

Miss Mackenzie answered the question—which utterly baffled me—without apparent difficulty:

"Indeed, sir. He has so many wondrous things there. . . ."

"No doubt." Holmes pulled a pencil and a scrap of paper from his pocket, and began to sketch furiously. "And among those wondrous things, is there a wooden machine that resembles—this?"

He placed the paper before the girl's eyes, which lit up in recognition. "Have *you* been there too, then, Mr. Holmes? I canna' remember what they called it—but they found the pieces of it scattered in one of the sheds in the castle, ages ago. Will's been at work on it for e'er so long. . . ."

"Indeed?" Holmes placed his pencil back in his pocket as I helped the girl up. "Well, Miss Mackenzie—I should say that he has completed the task. . . ."

∞

Chapter X

THE MARCH TO THE FIFE AND DRUM

I have often alluded to Holmes's tendency never to share all the pieces of a solution to a given crime until the moment when that solution reaches its fulfilment (in the early years of our acquaintance, I sometimes referred to this predilection as a "defect," an assessment that I have come to regret); and so it was with a familiar sense of expectant but resigned confusion that I set out into the Edinburgh night with him, following our delivery of Miss Mackenzie into the safe company of her family in the servants' hall. As Holmes had predicted, the once off-putting Hackett (who, thankfully, wore a patch over his injured eye during this encounter, forgoing the glass eye that had so puzzled and distressed me earlier) became quite a changed man at the sight of the girl, and even more when he observed that she was entirely safe—if somewhat distressed, still a little tipsy, and in need of a hot bath. Mrs. Hackett, particularly, was profuse in her thanks to Holmes and myself, saying that they all—the staff of the palace generally—had wondered if anyone from the outside world would ever come to do what they could not: reveal the disgraceful dealings that had gone on for so long in the west tower. Such statements may seem strange to those who know nothing of the life led by servants in a grand house (and no "house" is grander, in every sense, than a royal palace). But those who do will recognise the characteristic terror of losing one's position (and, perhaps worse still, of losing one's reference for a position elsewhere), and the openings that these fears very often create for persons clever enough to orchestrate a great scheme of theft, of exploitation—or, as in this case, of imaginative and lucrative fraud. As Miss Mackenzie had intimated, and Holmes had stated plainly, trust between the owning and serving classes in a great household is a highly delicate machine, wherein the corruption of a single part can lead to the replacement of the entire works; and this

explained why Hackett had never spoken to anyone of the doings in the palace generally and the
west tower in particular.

Holmes, of course, had done a great deal more
than guess at the extent of the corruption in
Holyroodhouse; and Hackett had somehow
recognised as much, and was therefore able to
relax his guard, if only partially and only for the
time being, the better to enjoy the safe return of
his niece. But what was understood if unspoken
between butler and detective would be fully revealed to me only later; for the time being, my
attention was focused upon our march toward
the great stone formation called Castle Rock,
atop which sat the massive walls and stone bar-
racks of Edinburgh's great and ancient fortress.
This journey began with our being escorted to
the main entrance of the palace by Hackett and
his apparently redoubtable son Andrew, the pair
of whom promised, at Holmes's urging, to in-
struct the women of the family to keep all the
building's doors not only locked but bolted that
night; as for Hackett and Andrew, they agreed to
keep watch at the gates of the inner fence until
our return, ready to re-admit us or to repel our
antagonists—whichever should come first.

"You need have no fear on that account,
Mr. Holmes," Hackett said bravely. "We've a

well-stocked gun-room here—and if I've but one eye, I yet have Andrew's two, and since he was but a bairn, he could shoot the eye out of a hare at fifty paces."

"Excellent, Andrew!" Holmes pronounced. "Then the eye of a scoundrel should present no challenge." The pale-skinned giant of a youth blushed and then smiled, at which Holmes moved closer to him, eyes full of serious purpose. "I do not jest, my boy—should Will Sadler return here this evening, you must warn him off; and if he will not go, you would do better to put a bullet in his brain than to allow him near your cousin. For such, I can assure you, is the fate he plans for her."

Young Andrew's skin regained its usual pallor at that, and he scarcely managed to mumble, "Aye, Mr. Holmes," in reply; but he took greater heart when Holmes clapped his shoulder.

"Fear not," said my friend. "If I doubted you for an instant, I should not go. But I have seen something of the mettle of this family, and I know you are more than equal to your assignment." Andrew smiled once more, with real gratitude and admiration—and that was all Holmes needed to see. "And so, Watson!" he declared, turning and striding quickly toward the western gate of the palace's inner fence.

I smiled encouragingly to Hackett and his son, then turned to follow Holmes; but Hackett caught my arm as I did.

"You must no' think yourselves safe, Doctor," said he, "simply because you leave this place. The Fife and Drum is Will Sadler's lair, as sure as if he were a wolf among his pack."

The military man in me, which had bridled at Holmes's comments on the train, was momentarily roused again at the suggestion that British soldiers would defend the rogue Sadler; but the earnest expressions in both Hackett's and Andrew's faces made my indignation pass instantly, and I thanked them both before hurrying along to join Holmes.

This short, hurried walk was interrupted when my eyes caught sight—again, it seemed, almost involuntarily—of the palace's west tower, that seeming repository of all that was evil, past or present, about Holyroodhouse; and I confess that, as I stared at its baleful turrets, my step slowed once more, and my mind fell to wondering.

Were we truly protecting Hackett's family from the palace's most terrible dangers, by advising them to barricade themselves within its walls? Or had we not, in fact, done the work of the creature that was actually our most terrible enemy, by placing four innocents at his other-worldly mercy?

This unexpected moment of horrifying doubt was mercifully brief; a call from Holmes brought me outside the gate at a run, and once we were among the winding streets of the capital (for Holmes would not risk, even at the late hour of ten o'clock, our being sighted along the open stretches of High Street, the most direct route to the Castle), my friend broke the silence of our progress by rather pointedly and relentlessly whistling; and it was only after the first few minutes of the sound reverberating off of the cobbles beneath us and the stone houses around us that I realised he was offering up the same tune that the mysterious visitor had hummed during his visit to Queen Mary's rooms in the palace. I was on the verge of reminding Holmes of his rather limited ability to carry a tune on anything save a violin, when it occurred to me that I knew the piece in question.

"Good Lord, Holmes!" said I. "Verdi!"

The man finally ceased his squeaking and nodded in satisfaction. "Verdi, indeed, Watson—to be precise, 'Va, Pensiero,' from his *Nabucco.*"

"But—*Nabucco* is a comparatively recent opera, surely."

"Comparatively—first performed at La Scala, in '42."

"And yet our centuries-old 'ghost' apparently knows it?" Genuine relief gave my query a certain hauteur, I will admit.

"Not only knows it," replied an amused Holmes, "but is aware—or has been told—that Miss Mackenzie does *not* know it, and cannot therefore determine that the person humming the tune is many things, but no sixteenth-century wraith. Which tells us . . . ?"

"That the impostor is intimately familiar with the staff of the house—it is reasonable, perhaps, to assume that the maids employed therein do not spend their evenings off at the opera, but it is certainly not *safe* to do so. Firsthand knowledge of them would be vital."

"Indeed, Watson. There are many ways to come by such knowledge, of course—William Sadler could doubtless have had it from Miss Mackenzie herself, but one doubts that Sadler is *himself* a particular devotee of Verdi. Thus we begin to detect multiple hands at work here—as, indeed, the nature of the injuries to both Sir Alistair and McKay would indicate."

"Yes, that thought had occurred to me during my examination of the body. It is even unlikely that there were but two: An excess of fifty wounds, unless we are dealing with a madman, speaks in favour of as many participants as we may reasonably hold under suspicion."

"As does another factor," replied Holmes. "And it was among the reasons why Rizzio met his fate as he did—I speak of guilt, or, rather, the dissipation of it. There can be no sacrificial lamb among conspirators, so long as they all draw blood. As in the case of your own army execution squads— who can say who fired the deadly shot, or dealt the mortal blow?"

"This seems an unnecessarily melancholy consideration, Holmes," I said, pulling my friend onward. "Especially in-so-far as Miss Mackenzie is concerned. For, if we are looking about for new hands to implicate in this bloodshed, we need not concern ourselves with affairs of state, but can look at once to the brother, this Robert, who the girl seemed to have felt was so much her protector."

"And he may have been, Watson," Holmes replied, his voice quickening with his steps, "to the extent that her protection did not conflict with the goals of their criminal consortium. There are those who delight in deceiving and destroying young women—Baron Gruner was one of the worst, of our common acquaintance—and then there are those criminals who only destroy reluctantly, to preserve the safety and integrity of their operations—but who destroy, nonetheless. And, in my heart, I confess to an even deeper loathing, in certain ways, for the second type. Let us by all means try to understand the criminal mind, Watson—but let us end these attempts to rationalise criminal behaviour, whether that behaviour be manifested by high statesmen or by low confidence tricksters, who make women their pawns! Let us have no more solicitors and barristers who come before judges and declare, 'M'lud, I do acknowledge that my client despoiled and later strangled Miss So-and-so, but I ask you to consider that he showed her great tenderness until that day, and that he only murdered her, with great reluctance, because she threatened his livelihood.' For what is all that supposed tenderness, save a trap—a reason for the poor female to believe she may trust that the man in question will honour her interests, come what may, when he knows full well the limits of his honour. No, Watson! I say, let justice fall equally hard on both of these brothers, if both be implicated—and on any of their other confederates, even if they be nobly born!"

"My dear Holmes," I said impatiently (for the true meaning of his last words was as yet unsuspected by me), "your interest in arguing such matters, when you know perfectly well that I *have* no argument with you, remains one of the great mysteries of our acquaintance. I made my remark simply out of concern for Miss Mackenzie, who will doubtless be further crushed when she discovers not only that the man to whom she entrusted her heart is a vicious miscreant, but that his brother, who, at least, she felt safe in thinking a friend, is ultimately no better."

"Oh. That." Holmes passed a hand impatiently through the air. "That cannot be helped," he pronounced simply, once again displaying how brutally shallow his understanding of the feminine mind could sometimes be—save for the most *devious* feminine minds, of course. "Ah! And here we are," he continued in the same tone, upon spying the pub: as if the little that had been left of a perfectly decent young woman's happiness and faith in humanity had not been disposed of in the most short-handed manner.

The Fife and Drum was a cramped, ancient den, carved, literally, into the stone of Castle Rock, and facing onto one of the maze of very small streets that ran up the promontory's face at several points. The place thus appeared not so much separate from as a part of the great, prehistoric mountain of stone: Its walls were composed of the bared insides of the Rock, and the leaded panes that interrupted the walls in only a few spots had sagged with age, whilst simultaneously growing clouded by years of grease and nicotine-staining, so much so that they no longer merited the title of windows. The thick door, planks held together with iron banding, gave way to my push with a loud squeal that made any additional bell quite unnecessary; and having been thus announced, we entered, making no plan for what we should do if we were faced with hostility from the moment of that entrance.

Fortunately, the scene that we discovered inside was not unlike many of the better garrison bar-rooms I had frequented in my life. If the appointments were as squalid and poorly maintained as the exterior of the place, the loud laughter of honest soldiers glad of a few hours' break from boredom and drill more than made up for the lack, and gave the middling-sized, low-ceilinged room a cheery air. I had and have seen my share of ugly occurrences in such places, of course, for there are more than a few bottled passions that soldiers seek to uncork when the pressure of army life becomes too great; but far more often one will find that the opportunity to enjoy unfettered joviality with comrades and a few female companions produces a wholesome effect, first upon the men and then, in turn, upon their visitors.

If such a welcome was not immediate upon our entrance, it did not seem to me that it would be difficult to prompt. Quickly scanning the sea of faces before me, I recognised only one pair of male patrons—in the corner to the right of us, hard by a stone fireplace and amid a sea of uniforms— whose irregular appearance revealed them as being not in active service: clearly our men. Both were approximately thirty years of age, handsome and so similar in appearance that they could have been nothing but brothers. They were of that dark-haired and rather romantic type that one sometimes finds in the North, as well as Scotland: the type upon whom female novelists have spent more words, perhaps, than sober appreciation would warrant.

The first of the two, whom I took to be Robert, was a respectable enough specimen, with a good-natured face and an expression in his brown eyes that I could well imagine inspiring trust, especially in a lonely and rather frightened young woman. Had he been standing, I should have thought him to be just better than six feet in height: Holmes had long ago acquainted me with the fundamentals of the esoteric science known as anthropometry, the method of identifying per-

sons by their body type and parts; and a facet of
that science (one of the few aspects I had actually
remembered, if the truth be known) was the pro-
portional method of taking a man's measure
whilst he was sitting down. This first fellow also
bore the rugged stamp of an experienced gillie,
which was perhaps the clearest indication of his
identity. The other of the two, meanwhile, was
clearly the rogue we had come to engage.

He seemed to have all of his brother's physical
power; but where his brother's aspect was amiable, Will Sadler's every feature might have been
hewn, like the pub itself, out of the very rock that
surrounded the place. Set against all that darkness and angular strength, however, was a pair
of sparkling blue eyes that would have fit as well
in a woman's face as a man's, and which doubtless had the power to lower the defences of even
the most sceptical among the fair sex. It was a
phenomenon I had seen many times, this ability
of certain unprincipled men to use some seeming softness about their features—usually, as in
this case, the eyes—to disarm women, and I had
always despised it; but when I thought of that
girl back at the palace, who had been seduced by
those eyes and then abandoned by the man who
possessed them, my dislike evolved into—well, I
can only say that those muscle groups with which

one generally inflicts a sound thrashing must have grown involuntarily tense, for Holmes put a hand to my arm, urging me away from the corner in question and towards the bar on our left.

"Steady, Watson," he said. "We are here to bait the trap, not to spring it. Let us take rather another tack."

"You have another in mind?" said I, angrily.

"*You* possess the military experience," said he. "Is there not some way of establishing a quick rapport?"

I gave the matter just a few seconds' thought. "Indeed there is." Gaining control of my rage, I asked, "Would you suppose that any of these men, or either of our adversaries, know your face?"

"I cannot think how they would."

"Good. You know enough of the Afghan campaigns from my reports of them to impersonate a veteran officer—and so, follow where I lead. . . ."

The barman, a good-natured fellow with a kindly grin and arms like the pistons of a large steam press, approached us.

"Gentlemen!" he called over the din. "What can the Fife and Drum offer you?"

"Whatever whisky you judge your best, sir," I replied, my bellicose mood displaced by enforced joviality. I turned to my right and added, in a loud voice, "And a large measure of the same for

any man who has seen the North-West Frontier—
two for any who have, like my comrade and myself, felt the sting of Jezail bullets!"

As most of the faces in the room were young, I
did not expect a mob-like response to my offer—
nor did I desire one. Half a dozen career non-
commissioned officers, all somewhere between
forty and fifty years of age, rose with great en-
thusiasm and headed towards Holmes and myself, hands already extended. We exchanged unit
names and years of service: Holmes became
"Captain Walker" of my own regiment (whose
thin stature, so at variance with the other men
in the room, I explained by saying that he had
been afflicted with chronic malaria while in the
Sudan—knowing that Holmes could at least
provide a first-hand account of that region, if
pressed), while I myself assumed the role of "Ma-
jor Murray," using the name of my old orderly
and keeping to one of my old regiments, the
Northumberland Fusiliers, but cautiously failing
to include the fact that I had been a surgeon with
it—"surgeon" being a word that can produce an
even more mixed effect on a group of soldiers
than it tends to do on civilians. Our elite little
gathering, after another round of whisky, drew
some younger hangers-on, those who had never
seen action and longed to hear tales of it; and it

was nigh on closing time before anyone thought to ask what we were doing in Edinburgh, as well as in the Fife and Drum.

"Well, sir," I said to the leather-skinned colour sergeant who had asked. "We came to see the sights, in this fine city, and diligently completed our mission—or *thought* we had done so. But this afternoon, I was speaking with my friend Walker, here, in the hotel bar of the Roxburghe" (I deliberately cited one of the city's oldest and most elegant hotels, on Charlotte Square) "or rather, truth to say, I was wearying him with another lecture concerning my lifelong fascination with matters of the world beyond, when the bar steward quietly slid *this* beneath my nose. . . ." From my pocket I pulled Holmes's little pamphlet, which I had never returned to him. "The fellow informed me that if I wished to know more, this was where I should come. And so, here we are—although I confess, had we known that such good company was to be had, we should have come long before this, 'secret tour' or no!"

It was a calculated gamble, one that I must admit I enjoyed embarking on without Holmes's advice or consent. I had speculated that Robert and William Sadler must have been highly discriminating as to their clientele, which was almost certainly made up of wealthy visitors to the city (over-exposure among the citizenry seeming a quick road to ruin). Such visitors would usually be found in Edinburgh's better hotels; and among the employees of such establishments, no one was more capable of judging a given guest's capacity for discretion concerning illicit activities than were bar stewards. At least some of these men were likely supplying the Sadlers with appropriately wealthy and tight-lipped customers, in return for a share of their proceeds; and, unless I was very wide of the mark, among this group of secondary players in the elaborate fraud that we had uncovered at the palace was a jovial but rather rakish fellow at the Roxburghe, a barman whose acquaintance I had made almost a year earlier, when I had made a brief trip to Edinburgh to attend a series of lectures at the medical college. The man had at that time made it clear that whatever entertainment one might be looking for, he could arrange it, a claim that I had been given good reason to respect. But as to the assumption that he was involved in the Sadlers' ambitious and dangerous doings—there, my thinking could have been disastrously wrong, and when my little performance was over, a sense of apprehension seized me for an instant. The instant, however, was brief: So effective had my efforts at ingratiation been, and so apparently correct my assumptions, that the crowd about us only roared with laughter and sent up a rousing cheer. The old colour sergeant turned to face the corner behind us, and set the game fully in motion by bellowing:

" 'Ere! Rob—Will! Up you get, here's more fellows as would like to fill your pockets!"

The two young men that I had spotted upon entry rose from their seats quickly. "Likely Will" bounded our way with a few quick steps of his long, powerful legs, while his brother followed at a far less enthusiastic pace: I had measured their heights correctly, but their apparent strength was both surprising and a bit disconcerting. The eagerness with which the lead brother moved, however, indicated first that the pair had formed no suspicions about us, and second that this pub was entirely safe territory for them—the latter a fact that bore those same implications about at least some of the other men in the establishment that I had earlier resisted, but which I was now forced to acknowledge as dishearteningly accurate. But, telling myself that the greater number of the soldiers present could not possibly have had any idea as to the full extent of what their civilian friends were about at Holyroodhouse, I pressed on. Holmes, meanwhile, remained for the most part a silent partner—and there was no little satisfaction for me in *that* fact, as well.

The colour sergeant made introductions, and from the first, the brothers were so apparently charming as to more than justify their reputations: They evidently fell into that narrow category of men that are almost as ingratiating with their own sex as they are with women. But on further acquaintance, as the gillie's full involvement in the schemes at the palace became apparent, one could detect a rather forced air to his joviality. Was this a long shadow being cast by recent events at the palace? One rather hoped so, for Miss Mackenzie had not been wrong: Robert Sadler did seem a genuinely decent fellow, with the apparently solitary flaw of having allowed himself to be led into mischief by a more dynamic brother—hardly a unique failing, but one that, in this case, had proved fatal, for Likely Will Sadler's dynamism tended towards ruthlessness, his mischief toward murder. But, I told myself, we must not allow congeniality, sympathy, or any other factor to mitigate the severity with which we held the pair responsible for such outrages as we had seen: If these were indeed our men, then in the few but vital moments that we would spend in the pub, it was imperative that we attend to business, first, by ensuring that we not stray an inch from the roles we had created for ourselves, and, second, by establishing enough camaraderie with the men to allow Holmes's overall plan (whatever it might be) to come to maturity.

"I must tell you right away," I announced to the pair, after they had explained how it was that they were connected to the palace, "that the ancient crime at Holyroodhouse has always fascinated me—is that not so, Walker?" Before Holmes could do more than nod, I charged on: "Yes, many's the night on patrol that I have tried poor Walker's patience"—and here I shot my old friend a meaningful glance—"telling and retelling every detail of the business. But I confess that I knew nothing about this legendary wraith of which your advertisement speaks, and certainly never dreamed of the possibility of seeing evidence of such a phenomenon!"

"We're just simple working men, sir, and of a mind to keep things quiet," said Likely Will Sadler, with a contrived self-effacement that, I was forced to admit, was effective. "Too many visitors, and sharing the secret of the palace would no' be possible. But if we limit the business to those who—like yourselves—are gentlemen of genuine interest and education, we can hope to go on as we are, making this remarkable phenomenon"—and there was a strange, an almost rehearsed quality about the way in which he said these last words—"known to others. As I'm certain you appreciate, my brother and myself are both loyal subjects of the realm, no one more so than Rob, here—the Queen loves him near as much as he is devoted to her. We've no wish to present her with any further difficulties. But—well, sir, the truth is, some things belong to *all* the people of a nation, is how we see it, and this is one of them."

"Aye—but, as Will says, gentlemen, never let our loyalty to the Queen be doubted." Robert Sadler's urgent tone seemed to me to go beyond playacting. "If sharing the secret were ever to pose a danger to her, or create an uproar such as has been caused of late by the murders of those two poor men—then we'd put a stop to what we're doing. Aye—in an instant, we would."

"Well said, well said," I replied. "Another dram on that, for both of you. And then we will speak no more of it—for it's a bad business, and I've been put in far too convivial a mood for such!" General agreement to this assertion was voiced, many glasses met in a toast to it, and then I added, most offhandedly, "You did not *know* the unfortunate devils, I trust?"

Again, a moment of apprehension—would

they detect deeper purpose in the query? But our
performances, it seemed, had been note-perfect,
and neither of the brothers showed even a trace
of uncertainty as they protested complete ignorance of almost all particulars of the crimes.

"We'd see them, now and again, of course,"
said Will Sadler. "Rob more than myself."

"And a better pair of Scotsmen this country has
never produced," Robert pronounced. "Sir Alistair
was a true gentleman—all condescension and fel-
lowship. And Denny McKay—well, you can do
no better than to say that, for a Glasgow lad, he
had nary a fault to him. A terrible business. . . ."

Holmes and I exchanged a quick look: Was
this young man, in fact, the master deceiver of
the family, rather than Likely Will? For his sor-
row seemed utterly genuine.

"And so we shall let it rest," said Holmes, perhaps wishing to stay to the business at hand.
"We shall wish them peace and justice, and then
return to our own affairs, as the living must."

In a gesture that I thought must, at last, be sure
proof of their base infamy, both brothers nodded,
raised their glasses, and declared, "Peace and
justice!"—as though either Sir Alistair or McKay
would ever have needed either, had Fate only
steered them clear of these two devils!

Holmes quickly pressed on to the business of

just when we could hope to be taken on our ghostly tour. Will Sadler asked whether the following night might suit us, and Holmes replied that we could easily return to the Roxburghe and arrange an additional night's stay. Similarly, we could procure the stated and princely fee of fifty guineas at the hotel with little trouble. As to our rendezvous, however, Holmes said that he assumed the brothers did not like to conduct their business in the open glare of a hotel lobby, an assumption that proved sound: It was arranged that we should meet at eleven o'clock, near the gate in the park's outer fence that was closest to the palace, and that we would proceed from there.

Several more rounds of whisky were required to extricate us from the pub, and even at that, our exit through the ancient plank-and-iron-band door was delayed by a final question from Will Sadler:

"By the way, Captain Walker—the barman at the Roxburghe you mentioned—which one was it? So that we can be certain he gets his due."

I turned along with Holmes to face the questioner; and discovered for the first time, in his features, the cool, cruel gaze of a man capable of the kind of injuries we knew to have been inflicted on the palace victims. A sudden and terrible anxiety gripped me, for the cunning fellow had been shrewd enough to question Holmes—who could have had no idea as to the identity of the barman—rather than myself; or was I being overly suspicious, and was this, for the first time in the entire affair, a simple and genuine coincidence? Whatever the case, I did not waste a moment stepping in:

"Good God, Walker," I came near to shouting, "but you held your whisky better on the frontier—the man's name is Jackson, you know it as well as your own, or you did last evening at this same time!"

Holmes nodded, holding Sadler's scrutinising gaze: "Indeed so, Murray. But then, we were in rather an augmented state of awareness last evening, were we not?"

Sadler nodded once; but I grew only further unnerved by the subsequent speed and ease with which the appealing liveliness of his light eyes and his easy smile returned. I now saw that this was an antagonist humbler in his origins, but every bit as formidable, as some of the worst killers we had ever faced. Relieved was I, therefore, when we finally exited the pub and descended Castle Rock, more intoxicated but no cheerier than we had been when we made our way up, and surrounded by darkened houses and shops that

suddenly seemed less asleep than utterly devoid
of life.

Once on the streets below, Holmes steered me
forcefully in a north-westerly rather than an east-
erly direction, suggesting that it would be in our
interests to at least be seen entering the Roxburghe Hotel:

"I would count it as given," he explained, "that
some agent of the Sadlers, if not one of the brothers themselves, is following us even now, to verify the story we have told them. We can easily
lose the fellow in the crush of so busy a lobby as
that at the Roxburghe—and besides, Watson, the
cool night air will be beneficial for you, after your
performance in the Fife and Drum."

I nodded, rather glumly. "I realise that I must
in fact *be* inebriated, Holmes," said I. "But I have
rarely felt so low-spirited."

Holmes attempted sympathy. "You are disturbed by the possible connivance of British soldiers in this affair?"

"In part, certainly."

"As well as the apparent treachery of this Robert Sadler, who seemed to be Miss Mackenzie's
protector—whom she herself certainly regarded
as such—but who was evidently plotting her return home in disgrace, or worse?"

"Indeed. But there is more. I accept that Rob

Sadler assisted his brother in his hideous crimes, if only because those acts required at least two pairs of strong arms and hands for their success-ful completion. Nor is the motive obscure: Be-cause they were assigned to rehabilitate the west tower of the palace, first Sir Alistair and then McKay must have become aware of the lucrative farce that was being played out there on an al-most nightly basis, which would have come to a disastrous end, as would the freedom of the Sadlers, had those two honest men been allowed to tell the Queen of their discoveries. And yet, as I say, there is something more. . . ."

Seeming to grasp my line of thought, Holmes produced his pipe, and began to pack it with shag. "There is indeed 'something more,' Watson. We have almost all the necessary pieces, but one remains rather pointedly missing."

"I know as much, and yet I cannot put my fin-ger on it," said I, glad for the chance to exorcise this nagging doubt. "I do not, as I say, deny that these men committed these crimes—and yet, why the method, Holmes? Where was the need to so mutilate the bodies? Imagine the families of the poor devils, their wives, their children—how must they feel on being presented with such des-ecration?"

Holmes arched an eyebrow. "An odd choice of words, perhaps, Watson. . . ."

"I am a doctor, Holmes; thus, not so odd, I think. No, I will stand by it—desecration."

"Very well, then—but call it what you will, old friend, it is far from mysterious."

"Oh?"

"Indeed. You may demonstrate it for yourself, if you like: Ask the next ten Scotsmen we meet who is responsible for the murders. The opinions— the *official* opinions—of the Scottish press aside, I will wager you that at least half those you canvass will tell you that the spirit that is known to haunt the old west tower has been at work. Some may know Rizzio by name, and some, like Miss Mackenzie, may know him only as 'the Italian gentleman'; but of those who are aware of the tale—and they are many, in this city and country— most will truly believe that, whatever his name, the ancient spirit is abroad seeking vengeance. And this effect can only have been increased by the added feature of McKay's body being not only in a spot where no human could seem to have put it, but so thoroughly run through and crushed as to also indicate the work of a super- natural force: What *natural* power could create such an effect, after all?"

I was rather taken aback. "Are you serious, Holmes? *Half* the population of Scotland believes a murderous ghost is at work?"

"You think my estimate extreme? I can assure you that, despite the natural scepticism of the Scots, it is not. Among *any* group of human beings almost anywhere in the world—and I include England, now—you would find roughly the same results; and you would find, furthermore, a desire to *view* the supposed haunt of the wraith in question, a desire which the murderers doubtless factored into their calculations, as well. We are a species particularly averse to the notion that physical death puts an end to the spirit—how many cases have you and I investigated that prove such an assertion? Thus *dread* will not be the impulse that makes those you interview give such apparently ignorant or superstitious answers—quite to the contrary, it will be *hope*. They will *wish* 'the Italian gentleman's ghost' to be responsible, for it will confirm their fondest desire, at the same time that it frightens them. Even Miss Mackenzie, I suspect, has taken some secret comfort from all that she has been through, terrifying as it has undeniably been."

"Then—these two brothers—they *relied* upon such a reaction, when they re-created the circumstances of Rizzio's death?"

"Indeed, Watson. They did so in the first instance, and then even more elaborately when they positioned McKay's body—a clever bit of embellishment to the legend. And in so doing, they created for themselves a unique power, as the only people who seemed able to come and go from the tower without injury."

"Yes, Holmes, and I have been meaning to ask you about their comings and goings. How has the Hamilton family never once—"

"Not now, old man," Holmes warned, as we came upon a group of guests that were assembled, even at that late hour, outside the century-old elegance of the Roxburghe Hotel, just across from the calm, green expanse of Charlotte Square. "Such details will explain themselves, in time— but we have our own bit of subterfuge to bring off, just now...."

On entering the lobby of the Roxburghe, Holmes and I determined that we would quickly branch off: himself, to dole out a bribe to the young man at the registration desk (an amount large enough to ensure that anyone enquiring as to whether persons answering to our assumed names were indeed staying in the hotel would receive the desired answer); I, meanwhile, would seek some side or back exit, by way of which I might return separately to the palace grounds.

Thus having divided our defensive resources, we would be especially dependent on Hackett's pledge to keep a sharp lookout for us at the west gate to the palace grounds that night; and when we did finally present ourselves at that rendez-vous, mere minutes apart, there indeed the butler was: faithfully at his post, keys in hand and ready to guide us back to our rooms. (How wrong, how very wrong had I been about the fellow when first we had arrived!)

And in this way was the climax of the case carefully arranged, by the most astute mind that could possibly have undertaken its appointment. And yet, as I made ready to finally clear my head for the next evening's action by getting a solid night's sleep, I could not help but wonder if Holmes had in fact told me all. His sudden dis-section, during our stroll to the Roxburghe from the Fife and Drum, of the superstitions of hu-manity regarding ghosts did not sit comfortably alongside his own earlier insistence that he him-self believed in the power of phantoms. Once again, as at many similar passes during earlier cases undertaken throughout my years of work-ing alongside Holmes, I was forced to realise that I simply did not possess all the elements neces-sary for a full understanding of the situation as it stood; and so, despite the considerable consumption of whisky that the evening had required, sleep ultimately proved a long time in coming.

Particularly as I imagined (and it is not an easy thing to confess) that somewhere off in the distance I could detect the slow, inquisitive step that I had first heard earlier that evening: the restless rambling that my rational mind knew must belong to one of the criminal brothers—who was likely preparing the west tower for our visit the next night—but which the superstitious side of my nature told me belonged to "the Italian gentleman," who might, who *must*, view our coming invasion of his haunting ground with the greatest disfavour. . . .

"*Poignarder à l'écossais,*" I murmured, as I rose, pulled the Palm-protector from my jacket pocket, and slipped it beneath my pillow. "Not if an English bullet has anything to say about it. . . ."

Chapter XI

THE SECRETS OF HOLYROODHOUSE

The following day began with precisely the sort of event that one most dreads after an evening's overindulgence:

"Watson!" It was Holmes's voice, not any footman's, and his urgent tone was unmistakably genuine. "Rouse yourself, old friend! The game has commenced ahead of schedule—indeed, I fear the rules may have changed altogether!"

"I certainly hope some such calamity *has* occurred," I muttered sourly, as Holmes fairly tore the curtains from my windows and I forced myself into my clothes. "For your sake!"

"Do forgive me, Watson, but—ah! Here is Mrs.

Hackett, with your breakfast. Eat quickly, while I reveal this sorry intelligence." Holmes waved a telegram through the air once quickly, and I eagerly tucked into another of Mrs. Hackett's first-class Scottish breakfasts. "It is from Mycroft—"

"Holmes," I said suddenly, indicating the head housekeeper and temporary cook with my eyes.

"Oh!" answered he. "Fear not—Mrs. Hackett is entirely in our confidence, along with her husband and son. And we shall need their help, it would appear—Mycroft returns alone, or rather I would that he *were* alone. His intelligence officers have discovered what they consider further evidence of a connection between German imperialists and Scottish nationalists—evidence which, of course, was almost entirely of Mycroft's manufacture. He has left most of them behind to augment Her Majesty's safety—he is now aboard the same train that brought us here, in the company of none save that rather dyspeptic young army officer and Lord Francis."

I shrugged carelessly, allowing the breakfast to perform its characteristic miracle on my exhausted body and abused nervous system. "What of it? I grant you that Lord Francis is hardly likely to be of any great use in a crisis—but then, what crisis is Mycroft likely to encounter before he arrives here?"

"The crisis of Lord Francis himself," Holmes answered, stubbing a cigarette out rather pointedly in my small butter tray. "And I only wish I had made such more plain to—"

"Holmes!" I cried—for I had wanted that good Scots butter. "Of all the infernal—" Suddenly his words burst through the fog that had enshrouded my brain. " 'Lord Francis himself'? Holmes, whatever are you talking about?"

"In part, at least, about this," answered he, producing what seemed an ordinary folded handkerchief. I opened it as I continued to dispose of the breakfast (in-so-far, that is to say, as one *may* dispose of a breakfast, without butter), and found myself staring at a small collection of hairs, apparently human, the exact colour of which I would have been hard-pressed to name, in the glare of the late morning sun that poured through the wall of glass panes across the room. But against the white of the handkerchief, the strands created an overall impression of a particularly bright red—hardly an unusual commodity, in Scotland.

"I suppose it has some importance?" asked I.

"On its own, it has some," Holmes replied. "In conjunction with this"—he pulled a second white kerchief from his pocket—"it has considerably more."

Opening the second packet, I discovered the bits of fuse that Holmes had so carefully gathered up from our train compartment the night before. "The bomb fuse?" I asked.

"Look closer, Watson—in my haste, I swept up more than just the spent fuse. . . ."

And, indeed, he had. Apparently without intending to, Holmes had also gathered up bits of dust and gravel, blown into the car from the bed of the railway line, along with particles of engine cinder—

And hair. Hair of the same peculiar colour as the first few he had shown me. Hair of a colour that I now recognised: "The madman from the train!" I exclaimed. "This is *his* hair, I am sure of it!"

"Certainly, Watson—but how did I gain the second sample?"

"I cannot imagine—unless the fellow has been apprehended—"

"The fellow is far from apprehended. Although he *has* been closely observed, over the last twenty-four hours—by my own brother."

"Mycroft? But Mycroft has been at Balmoral. He would never take a lunatic of such sentiments—nor one, I should hope, of any other sentiments—into the royal presence."

"And if the 'madman' has been in that presence many times on his own? If he is, indeed, well known to Her Majesty?"

I gave the matter a few minutes' thought; and then my very active jaw came to a full stop amid a mouthful of egg and Scottish salmon. "Good God—you don't mean to say—but you do. And worst of all, I begin to see it myself, now. . . ."

Holmes carefully refolded his handkerchiefs, looking quite satisfied. "I have warned you about this sort of thing before, Watson. I recognised him at our very first meeting outside the palace—he is an amateur, after all, and utterly unacquainted with the science of anthropometry. His sole concern was to disguise his face and head, and he believed that the rather crude theatrical properties from which these hairs are taken—along with the adhesives and astringents that he used to disfigure his face—would fill the bill. But the eyes themselves, his skull, his build—none of these could be concealed so readily."

"But—how did he get here? He was back at the palace before we ourselves arrived!"

"Fast horses, carefully staged, are still speedier than trains, Watson, if the rider is expert and can travel over rough country. And Lord Francis was doubtless bred to the hunt."

I considered the point. "Yes. That is certainly

true. . . . But—*why*? Why would he? And how—where—did you find this second group of hairs?"

Holmes shrugged and lifted his head in Mrs. Hackett's direction. "As you know, Watson, it seemed to me from the very start that the great bitterness evidenced by Mrs. Hackett's husband and son was only *deflected* in our direction, from some secret target. That target, I can now tell you, was and remains Lord Francis."

"Indeed, sir," Mrs. Hackett said, her voice and manner far calmer than they had been just a day before. "And, while we are alone, I wonder if you'd mind me asking—what made you believe as much?"

"A wealth of small points, Mrs. Hackett," replied Holmes. "For instance, shortly after we arrived, your husband made sure to tell us that you had not only turned down our beds but warmed them; a detail, perhaps, but hardly a meaningless one. Had we been utterly unwelcome, you could easily have spared yourself that effort, and left us to the cold comfort of unwarmed linens."

Mrs. Hackett blushed and then smiled, in embarrassment, appreciation, and perhaps even a bit of amusement: Clearly, this woman who I had initially thought the nervous, fairly simple wife of a cruel husband was, in actuality, as perceptive and capable an arranger of complex, dangerous dealings as was Hackett himself, and would prove a reliable ally in whatever difficult events were to come.

"Oh, he is a wicked, wicked master, Doctor," Mrs. Hackett pronounced, with as much disdain as fear, "but he is a Hamilton—the noble and ancient family charged with Her Majesty's care in this palace, as well as with that of the palace itself. How could my husband or I ever speak a word to strangers? Lord Francis had made it clear enough what we might expect. But Mr. Holmes was good enough to remove him from the house, if only for a day and a night—and that, praise God, was time enough for us to finally do some of the things that had needed doing for so very long. And I began by fetching the hairs that Mr. Holmes said he needed—"

My head had been almost spinning during this remarkable revelation, and to stop it I finally dropped my silverware rather forcefully onto the breakfast tray. The resultant noise silenced my two visitors. "A moment, if you please, both of you. Now, then—*you* are saying, Mrs. Hackett, that Lord Francis, far from being the amiable host he appears, has been a sinister tormentor of the staff in this house for years on end?"

"Aye, sir," the woman said. "That—and far worse. My niece's honour may have been lost to

Likely Will Sadler's deceiving tongue—but it would have been lost to far worse, as have other serving girls', had Lord Francis been allowed his way. But from the first, he was made to understand—by one in a position to tell him—that Allie was no' to be trifled with; and there were lasses enough, for his amusement, to be found among the rest of the staff. Some were even willing, God help them—although Lord Francis preferred them not to be. The evil monster. Yes, he preferred them to resist, so that he could use on them the same crop with which he has often driven his horses to their deaths, the poor beasts—"

"And *you*, Holmes," I interrupted, unable to bear any more of this litany of foul abuses of power by a royal agent. "You are saying that you knew his nefarious nature from the moment we reached the palace?"

"I am not saying that I knew its full extent, Watson—but I knew him to be the same man who had attacked us on the train."

"Who had nearly killed us with a bomb, you mean to say!"

"Certainly not. That device was meant to frighten, not to kill. Such may not have been the intent of the man who originally assembled it, nor of he who delivered it, but it was *someone's*.

As we noted at the time, the charge had been constructed by a person with access to advanced ingredients, but without the knowledge to assemble them correctly—such is not a description of Lord Francis. Indeed, had the device detonated when he threw it, the resulting explosion would have been far more destructive than he anticipated, and would almost certainly have resulted in his death, as well as our own—witness the terrific explosion produced by the similar creation which his minions merely hurled in the direction of the railway line, with the object only of halting our engine. *Our* 'gift,' however, had been tampered with *before* Lord Francis delivered it—the fuse was made long enough to allow us ample time to simply tear it out by the root, as we did."

"As *you* did, Holmes." The man rather decently waved off my correction. "Who, then," I continued, "was our angel of mercy?"

"You have only to consider the origins of the device, Watson," Holmes replied. "To begin with, remember the gun-cotton: There is but one place where one might procure it in this city—the garrison armoury at the Castle—and, even at that, one could only do so if granted free access to all areas, without rousing suspicion. We know that Will Sadler does various jobs relating to the restoration and maintenance of all sorts of arms, within the Castle's walls—but he is no modern artilleryman. Thus it is consistent that he viewed the gun-cotton as no more than harmless wadding, when he purloined it."

I weighed this analysis, realising that it had been only my own concern about the possible complicity of British soldiers in Sadler's scheme that had kept me from seeing as much on the previous night. "All right, then," said I. "Will Sadler built the bomb—but, certainly, *he* did not leave the fuse too long. Nor did the man who delivered it—which brings me to this business of matching hair samples. How did you manage *that*?"

"As Mrs. Hackett has said, it was necessary to remove Lord Francis to obtain such proofs—and I supposed that if Mycroft would employ a royal command, there would be no question of Hamilton's refusal. My brother cooperated, unknowingly and swiftly—after which, Mrs. Hackett and I had our choice of opportunities to go through the man's rooms, which we did earlier this morning."

"He keeps a closet full of such things, Doctor," Mrs. Hackett added. "One would think he was an actor on the stage!"

"An actor, yes," said Holmes. "But I fear his 'stage' is the whole of this city, where, in disguises far more effective and pleasing than that which he employed at the train, he has despoiled count- less young women—and perhaps done far worse. At any rate, I soon found the accoutrements we had seen, and a reading glass in the library was aid enough to confirm the match."

"Whilst I, in the meantime, was utterly taken in by the man's manner, and unable to provide any help at all," said I, taking my knife and fork back up rather contritely.

"Nonsense, Watson—had we *both* been imme- diately aware of Lord Francis's dual nature, one of us should doubtless have made a false step. Your genuine liking for the creature in his most pleasant guise kept his guard down—and con- tributed to the ease with which we were able to convince him to depart. Besides, you must not blame yourself *too* much, my dear fellow, for the fact of being taken in—after all, amateur or no, Lord Francis is among the best of this criminal type that we have encountered together. You will recall the man who called himself Stapleton, some years ago?"

"Of course," I replied. "The Baskerville case."

"Indeed. A comparable example—although I suspect that Lord Francis is Stapleton's superior in raw physical strength: Do not forget the manner in which he shattered our compartment window."

"I am unlikely to. And yet—his manner, Holmes, when we reached the palace! *Surely* his disguise on the train was more elaborate than a mere wig and whiskers—for he seemed such a smaller man when we met him in his true guise."

"The pure effect of posture and voice, Watson. The deliberate slouch of the shoulders, the effeminacy of the handshake, the coyness of the voice and obsequiousness of manner—all were designed to make us *see* him as a smaller, weaker specimen. And yet, recall more exactly: Was he not capable of looking me quite directly in the eye when I mentioned the effect of bloodshed on the palace?"

"Why—indeed he was! In fact, I remarked to myself upon it at the time: He seemed for a moment truly indignant, and to be capable of rising quite to your own appreciable height. Was that your reason for such a rude introductory remark?"

"Of course. However clever, any fellow who has become arrogant enough to rely on such rudimentary methods of disguise will surely allow himself to be drawn out by a ploy only slightly more complex. Once I had gauged his actual height and strength—the matter began to clear up quickly. He is a third son, after all; and the Hamiltons— while, as Mrs. Hackett says, an ancient clan, rich in their position—are nonetheless poor in their purse. There is little he can hope for from his rather humiliating post as caretaker of a royal lodging house—but of that little, I confess, Francis Hamilton has made the very most. Indeed, the only thing he lacked, when he concocted this scheme, was an effective lieutenant."

As Mrs. Hackett took my tray away, I lit a cigarette of my own and picked up a final cup of strong tea, protesting: "Ah! You mean lieuten-*ants*, do you not, Holmes?"

My friend looked somewhat hesitant for a moment; then, turning to the housekeeper, he seemed to silently enquire as to whether or not *she* wished to answer the question; and in doing so, he brought something back into my mind. "Wait just a moment—Mrs. Hackett? You said before that, had Lord Francis been allowed his way, your niece would have suffered violent dishonour—but that he was warned off, by one whose warning he would respect. And you, Holmes: You have yet to say who would have had reason to *deliberately* leave the bomb fuse long enough for us to be able to rip it out prior to the explosion. It seems that you are each trying to intimate some same fact—am I not correct?"

Holmes simply glanced at the housekeeper. "Mrs. Hackett?"

The woman gave a small curtsey, turned, and,

holding the tray with one arm, opened the bedroom door—

And there, standing in the hallway, was Robert
Sadler, his height and strength never so apparent.

"Holmes!" I cried, lunging toward the bed and
securing the Palm-protector that lay under one of
the pillows; but Holmes only placed himself
squarely in my line of fire. "Damn it, man!" I
urged. "Move, I've no clear shot at him!"

"That's precisely why I *am* standing here, Watson," Holmes answered. "I know your skill, even
with unorthodox firearms."

And then I noticed that, as Mrs. Hackett passed
out of the door and into the hall to set the tray on
a side table, she laid an affectionate hand on Robert Sadler's upper arm, and then guided him into
my bedroom. The man took one or two steps inside, eyes ever on the peculiar little gun, and
stopped.

I stood up straight, allowing the pistol to drift
to my side. "What the devil *is* going on?" I bellowed. Looking for some further way to express
my irritation at this rather indirect revelation of
the truth, I was able to produce only the rather
absurd question: "And is it *entirely* necessary that,
whatever it is, it all go on in my bedroom?"

"Neither necessary nor desirable," replied
Holmes. "Yours is the room most dangerously

positioned. So, if you will withdraw to the
dressing-room adjacent and finish preparing
yourself for the day, both Mr. Sadler and I will
explain the rest of what has transpired this morning, that we may transfer our operations to the
courtyard side of the palace."

I huffed rather theatrically as I followed the order, and once in the small dressing-room, called,
"I suppose you will tell me that this young man
is innocent of all wrong-doing in this affair!"

"Not *all* wrong-doing," Holmes replied. "He
was indeed a part of the original fraud."

"Aye, sir," added Robert Sadler, in quiet contrition. "I will ask no forgiveness, so far as the tours
of the west tower are concerned—in fact, they
were my idea, at the start of it all. And believe
me, there was no harm in any of it then. What
Mr. Holmes says of the Hamiltons is true: They
are hard masters, and the wages here would be
the true crime, were it no' for occasional and generous gifts from Her Majesty. But—well, we'd
had so many curious parties come to us, so many
wealthy types as had heard the tales of the ghost
of the Italian gentleman—and there is scarce anyone here, 'most all the year. . . ."

I emerged from the dressing-room, adjusting
my collar and tie. "These are hardly justifications,
Sadler."

"No, sir, true enough," he answered, quite whole-heartedly. "And I make none. But it's simply that—well, when Mr. Holmes surprised me this morning in the tower, while I was setting out the blood—"

"Ah! When you were renewing 'the blood that never dries,' I take it."

"Precisely, Watson," Holmes answered. "I fear my own night was passed beneath Queen Mary's old bed, in the chamber above that in which we found Miss Mackenzie. A cursory examination of the floorboards revealed a peculiar wood—I do not believe that I have encountered it before. But its grain was such that the 'blood that never dries' would only need to be renewed ten to twelve hours before each visit, in order for the correct effect to be achieved. In addition, while it was indeed possible that Robert, here, was an enthusiastic partner in the recent violence, his manner last night, along with Miss Mackenzie's protestations, revealed something else entirely. He displayed all the mannerisms of a man who, as the Chinese say, has leapt upon a tiger's back, and finds it difficult to dismount. But I admit to having been prejudiced, by the time we visited the Fife and Drum—by something Miss Mackenzie confirmed when we encountered her."

I quickly recalled one of the comments that

had struck me as obscure, at that time—and, in an instant, I was able to combine it with one of the first and most peculiar sights that had marked our stay. "The bird," I said, referring to one of Holmes's queries to the young girl; and then I turned round: "Mrs. Hackett, if I may—is it your husband's common practice to wear the patch that we saw upon his eye last night, rather than that rather ill-fitting glass eye that he struggled with so while taking my bags?"

"Indeed, Doctor." A new voice had entered our chorus: Hackett's, and as he entered the room I noted that the man was—as if to demonstrate the current point of the explication—wearing the patch. "I do sincerely beg your pardon for that display, sir. It was yet another attempt to signal to you gentlemen, in the hopes that you would not take matters in the palace at their surface value."

"Then you *did* lose your eye to Will Sadler's— what sort of a bird is it?" I moved closer to the man, and saw that, even with his patch in place, the cluster of scars reached out under it. "No falcon, that much is certain. A goshawk, perhaps?"

"Well done, Watson, well done!" Holmes said, as Hackett offered me an affirmative inclination of his head. "You see, now, why I mentioned the markings as being quite distinctive, and occupying an important place in the pattern of details we have assembled about Will Sadler. He is evidently preoccupied with all things medieval, and my certainty about Hackett's shielded sentiments made me curious—perhaps even suspicious—about the wound from the start. For it is not a terribly old injury, is it?"

Examining the man's face again, I said, "I should not think so. Not more than a year, certainly."

"Aye, sir," Hackett said. "It was when I first discovered what was happening in the west tower. Without thinking of what it would mean for all the palace staff, I declared that I would go to Lord Francis's father: This"—he indicated the patch, with scarcely contained rage—"was the young nobleman's response, or, rather, his order to Likely Will, although Lord Francis took much delight in watching Will torment the bird into committing the act. Blood and cruelty, Doctor—they are that 'gentleman's' food and drink. I should no' have cared, for m'self, but he said he would do far worse to little Allie, however his henchmen might try to protect her—and I believed him. . . ."

Glancing at Robert Sadler, I saw real and deep remorse in his expression. "It was then that I began to look for ways to end the business," Sadler said. "But we were already so deep in the mire. . . . With the right sort of audience, hundreds of pounds, even guineas, could change hands in a single night—the sort of money men will kill for, much less commit. . . ." He looked to the floor in even deeper shame. "But I *could* protect Allie— that much I could do."

"And it meant a great deal, son," said Hackett. "Ne'er think otherwise."

Robert tried to smile at the older man in response; and although the attempt was not strong, he clearly felt some measure of relief at Hackett's attitude.

"I shall continue to do so, Mr. Hackett," the young man replied quietly. "For as long as she will allow me to. . . ."

Was this, at last, the *true* reason for Robert Sadler's presence among all these people, that morning? Was he, had he been—despite all his fraudulent activities, and despite the terrible manner in which his own brother had misused and despoiled the girl—in love with Miss Mackenzie? A mere look at his face as he went back to staring at the floor told all—or seemed to.

"Does this mean that you have now abandoned your brother?" asked I. "And intend to work with us to bring both him and Lord Francis to justice?"

Sadler's answer was eager: "I know I have much to answer for, Doctor—but I beg you to believe that I could no' have played a part in those murders. What I said last night to you, I meant—

both as a way of appealing to yourself and Mr. Holmes, and as a warning to Will—I can follow him no longer, if such methods are to be his way of protecting his wealth."

I nodded, harbouring no real desire to be stern, but feeling that the statement—noble as it might have sounded—must not be allowed to go unquestioned.

"You have proved a master of chicanery, Mr. Sadler," said I. "And it might look to an outsider as though this is another elaborate trick. Even false affection for Miss Mackenzie would be an extraordinarily pleasant price to pay, to gain our support in your appeal to the authorities."

"I know, sir," he replied. "And I expect no mercy. I will take the punishment I am due—all I ask is that I take no other, and that the men responsible for those greater crimes be revealed, so that Allie *will* be safe—always."

"Well said, Sadler," Holmes announced. "Even Watson—who sees far deeper into matters of the heart than can I—must surely be satisfied with such an assertion."

I studied Robert Sadler carefully for a few more seconds before announcing: "Yes, Holmes. I believe I am."

"Good. And so—here we are! Or are we? We lack two of our company—"

"Allie and Andrew," said Mrs. Hackett. "They're preparing the master's and Mr. Mycroft's rooms. You said that all should appear regular when they arrive, sir."

"Indeed I did, Mrs. Hackett," replied Holmes. "And indeed it must—well done. Although I now worry that it may avail us little: I had intended to reveal all to my brother in a coded wire, before he commenced his return, so that we might catch these fellows tonight, *in flagrante;* now that he has left before I could dispatch that communication, I confess to being anxious that he may grow too talkative on the train, before he realises Lord Francis's true character. Our only advantage is that Mycroft *himself* knows comparatively little of the truth. But even that little—our dismissal of most of the household staffs, here and at Balmoral, as suspects, for example, or our ruminations over McKay's corpse—may be enough to alert so clever and ruthless a villain as Hamilton and inspire him to violence. Or even more probably, he will attempt to abduct Mycroft, and to bargain with us for his own freedom."

"But, Holmes," I replied, "you say your suspicions were confirmed *before* your brother departed with Lord Francis—why did you not tell him all, then?"

"It seemed a fair risk to take," said Holmes. "After all, I had only *some* of the answer, virtually no proof, and an urgent need to be rid of Lord Francis. I could not be certain that, had Mycroft known of his companion's treachery, he would not have revealed as much during their travels, or appealed to the Queen directly, before our case was ready to be made."

I gave my friend a stern eye. "You could fairly be accused of having acted in a most careless manner where your brother's safety, rather than your own, was concerned."

"It was necessary!" Holmes protested. "Mycroft is capable of far more self-defence than you suspect, Watson." It sounded, for an instant, as though the man was attempting to convince himself, rather than me, of this last fact—particularly in light of the dangers that he had himself only just enumerated.

"Let us hope so," said I. "And I suppose I must concede an additional consideration—had your brother known all, and alerted Lord Francis in some way, we at the very least could have depended on the villain not to return. He would be well away by now, would he not?"

"Forgive me, Doctor," said Robert Sadler, and we all turned to him. "But I don't think such is the case. It's the money, you see—we eventually made so much of it—*mounds,* indeed. And we could hardly go to a bank—"

Holmes made a noise of deep, amused comprehension, as I asked, "And so—you did what with it?"

"The west tower, sir," replied Sadler. "The Queen's old bedchamber—it's inside the mattress. And from what you and Mr. Holmes have said, Will may have started to remove it, even last evening, before we met at the Fife and Drum. He said nothing to me of it, but it's no' likely that he would, if his intent was to make off with it."

" 'The Italian gentleman,' Watson," said Holmes. "The spirit that walked abroad last night, humming a most anachronistic tune—which it *does* now seem likely that Lord Francis taught him."

"I care no' for the money, any longer," Sadler continued, "but Lord Francis will never let Will cheat him of it—and it matters little to a man like that *who* tries to stand in his way, I promise you. He *will* come here and claim what he believes is his, in this palace that he yet believes is the rightful property of his family. I've oft heard him refer to 'this tribe of German degenerates' when speaking of the Queen and her family—I honestly believe that the man may *be* mad, Mr. Holmes, nobleman or no. . . ."

Holmes's face had grown steadily darker through this speech—and it was not difficult to understand why. His brother was now traveling alone with this man that Mrs. Hackett had rightly called a monster (alone, that is, save for the presence of a young officer whose usefulness we had already been given good reason to doubt); and Mycroft was in this predicament because Holmes had, once again, put the solution to a case above all other considerations. It seemed, somehow, not only unlikely but quite impossible that so damnably clever a rogue as Lord Francis would not wheedle what truth Mycroft possessed out of the elder Holmes brother, over the course of even a short journey; and that from those few facts he would quickly divine something closely resembling the extent of his current peril. And if *I* suddenly felt anxiety of my own at this prospect, how much more must Holmes have been feeling?

I would never know; for he bore up under any strain he felt just as he did in all such situations and under all nervous pressures: actively.

"We can only concern ourselves, Mr. Sadler, with what we can do here," he said, "and your information will, I suspect, prove invaluable in this regard. Hackett—if you would, assemble your son and niece, and let us resume this meeting downstairs, *away* from these windows! We have a long day and night ahead of us—it is essential that we all know our parts by rote. Quickly, now!"

The order was taken seriously (even if Holmes's dread of the outer windows of the palace was as yet obscure), and before long we were in the royal dining-room below, which would serve as our impromptu headquarters throughout the rest of the day. I do not use the military reference lightly; for as the hours spun away, failing to produce any sign of Mycroft Holmes or even any communication from him, the sense of urgency grew, as did new doubts as to whether or not our antagonists would be able to produce new confederates to assist in the effort to safely carry off whatever disreputable lucre Likely Will Sadler had not taken the previous evening. Thinking of this, it occurred to Holmes that we ought to go up and examine the store of remaining monies, in order to determine how probable it was that our enemies would number more than one or two: If relatively little of the store was left, after all, it seemed at least possible that Will Sadler would let the rest go, in the interest of making good his escape. There was also the chance that Likely Will would honour his thieves' covenant with

Lord Francis, and that the *both* of them might depart, after dividing what had already been taken; Robert seemed to think this likely, although if the roles of the two villains had been reversed, he said, he would have voiced an opposite opinion. But, with the matter arranged as it was, there seemed momentary cause for hope.

And so, just after tea, Holmes, Hackett, and I assembled and began the ascent to Queen Mary's former rooms: the most ancient and untouched part of the palace, site of the supposed haunting by David Rizzio, and the reason for which Sir Alistair Sinclair and Dennis McKay had lost their lives in manners at once brutal and absurd. (Neither Mrs. Hackett nor Miss Mackenzie would, quite naturally, even consider making the trip; and we thought it best to leave Robert Sadler and young Andrew Hackett behind, to comfort and, if necessary, protect the women, should the matter come to a head before we were quite prepared.) With Hackett bearing a razor-edged gutting-knife and a torch, and myself, now, having raided the gun room of the palace for something more substantial than the Palm-protector (I chose a side-by-side twelve-bore, with a wide choke), we remaining three had some hope that we might approximate a considerable force, when we finally entered the rooms that had long ago provided the stuff of which our current troubles had been spun.

"Of course," Holmes said, as we began to ascend the stone circular stairs in the north-east corner of the tower, "all our reasoning is predicated on the notion that David Rizzio *has* played no part in all these matters. A presumption hardly proved, as yet. . . ."

Hackett attempted something like a smile in reply, although the effort was based solely and rather obviously on a desire to avoid the further appearance of ill manners; I, however, was under no such constraints:

"Given the predicament in which we all find ourselves, Holmes, and particularly given the possible peril in which *you* have placed your own brother, I should not have thought levity even a possibility."

"Levity?" the man answered. "I am perfectly serious, Watson."

"Are you?" I had not even the strength or the will to debate this increasingly, indeed, this *tediously* baffling issue. "Well, I suppose that we shall know the truth soon enough."

"Shall we?"

"Of course." With the light of the palace hall fading beneath us, Hackett ignited his all-too-dim torch, which cast fearsome shadows on the stone walls of the ever-narrowing stairway. "If," I continued, somehow feeling the need to whisper, "we find that the loot of the criminals is untouched, why, we will know that what we heard last evening was, indeed, your friend, the spirit of Signor Rizzio—who, evidently, continues to take an interest in the latest Italian music!"

I regretted the flippant remark almost as soon as I made it; and that feeling would deepen dramatically within a matter of minutes. . . .

∞

Chapter XII

"THE BLOOD THAT NEVER DRIES"

Immediately upon our entering the series of
rooms that had once been the private realm of
the last Scottish Queen, it became clear that the
century between her death and the expansion of
the palace by Charles II had been more than
enough time for the notion that there was something other-worldly about the chambers to take
root. It was not a hallowed feeling, precisely, for
Death does not always hallow the places it visits;
but the rooms were nevertheless overpowering
in their sense of tragedy, injustice, and even cruelty. Charles II—who had been forced, by the
tragedies of his own early life, to become a man

of greater personal sensitivity than most in our own age comprehend—had acted to prevent the physical collapse of Mary Stuart's chambers, but he had not tried to alter their essence, architecturally or otherwise; and none of the members of the various dynasties that had ruled Britain in the years since had meddled with this policy (beyond, that is, allowing it to degenerate into a state of out-and-out neglect). Thus, it was with a heightened sense of stepping back—no, that hackneyed phrase will not do, for in truth the feeling was more one of being grasped and *dragged* back—into a terrible past, one that was beyond the power of kings or commoners to change, that one now ventured into the upper reaches of the west tower. Time, to be sure, had continued to work upon the rooms; but one rather got the feeling that Time had been *allowed* to do so, since the decrepitude that it brought did nothing but reinforce the sense of brutal misfortune that was the legacy of and the memorial to the terrible act that had made the tower infamous, so long ago.

There was no ambient light of any kind: The window-shutters in each of the rooms—starting with the antechamber, into which the stone staircase disgorged us—had been closed and fixed generations earlier, and far more efficiently than in the rooms immediately below. They had then been covered with much heavier curtains, such that we continued to see solely by the light of Hackett's relatively small torch; although what we saw was, in truth, far less important than what we felt. The basic appointments of the chamber—panelled walls and ceilings, planked floors, rotted textiles, decrepit furnishings—were proportionally more unnerving than those below, the more so for being Tudor rather than baroque in style. And yet, as I inspected the appointments further, it occurred to me that there is, in houses, a certain moment at which decay seems to slow dramatically, so long as the building's walls and roof remain intact (as was the case with the palace's west tower); indeed, the process of decrepitude seems at some point almost to stop, as though not only Time, but vermin of every variety, have taken all they can take and destroyed all they can destroy, leaving behind what amounts to the bleached bones of a formerly warm, living habitation. And Queen Mary's rooms had, apparently, long ago reached this archaeological nadir.

So powerful had this impression grown, even before we had so much as reached the doorway to the ill-fated queen's bedchamber, that it required Holmes's practised eye to point an interesting feature out to me:

"A laboratory of decay, eh, Watson? All the elements—dust, detritus, cobwebs. . . ."

"You have a point, I suppose, Holmes?"

"Only that we seem to be remaining remarkably free of it all."

And then I stopped, looking up and down my clothing and lifting a hand to feel the top of my head. "Interesting," said I. "And look behind us—Hackett, flash your torch this way, will you? See how it has all been carefully cleared and maintained—almost like a pathway through some dark jungle."

"Aye, Doctor," Hackett replied. "Many of their customers are wealthy folk, who come here after an evening's dining and entertainment—the master makes sure that they don't have to complain of cobwebs or spiders on their clothing, even if they see such all around them. Dust, as well—if you look at the floor, you'll see that he keeps the path free of anything that might tarnish the ladies' shoes."

"It was the first proof that we were indeed on the correct trail, last night," Holmes added. "I collected more filth under the bed than I did out here, where it seems so plentiful. Lord Francis and Likely Will are able artists of fraud, I will allow them that much."

I turned to face, at last, the fateful bedchamber. "Very well, then, Hackett—let us see all that we have come *to* see. . . ."

Inside the bedchamber, I was particularly un-nerved to discover that a gaming table still sat by the window seat, with other chairs gathered round and dust-covered cards of a very old style, as well as ancient crockery, lying atop it. Obvi-ously, it was another sham dreamed up by the criminal trio; but I imagined its effect was quite potent, for one could not help the feeling that one was staring at the remains of a diverting game, an amusement that had been interrupted centu-ries ago by those brutish noblemen, some in full armour, all intent on murdering a poor soul who had never done them any harm. We walked slowly to the very low doorway into the Queen's little supper-room, situated in the north-west tur-ret of the tower: One could still see that it must have been a charming, warm little chamber, where the queen might have suckled the infant that would one day become the first man to com-bine the crowns of Scotland and England into one legitimate honour (although, as I knew, James had actually been born in Edinburgh Castle, per-haps because the queen feared some new trag-edy of the type against which the Palace of Holyrood had already proved so terribly inse-

cure). I was about to step into this, the first inviting part of the west tower that I had encountered,
when Holmes caught my arm.

"Mind, Watson," he said, pulling me back.
"Sadler has gone to a great deal of trouble to re-
new that pool—it would be a shame if you were
to thoughtlessly track it all over the tower. . . ."

Looking down, I could see that, just where I
had intended on putting one foot, there was a
glimmering, rather sticky pool of blood, the crim-
son of life in its colour having given way to the
claret-like depth of age: It had been there, I esti-
mated, at least through the day.

"'The blood that never dries'?" said I, in an
especially hushed tone.

"If it is not," replied Holmes, smiling, "then I
should not care to know what it is."

I nodded, and then looked back at the small
pool. "Is it human? I suppose you have conducted
a re-agent test already."

"I have not bothered," said he. "Whether it is
human or animal is not really our concern, and is
something, too, that we shall likely find out soon
enough. Although, if it *is* human, I suspect that
we may be able to fix a string of new crimes to
our antagonists."

"You do not think they would have used the
blood of their two murder victims?"

"They *cannot* have done so for all of the several years during which they have been engaged in their enterprise."

Hackett spoke up: "Pardon me, sir, but young Rob *did* make a practice of storing the blood of any animals he culled within the park, if it could pass for human—I know as much because I found a bottle of boar's blood, once, in one of the coldest of the cellars. He told some tale about his mother using such for blood pudding, but he was lying, there was no doubt of that—and I never found his hiding places thereafter."

"Ah," said Holmes, starting to pull the disintegrating old spreads from the bed, "but that was before Lord Francis took absolute control of the endeavour, Hackett! I have no doubt that if the incentive for profit was sufficient, that man would have preyed upon this city's less fortunate for the satisfaction of *all* his base desires, carnal and pecuniary; yes, he would fit the role of a latter-day ghoul, not waiting for bodies to be in the ground before draining their blood for his own purposes. . . . But for now, let us see. . . . Here we are!"

The bared mattress of the bed bore a carefully bound-up slit in one of its sides, and when Holmes removed the leather lacing, *something*—ancient straw, horse-hair, goose-down, what have you—

ought to have come spilling out of the side. But nothing at all emerged—not, that is, until Holmes put his hand into the slit and removed a bag of coins. Opening it quickly, he made a noise of appreciation and said, "Quite a collection. Various nationalities and denominations . . . but for the most part"—he withdrew a coin—"sovereigns. A wise choice. . . ."

"And how many bags would you say the bed contains, in all?" I asked.

Holmes inserted his arm nearly up to the elbow, then said, "I can only tell you, Watson, that I am glad I passed the night *beneath* the bed, rather than *upon* it. But perhaps you would care to . . . ?"

Shrugging once—for I did not, to be honest, begin to suspect what he was hinting at—I turned round and rather cavalierly threw myself onto the mattress: not the *most* painful experience I have ever endured, but certainly one of the most shocking, given what one expects of even aged, dilapidated beds.

"Good Lord, Holmes!" I cried, getting to my feet as though I had leapt into scalding water. "It's everywhere—almost the entire surface of the thing!"

Holmes nodded. "And nearly to the bottom," he added, examining to that depth.

Even the normally imperturbable Hackett went

wide-eyed with wonder. "The devil," he said, in a faint whisper. "I never dreamed it could be so much. . . ."

"We would be hard-pressed to say just *how* much," Holmes replied, "but I should not put it at any less than a considerable fortune. Certainly, Dr. Watson and I have known men to kill for only a portion of this collection—how easy must it have been for one such as Lord Francis to do so, when the business was putting him so close to achieving the wealth that he evidently feels is the proper due of a man with his pedigree."

" 'Close?' " said I. "My dear Holmes, you must be joking—there is a princely sum here, certainly!"

"You forget the need to split that sum three ways," answered Holmes. "No, Watson," he went on, replacing the sack that he had removed, lacing the opening back up, and stepping over to where I was standing. "If such a man's lust for wealth *can* ever be sated"—Holmes glanced down at the glistening pool of blood on the floor—"certainly, *this* store would not be enough. Not so long as his partners are alive. . . ." Reaching down, Holmes dipped a finger into the thick pool and then rubbed the substance between the finger and its opposing thumb, examining the stain it produced. " 'The blood that never dries,' " he murmured; and then, after remaining silent as Hackett and I replaced the spreads that had covered the bed, he turned to me. "You have not yet noticed it, Watson."

"It? The blood?" I looked at the pool, then about the room. "What is there to notice, save that—that—" I felt my brow screw up in some confusion. "Just a moment, Holmes. . . ."

"Well done, old man."

"It—it's not in the right location."

"Indeed—given all the distractions you've endured, you have shown admirable speed of perception."

"Excuse me, sir?" said Hackett, obviously interested but quite perplexed.

"The blood, Hackett—it shouldn't be here."

"Well, of course, sir—"

"No, no," Holmes clarified. "It shouldn't be *here*, Hackett—in *this* spot."

"The Queen's party were dining within the *smaller* chamber, there," said I, pointing at the very supper room that I (not yet recalling the full details of the story whilst in the spot) had found so charming. "Darnley and the nobles came up the hidden stairs, which must be—"

To spare me the effort, Hackett simply moved to one wall and placed a hand on the border of a wooden panel, which drew away (as I had heard its corresponding number one floor below do when I discovered Miss Mackenzie) to reveal the privy stairs that led down to what had been, before Charles II's renovation of the palace, Darnley's rooms.

"Thank you, Hackett," said I. "And so the men appeared from these stairs—seized Rizzio in the supper-room—and dragged him to the larger stairway before killing him. This 'blood that never dries' was never here to begin with!"

Hackett looked mystified. "And yet it *has* been, sir—aye, even before Lord Francis was ever born. My own father worked in the palace, Doctor, and told us of the stain. I saw it, in my youth, with my own eyes."

I looked to Holmes to find him still examining the blood on his fingers, but nodding, now, with the deepest intellectual satisfaction. "At last," he mused. "Hackett—you have provided the proverbial missing link in our antagonists' chain of crime. For no confidence scheme such as this one can *ever* be created out of *pure* legend. In order for an entire city—indeed, an entire nation—to have believed that the blood of the wrongfully slain Rizzio was reappearing every night, there must have been some sort of a factual foundation upon which to build."

"But—what was it, Mr. Holmes?" Hackett asked anxiously. "What *did* I see on the floor, all those years ago?"

Holmes merely lifted his shoulders. "So many things may pass for blood, Hackett: We might find that the unusual floorboards of this regal bedchamber were cut from an exotic wood, one whose oils and tannins do not truly dry for centuries—there are several such species. Or, more likely, some early and untraceable leak in the turret roof kept one spot not only moist but stained, as the water carried with it various forms of soil, dust, soot, and vermin excrement. Perpetual leaks and stains are known in nearly every ancient house—and are why many are demolished. But the important truth is that there was, indeed, a stain! And what, for many generations, *was* a stain, could easily *become*, if the perpetrator was clever enough about his business, a 'pool'— for, as I have already told Dr. Watson, it is in the nature of mankind to *wish* to believe such stories. Yes, we have a complete structure of our legend now—"

Holmes's moment of triumph was cut short by a voice, sudden and shrill, drifting up the stone stairway without: It was Mrs. Hackett.

"Mr. Holmes—you must come down at once, oh, please, you must!"

Holmes moved quickly to the antechamber doorway. "What is it, Mrs. Hackett? My brother?"

"Oh, indeed, sir!" came the reply. "And in ever such a state! He looks as though he shall expire, sir!"

Fascinated as we all had been by our discoveries, we fairly fell over one another getting to the winding staircase—although it was, of course, Holmes who quickly moved to the fore, concern for Mycroft at last showing in his legs, if it had not in his earlier manner.

Chapter XIII

THE LINES ARE DRAWN. . . .

We did not, thankfully, find Mycroft Holmes on death's door when we descended to the dining-room—although it was easy to see why Mrs. Hackett had thought him so. Upon reaching Waverley Station, Mycroft had been surprised to learn that not only had Lord Francis failed to ensure that a carriage from the palace was waiting to retrieve them; he was not planning to return to Holyroodhouse at all (not directly, at any rate). And although the military intelligence officer had eventually secured a hansom, the driver of said cab had ultimately proved unable to face down his fears and deliver his passengers—who had already been exhausted by more than a full day's continuous travel—the whole way to the palace entrance: Mycroft and his escort had been deposited instead at the edge of the park, and from there had been forced to walk. The remaining leg of their trip was less than half a mile—but such was a greater distance than Mycroft's legs normally traversed in a week, and it had generated enough exertion to quite take the wind from him, whilst simultaneously covering his brow with perspiration and ultimately making the poor housekeeper believe that his wheezing and gasps were signs of some mortal physical crisis.

Mycroft's journey back from Balmoral had otherwise gone without incident, despite his having revealed, as Holmes had feared, all that he knew concerning the investigation at Holyroodhouse— and when he learned how fortunate his journey's seemingly innocuous conclusion had in fact been, he settled into an odd brew of relief, amazement, and anger: relief, for reasons various and apparent; amazement, that he had suspected nothing in Lord Francis's manner that would have indicated the real nature of the latter's activities; anger, at both himself and his brother, for having allowed Lord Francis into the royal presence at all. Immediately, Mycroft dispatched our dour old friend from military intelligence into the city, to try to locate the young lord of Holy-roodhouse; but, following the man's departure, he continued to upbraid himself for ever having taken Lord Francis to Balmoral. Holmes did his best to insist that his brother should feel no responsibility for this seeming risk, that he himself deserved to bear the entire weight of whatever danger had existed; but that it had been, in the first place, necessary to our forming a better picture of what had been happening at Holyroodhouse, and in the second, no real risk at all, being as it had been safe to assume that Mycroft could be relied upon to attend to the Queen's safety more sensibly than any man alive, even if he for some reason did *not*, during the trip to Balmoral, begin to understand Lord Francis's true nature.

"But how could you think that I *would* determine Hamilton's devilry, Sherlock?" Mycroft demanded, once Mrs. Hackett had produced a decanter of dry sherry and several glasses.

"You will forgive me, Mycroft!" Holmes nearly shouted in reply, in that tone of irritability that often comes over those who have found that a close relation who they thought in mortal peril has come through it safely. "But I believed the face that this man presents to the world to be so false that persons of common sense *must*, after a time, find it transparent—as the staff of this household evidently did long ago. And yet here are you and Watson both, telling me that you found nothing objectionable in it—"

"My dear Holmes," I interjected, with no little irritation of my own, "I had known the fellow less than a day, and your brother had not had his acquaintance for very much longer. As you yourself said to me on the train, we do not all share the same skills and strengths—so I hope you will forgive our less than encyclopaedic knowledge of the criminal type, its permutations, and the most arcane methods of detecting any and all such."

"Well said, Doctor," added Mycroft, after sweeping down three full glasses of sherry like so much water. "Had I spent as much time crawling through gutters and opium dens as have you, Sherlock, I might perhaps have marked a certain disingenuousness in Lord Francis—"

"Hyperbole will not pass for argument, Mycroft," Holmes answered, trying very hard to regain an even tone. "You might easily have formed a suspicion that your estimate of the man was wanting long before you even arrived here."

"And pray tell me, comrade of my youth," said Mycroft, his fourth glass of sherry bolstering his confidence, "how I should have done *that*."

"By analysing what you already knew!" rejoined his brother. "This case was plainly unconnected to any international or political plots, from the very beginning."

"Eh?" Mycroft's head snapped around at an unusual pace. "Now you go too far, Sherlock—really you do. How can you possibly claim as much?"

"Brother—" Holmes took a dining chair, turned it to its side as he placed it before his brother, and then sat with his arm dangling over the straight back of the thing. "Surely, *surely* you must, at the very least, have seriously doubted the notion that all of these attempts on the life of the Queen of which you have told us have been somehow connected to one another."

The query seemed at the same time a plea; and it forced me to remember Holmes's original opinion that the "entire notion" of a long string of connected assassination attempts was in fact "too much"—"too much" to be considered seriously, yes, but also "too much," or rather *too many*, in the literal sense. And, apparently, his brother had felt the same way, at least in part: Mycroft breathed deeply, frowned, and said, in a less than forceful tone, "The belief in such a connection was and has long been that of many to whom the Queen has entrusted her day-to-day security. And I believe such men—whose names, you understand, I shall not mention, in this context—to have always been honest in those opinions. In addition, in order to obtain the cooperation of Her Majesty in any way towards schemes that I thought might enhance her *actual* safety, it has proved necessary to accept certain fundamental terms of operation based upon those opinions."

"Including the absurd?" Holmes said. "Mycroft, you have had nine attempts on Her Majesty's life, all committed by youths or young men within a few years' age of each other—an age, in short, when most such fellows are more anxious about their ability to make a mark on the world than they will ever be. That mark seems, at that age, so difficult, so complex, as to be impossible to achieve—and yet, to the disturbed few, there is always the method of creating one's own fame by destroying, or merely attempting to destroy, one who already possesses such dynamic stature. The modus operandi in each case was also so consistent, so idiosyncratic, as to lead to the inescapable assumption that they read of each other's attempts and imitated the same—assuming, that is, that the water supply of English schools has not been tainted by some peculiar fungus that induces an urge towards assassination! Finally, and again in every case, the punishment universally meted out was such as would only have offered encouragement to any future aspirant. He might have his momentary notoriety, and then, for his pains, be transported away from the very cause of his anguish: The anonymous crush of life on our little island. You *must* have known that in our age, when the popular press makes celebrated beings of the most infamously banal souls, such a quest was, in most if not all cases, sufficient motivation for these supposedly 'deadly' attacks on Her Majesty?"

"Yes, I have indeed considered all that, Sherlock, of course I have!" Mycroft replied quickly. "And a good deal more along such lines, besides; but, as I say, those more intimately involved with the Queen's daily safety have not done, nor would they ever do, likewise. Remember of whom we speak—men who, while personally valiant and loyal, are ill-tutored in anything, save gamekeeping." He lifted his glass in Robert Sadler's direction. "You will forgive me, I am sure, young man."

"Aye, sir, indeed," replied the fellow. "If there's one thing for which I wouldn't like to think myself responsible, it's the safety of Her Majesty— I've no' the training for such, and have often wondered, when she stays here, why *she* does no' seek out more gentlemen such as yourselves." His head dropped for a moment. "If only to protect her home from the likes of my brother and myself. . . ."

As I turned back to the Holmeses, my eyes

lingered just long enough on Sadler to catch a quick glimpse of Miss Mackenzie offering some condoling whispers to her one-time protector; and I wondered if, already, the gravity of the situation was not inducing a shift in her affections from one brother to the other.

"Well said, my boy," Mycroft replied. "This, in addition to all else that I have heard since my return, marks you as truly penitent. And so, there you have it, Sherlock—whatever *my* opinions, the Queen's own simply would not allow, as I have told you already, for their implementation. And then, as well, this last attempt on Her Majesty seemed as though it might, in fact, represent a departure from the others: There existed the possibility, at least, that an attentive foreign secret service, such as the German emperor is known to employ, might seek to capitalise on Scottish Nationalist ambitions by enlisting a young assassin who fit the pattern of the other youths, and encouraging him to make another attempt, based in deeper motivations. If he failed, his case would be treated as just another in a long line, and he should likely be transported without serious interrogation; if he succeeded, as you yourself have said, the one effective brake on the Kaiser's ambitions and behaviour would be removed. It would have been irresponsible for me *not* to consider the possibility that such was happening!"

"Indeed, Mycroft," Holmes said, "save for one qualifying consideration: Dennis McKay, or, more properly, his murder. Had German agents been manipulating some young and impressionable nationalist from Glasgow whose family was *known* to McKay, do you not think that the plot would have been found out by that older leader of that group—who lived in the very same city and was perhaps of the boy's personal acquaintance—and reported to the police, so that their movement would not be associated with so spectacularly unpopular a crime? And yet, Robert tells us, McKay was not murdered for *any* reason involving politics or political vengeance."

As Holmes looked to him, Robert Sadler spoke again. "No, sir. My brother and Lord Francis decided to do away with both Sir Alistair and Mr. McKay because they'd found out what we'd been up to in the tower—Sir Alistair by accident, during his explorations of the various rooms, and Mr. McKay because he never believed that Sir Alistair had met with any accident at all, and kept to poking about, even after the police seemed ready to give in. Both Lord Francis and Will knew, by that time, that I would never have joined them in any such schemes as murder—that I would, in fact, have tried to stop them; and so they made sure that I was well away from the palace when the acts were committed."

Mycroft Holmes appeared increasingly displeased and uncomfortable. "Sherlock, of course each of these considerations played some part in my thinking—but when we are talking of the safety of the Queen, one can be forgiven, I think, for errors caused by overzealousness!"

"Perhaps," Holmes replied dubiously and, I thought, rather ungenerously; and in so doing, he reminded me yet again of how simplistic his political opinions could sometimes be. "But, whether or not they are forgivable," he went on, "they remain errors, and must not become the basis of further misconceptions. Let us simply agree that politics and the loyalty each of us owes to the Crown"—and here he shot Mycroft a look that said plainly how much he was understating the issue, for the sake of his brother's pride—"blinded you to the true dangers and evils of this house—and let us further agree, now, to eliminate politics from our plan to finally terminate the criminal careers of Lord Francis Hamilton and Likely Will Sadler."

Mycroft gave a firm nod of affirmation, setting his sherry glass aside; and before long, we had indeed moved on to the question of how best to vanquish our foes:

The principal difficulty facing us was that we still had no definite proof with which to approach the local police, Scotland Yard, or even the garrison in Edinburgh Castle. Nevertheless, we quickly did make just such approaches: Holmes ventured off to the police, while Mycroft and I ascended Castle Hill once more, to enter the mighty fortress on its summit. Our luck here was as predicted: My worries that the activities of Will and Robert Sadler had in some way been tolerated, if not actually facilitated, by members of the garrison were obviously shared by its commandant, who had no desire to delve any deeper into the matter by "exceeding his authority" and involving his command in what were, to his way of thinking, matters at Holyroodhouse that were clearly the province of the police—particularly not, at any rate, while the Queen herself was at Balmoral. (We could have wired Her Majesty, of course, and elicited a royal command for military cooperation; but by the time we completed this process, the affair would likely have been decided—in one way or the other.) Rather than seize the initiative, the garrison commander referred us to those same police; and it was a measure of how limited our tactical choices had grown that neither Mycroft nor I could think of anything to do save follow the referral.

Our trip to the headquarters of the local authorities in order to lend support to our comrade was cut short, however, when we encountered the exiting Holmes, who related the opinions of the senior officers of that force concerning our decision to leave them out of our inquiries and efforts. When we had some "actual evidence," Holmes had been advised (such evidence going unnamed, but clearly not including tall tales of a gillie or supposed "hair samples"), this reaction would of course be tempered; but the officers had obligations enough to attend to in Scotland's capital (not least their own investigations into the deaths of Sinclair and McKay) without taking the time to chase about after men who could not be definitely implicated in the proceedings, or even certainly stated to be any longer in Edinburgh.

Incredible as it seems, then, even in retrospect, our small band was to be left to defend our own lives, as well as the honour of Holyroodhouse, alone. Holmes and I had, of course, faced long odds before; but the odds in this situation had dimensions that seemed to transcend ordinary notions of length, and to stretch into the past—into History itself.

Chapter XIV

. . . AND BATTLE IS JOINED

By the time that Holmes, Mycroft, and I returned to the palace, darkness was fast descending, upon both the parkland around us and our spirits. It would be for Mycroft to transform the moment, by attempting to marshal our small force into an optimistic unit that could offer a carefully coordinated resistance to what we were sure would be an attempt by Lord Francis and Likely Will to retrieve their hard (if illicitly) won treasure that very night. It now seemed beyond question that this was why Lord Francis had not accompanied Mycroft back to the palace upon the pair's return from Balmoral: Although he could not have known how much we had learned of his own and his henchman's activities, the knowledge that we were investigating more than merely the obvious explanation of the murders of Sinclair and McKay would have offered two reasons for him to take flight: to avoid apprehension, and to ascertain the disposition of his own forces from Likely Will. But the crystallisation of our certainty as to our enemies' plans came shortly after our arrival back at the palace, when Robert Sadler made an almost off-handed reference to his brother's having ascertained Holmes's and my own true identities the night before, through the method we had most feared: betrayal at the Roxburghe Hotel. So concentrated had I been on the necessity of bribing the desk clerk that I had flatly forgotten that although I was acquainted with the barman Jackson, he would require similar remuneration for his silence; lacking it, he had given us up without even realising it. Sadler had thought we must have known as much, based on our certainty that Likely Will and Lord Francis intended to break and enter; and while this new intelligence did nothing to affect our plans (thus making the fact that we had learned of it so late almost meaningless), both Robert and I found an extra measure of responsibility difficult to escape.

Having joined forces, Likely Will and Hamilton

almost certainly intended, now, to move against us as quickly as the cover of night would allow, armed not with the noisy weapons of our own age, but with the rather frightening array of creatures and devices that we knew Will Sadler to keep among his private collection, all of which could be used to great effect without the police in the city ever hearing a sound. Hackett and Andrew were therefore instructed to secure all the gates of the iron fence that surrounded the inner grounds of the palace with new chains and locks, locks to which our opponents would (we hoped) possess no keys and which they would be reluctant to demolish with further charges of gun-cotton and black powder. The rest of us, meanwhile, readied firearms, hand weapons, torches, and medical supplies; and as we did so, nearly every one of us remarked (and I think, to lesser or greater extents, actually felt) that our efforts to prepare an effective defence of the royal residence against so peculiar an enemy were indeed drawing us backwards in time—back, towards the era of the Scottish Queen and David Rizzio themselves.

This feeling was heightened when Holmes again and much more emphatically urged that our movements about the palace be confined to those inner rooms whose windows faced onto the courtyard, rather than those that looked out over the abbey ruins and the lawns: Holyroodhouse had not been designed as a fortress, said Holmes, and the wide, tall transparencies of its outer rooms allowed an entirely too tempting series of targets to be seen—particularly since the weapons we would soon be facing were silent, and would not offer us the usual modern defensive compensations of muzzle flashes in the darkness, which could be marked and fired upon. Many heads were nodded, and solemnly, to all this sage advice; but, as we would soon learn, no amount of verbal preparation, not even from Holmes, could truly prepare us for the primitive onslaught that was coming.

Our education commenced soon thereafter; and the first lesson was vivid indeed. Just as our watch passed the third hour mark, Miss Mackenzie began to manifest fearful symptoms of nervous strain: She claimed that she could hear footsteps, quiet but deep, reverberating throughout the palace. At first, when the rest of us assured her that this phenomenon existed solely in her imagination, she attempted composure; but not half an hour later, the sound of glass panes being shattered in one of the small chambers opposite the dining-hall caused the night to be further pierced by Miss Mackenzie's uncontrolled screaming. Indeed, a general outcry went up from the rest of us, as well; it was only with a certain effort that we finally obeyed Holmes's orders to remain silent, and to extinguish the lamps and candles that were burning on the table.

"You may find such discipline demanding," Holmes whispered, "but our lives now depend upon just such self-control, in the face of deliberate attempts to sow panic among us." His wise words had the desired effect on all our party: Even Miss Mackenzie, although emotionally and nervously exhausted from days of similar events, tried as hard as her young heart would allow to overcome her renewed horror. "Hackett," Holmes continued, "you had best come with me—and if you have such a thing as a crowbar, and perhaps a chisel, be good enough to bring them!"

Hackett snatched up some such tools, and then the pair of them ran into the room opposite, the mere motion of their bodies in the small chamber almost immediately prompting two more bursts of breaking glass. Watching from the dining-room doorway, I was able to see at least one of the relatively small sashes of windows across the way, the grid of which stood out against the now-moonlit sky; and as I studied the area, I realised with a start what was happening:

"Arrows!" I cried, observing one such weapon

protruding from the surface of a table in the targeted chamber. "Holmes—Hackett! In heaven's name, be careful, for the moonlight has revealed your position to the archer!"

"You are nearly correct, Watson!" came my friend's voice. "They are not *quite* arrows, however, but something even more deadly, and at least one carries a message!"

I puzzled a moment over that statement, listening with the others as some hammering and creaking of metal against wood echoed out of the small room. Then I stood guard with a rather fine Holland and Holland .375 calibre Mauser-based hunting rifle, as the two of our party who had gone across the hall rejoined us.

In one of his hands, Holmes did indeed hold something akin to an arrow, but I now saw what he had meant by his qualification of it:

"A crossbow bolt!" said I, for such it was: a shorter, thicker missile than the arrows used with long- and re-curved bows, but more effective, in this case, because a crossbow's much greater power would ensure proportionally greater accuracy when the bolts passed through a barrier such as a glass pane—after all, medieval armor had once been unable to resist their force, so what chance did we stand in those outer rooms? This particular bolt was wrapped in what appeared to be writing paper, and as Holmes sat at the dining-table we re-ignited the various sources of light, and watched as he carefully peeled a note from the shaft.

"Your brother may know little enough of modern explosives, Robert," said I, "but his mastery of these older weapons is flatly terrifying—it cannot be less than fifty yards to the west gate, and though comparatively few trees obscure his line of fire, any one would doubtless be enough to interfere with less-skilled marksmanship."

"Aye, Doctor," answered Robert Sadler. "When Mr. Holmes says that staying to the inner rooms of the palace may save our lives, he does no' exaggerate: Will can clip the wings of a songbird with that cruel weapon—I've seen him do it."

As Holmes studied the note, which appeared to be very brief, his brow arched in confusion.

"What is it, Holmes?" asked I. "A demand for our surrender, no doubt."

"Such *is* what I had expected," Holmes replied, in a deliberately, indeed a purposefully, measured voice. "But it is rather more—*personal* than that. And entirely more fiendish. . . ." He glanced quickly at Miss Mackenzie, into whose features horror had flooded once again. "Mrs. Hackett,"

Holmes said, realising that a crisis was likely near, "I wonder if you might not return with your niece to the kitchen—"

"Nay, I will no' go!" the girl cried, leaping forward with impressive speed and snatching the note from Holmes before he had a chance to keep it from her. Staring at the thing, she backed away slowly, toward the hallway door. "Aye. . . ." she murmured. "Aye, I thought as much—I can no' bear it—but he means to have me—!"

"Who, my dear girl?" said I, moving very softly towards her.

"Hush, Allie, let us help you," Mrs. Hackett said. "There's no one—"

"There is!" Miss Mackenzie cried. "I warned you that I heard him! He's abroad again—do you no' understand?" Her plea was a terribly desperate thing to hear, even more so to see, for her whole frame began to tremble violently as she was making it. "I have left the place I was to be— I've betrayed him, and now it's *him* that's come—"

"Nay, Allie," said Robert, trying to approach and comfort her. "Will could no' have come near here, without our knowing it—"

" 'Tain't Will!" the girl fairly screamed. "It's *him*—I must go back to the tower, he said I was to be there, perhaps if I go, he may let me live—!"

"I don't like this business, Watson," Holmes said to me, quietly but urgently. "Have you nothing with which to calm her?"

I shook my head, feeling entirely helpless; but then I spied a sideboard across the dining-room, and, moving towards it, said, "Some more whisky, perhaps, Miss Mackenzie? You must try. . . ." Yet even as I poured out some of the liquor and attempted to bring the glass to the girl, she only howled the worse:

"No! That's how you coaxed me down here, to begin with! I must go back, do you no' see? I was to be there, and now he's coming for me—!"

Seeing that the girl was well past reason, Robert again tried to get a quick grip around her shoulders—but she even more rapidly pulled away once more. "No, Rob—this is one devil even you canna' keep out!" The girl continued backing towards the hallway door. *"For he was ne'er gone!"*

No doubt it was the shock caused by these words that momentarily rooted the rest of us to the floor; whatever the cause, Miss Mackenzie was able to suddenly rush from the room and dash out into the Great Stair and beyond, without any of us trying, at first, to stop her. Holmes then led the pursuit, and the rest of us did follow quickly; but before we could get to the fleeing girl,

she had run into the north-easternmost royal reception room, a long, wide space on the outer side
of the palace, which—especially as it was devoid
of interior illumination, like all the chambers thus
positioned, as per Holmes's order—commanded
an ordinarily excellent but now quite fearsome
view of the moon-lit, Gothic archways of the old
abbey ruins and the inner fence-line in the mid-
dling distance. Miss Mackenzie had evidently
been making for the west tower, intent on returning to the room in which we had originally found her, before something—something
visible through the wall of mullioned windows,
perhaps—had drawn her into this very dangerous area. And, when we continued our pursuit of
her into the room, we soon saw what that "something" was: Just as her lithe young form became
silhouetted against the window sashes and the
abbey beyond, she, along with the rest of us, looked
up in horror at the sky above those ancient ruins.

Through the near-darkness was hurtling a terrible sight: a streaking ball of fire, high above the
roof-top of the palace, at first indistinguishable in
shape. Soon, however, as its ascent crested and it
began to plunge towards us, the mass of flame
opened up, almost as if it were some enormous,
fiery flower, and it became recognisable as the
outstretched form of a human being. The sight

was ghastly indeed, and ghostly as well—yet it was not so ephemeral that it prevented us from realising that it was about to smash through the windows before us, and set the reception room, the eastern wing of the palace, and perhaps the entire building ablaze. This idea alone was enough to set even the brave Mrs. Hackett screaming in chorus with Miss Mackenzie, and to bring loud oaths of shock and disbelief from nearly everyone else present, including myself; only Holmes and his brother remained silent: a typical manifestation of their idiosyncratic and unflappable ability to concentrate their minds and formulate plans in the most apparently terrible and hopeless of situations. We all braced ourselves for what we were sure would be the devastation of the flaming horror, and Rob Sadler bravely seized the opportunity to charge forward and finally snatch the hysterical Miss Mackenzie from the window—

And then, as fast as it had appeared, the danger seemed to pass. The fireball impacted the exterior wall just above the window; and although this fact was in itself fortunate and remarkable, the collision of body against stone was accompanied by a sickening series of sounds that I soon recognised as the simultaneous snapping of an incalculable number of human bones. In an instant,

the still-smouldering form fell from the point of
its impact to the ground below, as Holmes called
us out of our terribly transfixed state and to action.

"Andrew—remain here, with the ladies.
Hackett—where is the nearest stair and exit?"

By way of reply, Hackett led the way at a run
that left Mycroft somewhat to the rear of Holmes,
Robert, and myself, down a hidden servants' staircase, narrow and cramped, in the east wall, and
thence to a doorway that led out onto the grounds
near the abbey ruins. From that spot we could
easily see the terrible pile of charred flesh that lay
near the exterior wall of the building, and we all
rushed to it without an instant's thought. Had we
known what awaited us, our zeal might have
been tempered; for the burnt corpse upon the
ground was far from unrecognisable, and, hard
as it may sound, such corpses are somehow less
terrible when they are those of strangers.

"Good God!" Mycroft Holmes exclaimed
breathlessly as he drew up to us. "Doctor—who—
and *how*—?"

But it was Holmes who answered: "The 'who'
is no great mystery, Mycroft—observe the pronounced nasal ridge. It is, if I am not mistaken,
your man from military intelligence."

I had covered my mouth with a handkerchief,

in order to be able to breathe as I ascertained the inevitable:

"Indeed," I soon declared. "And he is more than simply dead—nearly every bone in his body has been fractured by the impact. He must have hit the wall with a fantastic force—but as to what can have achieved that force, after propelling the body from the eastern line of the fence—"

"The same thing that smashed Dennis Mc-Kay's body against the stones of the abbey ruins in a similar manner," Holmes replied. "And that may yet inflict—"

Holmes grew suddenly silent when he noticed something about the dead man. "Watson," he said, "what is that, around his neck?"

I took note, amid all the charred flesh and clothing, of a small but heavy metal box that was fixed to the neck by a length of blackened chain.

"It appears to be a small ammunition box," said I, using my handkerchief to lift it free. "Such containers are built to withstand fire—there may yet be something within."

"There is no doubt of it," Holmes said, in dismal anticipation. "Why else employ it?"

Using a pocketknife, I managed to pry the lid of the box free, and found within the container, as we had suspected, an object that our attackers had evidently meant to keep safe from the flames.

Wrapped several times in damp rags, it was, in fact, yet another note; but the purpose of this one was grimly pragmatic.

" 'You have seen by now what fate awaits you all,' " I read aloud, my eyes following the moistened but clear typescript. " 'Either grim death, or madness. But escape is possible: Bring the contents of Queen Mary's bed to us at the west gate. And take no heart from all of your newly placed locks and chains! We can assure you, such paltry devices will prove most inadequate protection against—' "

We would later surmise that Likely Will Sadler had been observing us through some sort of field glasses or monocular during this incident, and that he somehow signalled to his confederates in other positions when he saw us studying the note—for just at that moment, I was silenced by a sudden and terrible series of sounds. An explosion thundered from the direction of the west gate, reverberating over the palace, the park, and the city beyond: precisely the sort of sound that we had thought our enemies too clever to risk, but that hubris—or, perhaps, desperation—had led them to hazard. After that, a series of shouting, even screaming voices began to resonate, one after the other, off of the stones of Holyroodhouse: The first of them shrieked in sudden, and most intense pain, a second bellowed vague orders, while a third merely railed in mindless panic.

Then, at last, we all stood to listen, as a new and a far more familiar (to say nothing of welcome) sound joined the din: several policemen's whistles, followed by the unmistakable bluster of bobbies in pursuit. They were not yet close—but they were clearly getting closer, and quickly.

"Keep hold of your rifle, Watson!" Holmes ordered. "This body has been a diversion, I suspect, under cover of which Lord Francis has penetrated the perimeter! We must stop him getting to the tower! Mycroft—take Hackett and Robert to the eastern line of the fence. You may try to reason with your brother, Sadler, but above all, you must stop him! Unless I am very much mistaken, several of our reluctant friends from the local police have decided, in light of these sights and sounds, that valour is the better part of discretion, when royal interests are so unarguably demonstrated to be at stake—they will likely arrive at our antagonist's position just as you do, Mycroft, and if so, you must reason with them!"

"Why not simply allow them to arrest these infamous fellows?" Mycroft asked.

"Because Will Sadler will not allow it, as Robert himself well knows—he possesses a fearsome engine of destruction, and should he turn it against the police. . . ."

"Aye, Mr. Holmes," said Sadler, terrible conflict raging in his features. "But, done what he's done, he's still my brother. I'll make it my business to get between them, and persuade him to surrender, Mr. Mycroft—if you will only force the officers to take him alive."

"I've no idea if I can do any such thing, young man," Mycroft answered, beginning to get his big body moving north-east. "But I shall try!"

At that, Hackett and Sadler followed Mycroft into the darkness. I, in the meanwhile, stayed with Holmes, whilst he, having watched them go, said, "I only hope that, timely as we have been, we have been in *enough* time, Watson! Quickly, now!"

I followed my friend as he raced around the south-eastern corner of the palace. "Holmes!" I called, making sure that I had chambered a round in the Holland and Holland. "What do you mean, 'enough time'? To prevent what?"

"Miss Mackenzie's death!" answered my friend. "Lord Francis intends to secure his riches and prevent the girl from ever repeating her tale— and he has enlisted a very reliable ally in the performance of this last detail!"

At the speed we were moving, the sudden twinge of nervous weakness that this remark sent coursing throughout my body was magnified greatly, and I nearly stumbled. Righting myself and hurrying on, I said only, "No, Holmes! You do not mean to persist in this idea that—"

Holmes threw a dismissive hand back towards me as he sped along the ancient wall. "Not now, Watson—say what you will, if we are not quick enough, David Rizzio will be offered *some* form of revenge, against one who is as innocent as was he himself!"

I meant to pursue the argument; but my mind was drained of coherent thought by the almost incredible sight upon which we came—or, more precisely, which burst upon *us*—as we gained the southwestern corner of the palace and could finally see the west gate. The gate itself was afire; but that unexpected phenomenon was as nothing in comparison to the sight of yet *another* human form enveloped in flames. This one was still alive, and dashing madly about the grounds inside the mangled, sagging iron bars and scroll-work of the gateway, releasing terrible, high-pitched screams, as though he (or was it she?) had been disgorged from that eternal inferno that roils beneath us.

Chapter XV

STRANGE DOINGS IN THE WEST TOWER

Both Holmes and I slowed as we approached this unfortunate creature; and I was able to see that the fire that was consuming the upper part of its body and head, along with its hands, was of a distinctly chemical variety, so brilliant were the flames and so high was their heat. I made ready to give Holmes my rifle and run to the piteous victim's aid—but my friend held me back for a moment.

"You would show as much mercy, Watson," said my friend, "and far more wisdom, if you put a bullet through his head right now."

" 'His'?" said I. "Holmes, you know who it is?"

"One who did not understand the nature of the explosive device with which he rent the gate," Holmes replied. "Just as he did not understand a similar device that he threw at our feet on the train."

"Lord Francis!" said I. "Of course—Sadler concocted yet another charge with the gun-cotton!"

"Yes—and neither man had any idea what they were unleashing."

I pushed the rifle into Holmes's arms. "I must attend him."

Holmes caught me again: "Nitric and sulphuric acids, Watson—he will be dead before you reach him, and you shall only succeed in injuring yourself."

I broke loose of the man's grip. "I am a doctor, Holmes—you must not detain me. . . ."

Although Holmes did give up his attempt to stop me at that, his analysis of the situation proved only too accurate. During the full minute it took me to reach the man, Lord Francis stumbled about the gravel pathway inside the ruined gate, still shrieking most piteously, waving his flaming hands through the air and trying to extinguish the fire on his face. It soon became apparent that the terrible heat was scorching his vocal cords, for the screams became first hoarse, and then nearly silent; and by the time I had gotten to him, there was nothing recognisable in the fellow, save his clothing and the two terrible eyes that stared at me, displaying at once dreadful comprehension of what was happening. I stopped, removing my jacket and intending to at least *try* to smother the fire; but another look at those gleaming eyes told me that they had, in the merest instant, ceased to see what was before them. With a terrible rigidity, Lord Francis Hamilton fell forward, arms in the air, hands and fingers formed into the characteristic claws of the burn victim, eyes and mouth fully open. He hit the gravel squarely, and the speed with which he did finally wrote a finish to most of the chemical fire, leaving only that same terrible stench of burning wool and flesh that had hung heavy over the murdered intelligence man.

Looking up at the gate, I saw that the flames that had similarly consumed it were suddenly dying away—and I noted that two faces had been revealed by the reduction in the firelight. The men's expressions were alike in their horror, although it was evidently not horror of the paralysing variety: They took flight quickly, leaving me to wonder forever if I had in fact recognised them as having been two from among the merry crowd of drinking soldiers with whom we had passed the previous evening. I have always elected to believe that I was mistaken; whatever the case, the several policemen who soon appeared on the other side of the gate, moving at a full run with their whistles blaring, took my mind from the issue.

After identifying Lord Francis's corpse for the officers, I left them to the unpleasant duty of watching over it, while I returned to the spot where I had left Holmes. All I found there, however, was the rifle I had been carrying. Looking about and calling my friend's name, I became suddenly conscious of something most unusual in the front façade of the palace:

Movement in the windows of the west tower.

On the uppermost floor, in the Scottish Queen's rooms, someone had torn both the heavy draperies and the shutters away, exposing the windows: And through them, I could just make out, by the highly erratic light of a long-tapered candle within, the distinctive if wavering outline of Miss Mackenzie's body. She had her hands clasped before her, as if she were standing in prayer; but the agitated manner in which she was shaking her arms and head, as well as working her mouth, suggested something very different. She began to move back, ever more perilously back, towards the glass of the now-exposed window panes; and as I helplessly began my own mesmerized walk

towards the tower (I do not know what I intended
to do, for if she were to fall, I could scarcely have
broken the plummet), I expected of course to next
see the form of whoever was so grievously tormenting her.

But the figure remained hidden from my view.
At first, assuming that it was Will Sadler, and
that he was attempting to so manoeuvre Miss
Mackenzie that her fall would appear a suicide, I
ran to various new vantage points on the lawn
trying to find one from which I might train the
rifle on young Allie's pursuer; but no location offered any better view into the tower than the
first. It then struck me that firing any shots would
be most risky: What if the person trying to sub-
due the girl was not an enemy at all? What if it
was Andrew Hackett—or perhaps even Holmes—
trying to rescue Allie from her own hysteria? But
surely neither Andrew nor Holmes would have
kept moving towards the girl when her retreat
was so clearly reaching a dangerous pass. Finally
my racing mind turned to the possibility (the most
frightening of all) that Miss Mackenzie was not
retreating from a real pursuer—whether friend
or foe—at all; perhaps she was retreating from a
figure that was an invention of her own frayed
nervous system and horrified imagination; a
phantasm of her mind's making, but one as real,

to her, as such visions often are to those who have been driven past mere hysteria and nervous exhaustion. Yes, I finally told myself, as her "assailant" went on being imperceptible from the ground; this was surely what was taking place—

And then one of the windows in a room just above the main entrance to the palace flew open, emitting, in a curious cloud, a heavy blanket, which billowed in the breeze and drifted slowly toward the ground. I watched it do so for an instant, then looked back up at the window to see:

Holmes.

"Watson!" he cried. "Rouse yourself, man! Take those officers—form a sling with which to catch the girl, for he means to drive her through that window, and I cannot reach her in time!"

"He?" echoed I, dumbfounded. "Holmes, who is—"

"*Now,* Watson!"

I was able to clear my head of questions and comply, less concerned with explanations, at last, than with the life of the endangered girl who, in a very few seconds, clearly *would* back directly through and out of the window, which offered no balcony or terrace to catch her, but only a straight and fatal pitch to the gravel path below the tower.

The policemen, having heard Holmes's summons, raced towards me, and together we did indeed use the blanket to form a broad sling beneath the window—and a good thing, too, for an instant later Miss Mackenzie screamed with the terrible recognition that she had retreated too far, and tumbled through the sash of the ancient window in a great burst.

The girl hurtled towards the earth, where I, with the help of the stout policemen (who thereby more than made up for their commander's having refused to help us earlier in the evening) succeeded in catching her in the thick, luxurious weave of the blanket. Though she was momentarily stunned, a quick review of Miss Mackenzie's condition revealed it to be otherwise sound.

"Upon my honour, Doctor," said one of the officers. "She's a comely enough lass. What can have driv'n her to it, eh?"

"I fear that I cannot tell you," replied I.

"Ach," said another of the men, "there's no great mystery here—that's Allie Mackenzie, Will Sadler's girl!"

General agreement on this point followed, along with statements that revealed awareness as to the girl's delicate condition—no doubt the result of bar-room boasting by Likely Will Sadler, in a further demonstration of his swinish character.

Further speculations along these lines were interrupted by Holmes:

"Watson! Get up the spiral stairs—I'll block the hidden passage! Don't waste an instant—and don't forget that weapon!"

He was gone again before I could confirm that someone *had* been in the tower with the girl; but the possibility of capturing whomever the threatening party had been put new resolve in my actions. After instructing the slightly bewildered policemen to look after Miss Mackenzie, I fetched the Holland and Holland and headed quickly for an extremely old doorway—so narrow that one needed to turn sideways to move through it—in the base of the tower. It opened only with tremendous difficulty and an enormous groaning sound; but once inside, I found that I was but a few short steps below the base of the stone spiral stairs. Up these I now sped, the sound of my boots on stone echoing all about me—but not so loudly that I could not recognise, about half-way up, that my own steps were being answered by another's, moving in the opposite direction. Assuming it to be Miss Mackenzie's as-yet-unidentified assailant, I halted and raised the rifle, bracing myself against the staircase's stone wall, in order to mitigate the pain that the recoil of a high-powered weapon could sometimes cause in my old shoulder wound.

As I waited, the approaching steps picked up speed, and I began to hear low mumblings accompanying them. At first, I thought that whatever words the man was speaking were simply being muttered indistinctly; next, I reasoned that the quick bouncing of sound off of curved stone caused their incoherence; but finally, I could not escape a far more obvious conclusion:

That the man was not, in fact, speaking English.

Trying to ignore this consideration—for, native or no, this fellow was certainly a confederate of Sadler's, and therefore to be treated as a dangerous opponent—I awaited the villain's arrival, keeping the rifle's iron sights trained on the centre of the stairs. Disengaging the gun's safety, I waited until what turned out to be his short figure was fully before me—and then, just as I was about to squeeze off a round, I noticed something:

Although I could see only a silhouette, even that limited image revealed a pronounced mass of flesh above the man's left shoulder; a growth that, under ordinary circumstances, I should have had no trouble labeling a hump. . . .

Whether out of horrified recognition of this detail, or out of concern lest the fellow escape, I quickly fired the rifle. The noise produced within that confined stone space was massive, a concussive assault on the eardrums so painful as to be almost unbearable—but not so disabling that, as the man turned to race back up the stairs, I did not hear him shout some terrified, obscure oath. I could not make out the exact words—but they did indeed have the unmistakable patter of a foreign tongue, and one such in particular: It was a Maxim gun–like verbal speed that I have only ever detected in a certain nation in southern Europe. . . .

"I've missed him," I murmured, not surprised by the fact, given the haste with which I had fired, but unwilling, all the same, to face the truth of what I had heard and seen. The fellow continued to race back up the stairs, and soon Holmes called down to them:

"Watson! Are you all right?"

"Quite!" answered I, although the rifle's recoil had indeed sent a stinging shock through my shoulder. "Stay where you are, Holmes! He is headed your way!"

"No!" answered my friend. "He is beyond me already—I see him, however!"

And then I heard multiple footsteps, a cacophony of new echoes and confusion. Grimacing and clutching my shoulder, I continued up the stairs at a run.

"Gaelic," I murmured to myself as I ran. "It might have been Gaelic. . . ."

And, indeed, the language I had heard the fugitive speaking might well *have* been Gaelic, for all I knew of that ancient tongue—save that I *did* know that it was generally spoken in obscure parts of Scotland, rather than in urbane Edinburgh. But it served as a way to avoid further consideration of the much more likely linguistic candidate that had already occurred to me, as well as to take my mind from the unwelcome sight that had registered in my mind immediately prior to my firing the Holland and Holland. Acceptance of the image became increasingly unavoidable, however, and the struggle to avoid it slowed my pace greatly, until I finally could not prevent a full halt. Drifting back against the stairway wall, I slid down its stone blocks to rest on my haunches and catch my breath. Only the sound of Holmes's distant voice—ordering someone to halt—roused me from this unsettling reverie: I stood quickly and continued up the stairs to the palace's main floor, dashing about the Great Gallery and calling Holmes's name. Receiving no answer, I returned to the stairs and ascended them again, running headlong into Queen Mary's rooms and calling to Holmes once more—with increasing desperation, I will confess. But still there was no reply; and in the deathly quiet of those paradoxically alive yet utterly dead chambers, my nerves (or so it seemed) began to play tricks upon me: I imagined that I heard music, an incoherent form of music, played upon some outmoded instrument—and the sound was emanating, I soon realised, from the Queen's old supper-room. . . .

I approached that location with the greatest hesitation; but approach it I did. The sight of the pool of "everlasting blood" near its entrance did little to give me heart; but rifle in hand, I pressed on, stepping ever closer to the sound of the eerie music, and finally spying, through the small doorway to the room—

Holmes.

He was seated close by the window through which Miss Mackenzie had tumbled, by the room's old dining-table. An ancient stringed instrument was perched across one of his knees, and several sheets of musical score were perched on the other. He seemed lost in a peculiar reverie, and the strangeness of both the scene and the rooms in which it was taking place had the effect, oddly, of freeing my mind of both speculative thought and fear: I moved towards my friend like one numbed by a quick blow.

"Holmes?" I said. "All's well?"

"Watson!" he said, in a rather arrestingly cheerful voice; but he did not turn. "Yes, quite well—and with you?"

"Yes," said I, setting the rifle down. "But—" It was difficult to know what subject to speak of: There were so many that I wished to avoid.

"What of Miss Mackenzie?" asked Holmes, who did not seem to share my trepidation.

"In a swoon, but she will recover fully."

"You and your partners in that exercise are to be congratulated—you executed it flawlessly."

I tried to say something, but found myself only nodding. And then, as I stared at the old wooden walls around us, I suddenly thought to ask: "Should we not see to Mycroft and the others?"

Holmes chuckled. "My brother will be doing *us* that favour, I suspect, quite soon. I was able to chase the man we were pursuing from this room—I can only suppose that he was trying to retrieve as much of their loot as he could—and down towards the others. But I had no hope of catching him, for he is as agile as an ape. I did, however, take the precaution of checking on Mycroft's position prior to returning here, from a window in the north wing. They are all quite well, and several more policemen are even now pursuing Likely Will Sadler. As well as searching the palace grounds for the—*confederate* that you and I came so close to apprehending."

"Ah," I noised, greatly relieved; for it seemed that we would not have to further discuss the subject of the mysterious fellow (or *was* he, in fact, so very mysterious?) who had escaped us both. "And so—the matter is concluded?"

"Insofar as this palace is concerned, I believe we may say so—yes. And I should not wonder if we are not *both* the proud owners of elegant tie-pins before long. Your Queen will be grateful, Watson."

He continued to pluck and toy with the old musical instrument, forcing me finally to inquire: "Holmes, what *is* that thing?"

"This? You do not recognise it?"

"Evidently not."

"It is a lute, Watson. The favoured instrument of medieval balladeers—among others. . . ."

"And what is that music you are attempting to play on it?"

Holmes held up the long, lined sheets of paper, bowing his head. "This—is rather curious. A handwritten transcription. I found it atop the bed just now, along with the lute." He looked momentarily puzzled. "Yet I did not notice them last night. . . ."

And with that, evidently satisfied that he had

properly tuned the thing at last, Holmes began to play the lute again, keeping his eyes fixed on the sheets of music. The tune seemed obscure, at first; but then—

I was on the verge of naming it when Mycroft Holmes appeared at the doorway of the bed-chamber without. "Sherlock!" he cried. "And you, too, Doctor! In the name of Heaven, did you not, perhaps, think to let us know that you were well? And what of . . . of . . ."

Mycroft's words trailed away as he looked about and began to grasp just where he was. His heavy jowls rippled as he nodded several times in profound comprehension; and then he slowly approached the low doorway to the little supper room. "So," he said, his voice quite controlled now. "These are—*her* rooms?"

"They are, Mycroft," Holmes called. "And if you are not careful, you shall place your left foot into 'the blood that never dries.' " After his brother had performed the fairest approximation of a leap that his heavy form would allow, Holmes contin-ued: "It is likely taken from a pig or some other livestock, and has been there for better than twelve hours—so do spare yourself the mess."

Mycroft continued to look down and at the floor, frowning a bit and clicking his tongue. "Do you mean to say that it was for a glimpse of *this* nonsense that so much money changed hands? To say nothing of three good men's lives being lost, while an honest young woman was ruined and nearly driven mad?"

"No, no," Holmes mused, still tinkering with the lute, the tune it was producing making me less easy with every passing minute. "All of these things occurred, not because of that puddle, but because of these rooms and this palace—it was *their* peculiar power that transformed an animal's blood into a bit of magic. Shadows into mad visions. Life into death. . . ."

Mycroft nodded in seeming agreement, then appeared to remember something: "Speaking of the girl," he said. "What has become of her?"

I indicated the broken window, and Mycroft's eyes went wide. "Fear not," I said quickly. "She is quite well."

"Rescued!" Holmes erupted. "By Watson and the local constabulary. It was a brilliant feat, Mycroft—I should recommend them all for royal recognition. Particularly Watson."

"Indeed?" said Mycroft. "Well, I shall first have to—confound it, Sherlock, *will* you desist with that instrument? Our work is not yet finished: Will Sadler is still at large in the park, somewhere, along with God only knows how many other accomplices!"

"Fear not. There is only one." Then, so softly that his brother could not hear, he added: "And we shall not catch him. . . ." Holmes suddenly did stop playing the lute. "The ancient engine of Sadler's," he said aloud. "You have secured it?"

Mycroft's features filled with evident disappointment. "We could not," he said. "I had thought it well guarded, but somehow—"

Holmes lifted his head, as if he had expected this news: "Somehow, it has mysteriously ignited, and is burning even now. . . ." He then sighed once, in resignation.

"How could you have known as much?" his brother asked.

Holmes shrugged, returning to the lute. "It is in keeping," he said, "with the events of the evening. No doubt Sadler doubled back on his pursuers and set fire to the thing himself."

Mycroft did not seem any more satisfied with this strained explanation than was Holmes; but then he looked about the room once again, rather more dubiously, and murmured, "We can only speculate."

"What 'ancient engine'?" I asked. "What are you two talking about?"

"That's right—Watson has not seen it!" Holmes's mood seemed to brighten considerably at my ignorance, or rather at the prospect of putting an end to it: He stood quickly, set the lute aside, and strode from the room. "Quickly, Watson!" he said, slapping the sheets of music into his brother's befuddled chest. "Before the thing has quite burned away!"

Following behind him, I paused when I saw Mycroft studying the music. "Doctor," he said, holding out one large hand and taking hold of my arm. "I know my brother well enough to detect when something is of significance to a case." He held out the music. "What *is* this?"

I thought hard for a moment of how best to relate the tale; but, finally, all I could say was, "Mr. Holmes—have you a taste for Italian opera?"

"Well—as much as the next man who works in Whitehall, I suppose."

It was not the soundest of affirmations. "Verdi?" I inquired further.

He shook his head. "Rather histrionic, for my blood."

Pushing the sheets back at him, I said only, "I should keep it that way, if I were you," and then moved on.

By the time I caught up to Holmes, he was halfway out a window in yet another bedchamber on the outer side of the palace. Opening the next window in the room, I took up a similar position— and saw, in the distance, a furious conflagration.

A great, crane-like structure, made of mighty timbers and constructed on a wheeled base, was afire just beyond the northern line of the inner fence; and around it, one could just make out several police officers, who, having apparently surrendered any attempt to stop the blaze, were milling about and laughing in nervous awe at the sight before them.

The scene recalled similar images from picture books in my youth, and as I strained to place them in context, I finally formed an idea of what the structure must once have been. "Holmes!" I called. "That is a medieval siege weapon, is it not?"

"A *trebuchet*, Watson," Holmes called, as he took a rather perilous seat in the sill of the open window. "It was my first suspicion, when I heard of Likely Will's tastes—you will recall, perhaps, that, using such devices, medieval armies were known to hurl plague-ridden human bodies into cities that they held under siege. A similar tactic seemed the only possible explanation for the mystery of McKay's body, its position and condition—and Miss Mackenzie, you will recall, confirmed that Sadler possessed such a thing. Nevertheless—I was glad to actually see it, for it was one of the more unusual explanations I have had to formulate!"

"Indeed," I replied, suddenly noticing that I, like my friend, was smiling at the sight. "But it does the heart good to see it destroyed, does it not, Holmes?"

"Most certainly."

"Shouldn't we join in the search? For Sadler, that is."

Holmes merely shook his head calmly. "The police will likely find him—though undoubtedly idiosyncratic, Sadler's was not the greatest malevolent force at work here. *That* power was embodied in Lord Francis—yet in truth, there is much about this affair that defies any simple or criminal explanation."

"You'll have no argument from me, Holmes."

My friend looked up, clapping a hand onto one knee. "And now, perhaps we—*Watson!*" His face had become suddenly horrified. *"Look out, man!"*

From somewhere out of the left corner of the same eye, I detected a rapidly approaching object, and instinctively pulled back within the building. Just as I did, the still-sore drums of my ears were once again nearly split by the scream of some angry and obviously bewildered bird of prey: In fact, it was an enormous goshawk, which trailed two long leather thongs from its outstretched talons. These last were expert blades of dissection with which the bird had evidently intended to disfigure me as it once had Hackett: Holmes's warning had been enough to alert me, and spare me that fate—but my heart and blood had been sent racing.

"Damn the thing!" I cried, looking about and realising that I had left the Holland and Holland in the supper-room. "Had I only remembered the rifle . . . !"

Holmes laughed once. "And do you now profess to be such a marksman that you can take down even a large bird with a lone bullet in the dark?"

I put my head back outside rather gingerly, in time to see the admittedly magnificent avian hunter gliding away into the moonlit heavens, away from the fire, the palace, and likely the hard taskmaster who had so cruelly wrenched it from the wild, breaking, if only for a time, its proud spirit.

"No, Holmes. I do not—and I am glad, in fact, that the pitiable creature has got away."

"Let that be the symbol of this case, Watson," mused Holmes, as the bird screamed one final time. "If, indeed, it must have one. A noble if ferocious spirit, bent to the unnatural, nefarious purposes of a depraved human mind, has returned to the elemental world where it belongs, a world where life and death can once again make a form of preternatural sense that we civilised humans cannot hope to comprehend." Holmes kept his eyes upon the vanishing hawk. "If nothing else, we have taken that lesson from this place—and, with luck, we will be spared any further acquaintance with it. . . ."

Chapter XVI

TWILIGHT ON BAKER STREET

The remainder of our stay in Scotland seems a time apart from those few strange and dangerous days in Holyroodhouse. Called to attend Her Majesty at Balmoral, Holmes and I felt that we must first do what we could to assist the police in laying hold of the remaining fugitives. True to Holmes's prediction, Will Sadler was soon apprehended, trying to make his way out of the country by sea; and, on appearing in court, the man attempted to portray himself as the helpless pawn of a malevolent nobleman, a tactic that, in Scotland, could generally be relied on to produce a sympathetic reaction from the courts and the public; but not in this case. Angry that Sadler had so cynically manipulated one of their oldest legends and superstitions, the people of Edinburgh demanded harsh justice for the offender. Likely Will's affability and friendship with many of the soldiers in the castle garrison, as well as his association with hotel barmen throughout the city, were forgotten (much to the relief of those men), and he was eventually given the chance to feel what Queen Mary once had: the terror of a long early-morning walk to a lonely place of execution.

But as to confederates, Sadler refused to the end to name any, even when he was told that such might bring commutation of his sentence. Perhaps, ultimately, he wished to protect his brother; perhaps he even had some deformed sense of honour; or perhaps, as I have always thought, he took with him to the grave stories that belonged there in the first place. . . .

Whatever the case, an entirely different sort of fate awaited Robert Sadler. Holmes, Mycroft, and myself made sure that the facts of what had occurred at the palace were so arranged, when related to the police, that Robert's brave change of heart would be recognised and rewarded, while any former complicity in the purely fraudulent (as opposed to murderous) parts of Lord Francis's schemes would be overlooked. As a result,

Robert's only "punishment" was to be allowed to escort Miss Mackenzie back to the western loch country of her youth, where, we could only suppose, the pair would one day quietly marry, once the remarkable girl had quite recovered from her ordeal—as well as the birth of her child, whose paternity Robert both accepted and proclaimed. At the time of the couple's departure from Holyroodhouse, Miss Mackenzie was already well on her way to this happier state: The characteristic spark had reignited within her eyes, and I confess to an older man's envy of Sadler's good luck—although "luck" in fact had little to do with the matter, for he had worked hard and risked all to earn Miss Mackenzie's trust and affection.

Both of the Holmes brothers were again called on to use all the force of their personalities and reputations when Lord Francis's father, the Duke of Hamilton, soon appeared and indignantly attempted take personal control of the family's business at Holyroodhouse. Together, Holmes and Mycroft blocked the Duke's perhaps understandable but no less arrogant attempts to revise the history of recent events as a method of discrediting tales of his son's infamous behaviour, and to halt his concurrent and similarly unjust efforts to lay blame on Hackett and his family for allowing discipline at the palace to dissipate to the point of chaos. Mycroft had thought recourse to Her Majesty in this matter might be necessary, but ultimately it was not: Both the Scottish press and Dennis McKay's friends within the Scottish Nationalist party proved ready allies, and under all this combined pressure the Duke ultimately (if rather suddenly) remembered the obligations of his rank: He graciously abandoned his activities, rewarded Hackett's family for their loyalty, and satisfied himself with having his son's name quietly overlooked during the prosecution of Will Sadler.

It was with matters at the palace well settled, then, that the Holmeses and I finally set out for the Aberdeenshire Highlands, a spot whose beauty was, for this commoner, truly awe-inspiring, although my companions seemed to take it quite in stride. I shall not write in detail of what took place in the Victorian Gothic masterpiece that is Balmoral Castle, for words are inadequate to the occasion; and, even could I find them, Mycroft (who knows of my penchant for recording the details of my adventures with Holmes) has advised me that intimate details of the functioning of the royal household are best left out of tales of murder and mischief, and I have gladly accepted this admonition. I *will* say, however, that, quite beyond condescension, Her Majesty displayed real and extensive interest in, as well as concern about our dangerous adventures; and that, in particular, she wished very much to know if we had seen or heard anything that might shed light upon the ancient legend concerning a wandering spirit in the palace. Whatever frank answers Holmes and I might have been tempted to give were artfully thwarted by Mycroft—and I can further report that Holmes's original and remarkable claim that his brother enjoyed complete informality in the Queen's presence was utterly vindicated: While he never took advantage of such when he was aware of the presence of others, I did once catch sight of Mycroft sitting with Her Majesty in one of the castle gardens—and had the pair been an elderly married couple in Hyde Park, they could scarcely have appeared more completely at their ease.

During the several days of trout and salmon fishing that followed our audience, Holmes and I had enormously good luck, for the streams and lochs on or adjacent to the various royal holdings in Scotland were well stocked and populated, and our hunger for simple recreation was almost inexhaustible. We did not speak of our adventure at Holyroodhouse during this time, beyond the occasional and meaningless reference, thus perpetuating one of the stranger human habits that I have, over the course of my life, been in a position to observe: The more remarkable and even unbelievable a set of events through which a given pair or group of people have lived, the less need they feel to speak of it. One might think that the sheer inexplicability of such matters would almost *require* conversation; yet it is that very quality which makes talk unnecessary. For there is, in the end, little if anything to say about such encounters and events: We each saw what we saw, or we believe we did, and argument or debate, analysis or conjecture, would each and all require further proofs—but these, God willing, we shall never obtain.

There *does* remain, however, one small postscript to the matter of the Italian Secretary. Not long after Holmes and I had returned to Baker Street and resumed that routine which passed, when one lived in Holmes's remarkable world, for "normal," we were one evening reviewing the day's late newspaper editions in our sitting-room, and smoking furiously. It was a habit of Holmes's to surrender to inactivity only reluctantly after an important (to say nothing of chilling) case; and I was lending him what assistance I could in the quest to find some new criminal matter on which to fix his activated mental energies. But the going was slow, the rewards few and frustrating; and the slower and more frustrating things became, the more both our appetites for tobacco seemed to rise, until, once again, we found that we had burned through both of our stores. I offered to make the trip to the tobacconists', hoping to avoid another unfortunate encounter between my friend and Mrs. Hudson; and as I pulled on my jacket and was exiting the room, Holmes humorously suggested that I save myself a longer walk by simply purchasing whatever marginally decent tobacco the small sundries store across the way was offering that evening.

Although I chuckled at this suggestion and dismissed it out of hand, I found that, when I had exited into the warm autumn twilight of Baker Street, I felt a strange desire and even drive to cross over and pass by the little shop. I had no intention of going in; I thought at most to offer the owner a greeting and pass on, although I could not say, even now, why this idea should have taken such hold of me.

Midway across Baker Street, I passed into the shadow cast by several buildings; and my eyes, accustomed to the sunlight out of which I had just passed, required a moment to adjust to what seemed, by comparison, almost darkness. As I moved along towards the shop in this state, I looked towards its entrance—

And I stopped suddenly. Ahead of me, walking aimlessly before the shop doorway, was (or so I thought) a young girl with golden hair (or was it simply the autumn light that made it seem so?) and a face that was a picture of innocence. Just how she was dressed I cannot now say; but it seemed to me at the time that she wore some wafting garment, like a delicate child's nightgown, and that, at its edges, this garment almost disappeared in the shadows beneath the building. I had the idea that she was singing quietly to herself, although I could hear no sound; and as I slowly resumed walking, my heart began to beat much faster than it had during any similar encounter with a child. And then the girl looked up and directly at me:

With a plaintive, almost sad expression on her young face, she urged me into the shop, which she herself then seemed to enter.

Now quite beyond rational thought, I hurried along and quickly followed where I believed the girl had led. Here, I found the proprietor standing behind the short glass counter, himself perusing some foreign-language newspaper. He looked up, smiled wide, and greeted me with the pleasant expression that was his custom—

But there was no sign of the young girl anywhere in the store.

"Well, Doctor," said the Punjabi man, "what can I do for you this very fine evening?"

I could form no answer, but continued to look about the store, increasingly urgently.

"Doctor?" the man repeated. "Are you quite well? Are you looking for something particularly?"

I held up a finger, and pointed about the well-provisioned room, desperately trying to find my voice.

"Do you require medical assistance, Doctor?" the proprietor said, alarm now filling his voice. He rushed around the counter, and stood by me. "Have you been taken ill?"

Shaking my head repeatedly, I was finally able to say, "Did—did not someone just come in here?"

No sooner were the words out of my mouth than the proprietor's expression changed—slowly, at first, but markedly. "Someone?" he said. "Someone who?"

"It was—" I felt some reluctance, but my fear got the better of it. "It was a young girl—she was standing outside, just now. . . ."

And that was enough: The shop-owner's face lost all sense of sympathy, and he waved a hand in my face, saying sternly, "No. No, no, no, Doctor! Please!" He indicated the door. "Leave my shop, please, sir—this is not worthy of a respected man such as yourself!"

"What?" I mumbled. "What do you mean?"

The man's manner was unflinching. "These are children's games, Doctor—and they injure my business! How can you participate in such things?"

I had begun to emerge from my haze, enough to comprehend what he was referring to—and suddenly aware that I had, indeed, upset him tremendously. Yet I could not help but insist, one last time:

"But—she was here! She beckoned to me—!"

"No, sir! Please, I will not tolerate it! Leave, sir—immediately!"

As my senses adjusted to the moment and the predicament fully, my shock and fear began to subside, to be replaced by embarrassment and sympathy. "I must—it must have been the next house. . . ."

The man's manner softened as quickly as it had hardened. "Ah. Yes—well, of course, Doctor, there *is* indeed a young girl in the next number."

I was aware of as much: I had been aware of it when I made my last statement. The only difficulty was that the young girl in the next house bore only a passing resemblance to the one I had seen. Yet in that strange light. . . . "I'm very sorry," I went on, regaining my composure. "I didn't mean to trouble you. I know you have had—difficulties."

"Yes," the man answered, even managing laughter, "and I thought that *you* had joined the ranks of the troublesome!"

"Do forgive me," I said, trying to match his jocularity.

"Speak no more of the matter, Doctor!" he said. "And I shall not. All this silliness—unhappy spirits—I have been here many years, Doctor, and I have seen nothing. For such a powerful people, you English can be very superstitious—not that I intend disrespect to the spirits of the dead! Now, then—did you need something?"

I quickly decided that a purchase might mend the situation. "Tobacco—the strongest you have. And I shall take all that you can give me."

"Ah! You and Mr. Holmes are hard at work, eh? I daresay you will not tell *him* that you saw a 'young ghost,' Doctor!"

That gave the fellow a good laugh, and by the time I departed we were fast friends again. I took up my parcel, accepted his warm wishes, and stepped back into the street; then, as I was look-ing about for approaching traffic, I happened to glance up at our sitting-room windows—

And would have sworn that I caught a quick glimpse of Holmes, suddenly moving away from the window that afforded the best view of the little shop.

When I arrived back in our sitting-room, however, he was just where I had left him: poring over the same papers, seated in the same chair. *Had* he seen what had transpired across the street? A part of me desired very much to know, although another part wished to forget the matter of the spirit world entirely, and to avoid further embarrassment of any kind.

And so I placed the package of tobacco on the table that held the newspapers, took my suit coat off once again, and set to rolling up my shirt-sleeves and filling my pipe without comment. As I was doing so, however, Holmes took the opportunity to say, in a very quiet and rather sympathetic voice:

"You asked me once, Watson, if I was serious about believing in 'ghosts'—the idea perplexed you so greatly, in fact, that you did not consider the actual statement that I had made." As he continued to speak, Holmes filled his own pipe with the new tobacco, and set it burning: "My actual words were, 'I give entire credence to the *power* of ghosts.' Perhaps you may ask, somewhat fairly, whether any claimed difference between the two is not mere word-play. But it is not. Within the study of crime, Watson, as within the study of *all* disciplines, phenomena occur that we are powerless to explain. We tell ourselves that someday the human mind *will* explain them; and perhaps it shall. But for now, the unexplained nature of these phenomena gives them extraordinary force—for they cause the behaviour of individual persons, as well as towns, cities, and nations, to become passionate and irrational. This is power, indeed; and what possesses power, we must admit, possesses actuality. Is it real? The question is the wrong one, and irrelevant, really—real or no, it is a *fact.*"

Holmes stood, his head surrounded by smoke that seemed to have a kind of solidity, and approached the same window again. "We believe; we act accordingly; others tell us that our beliefs are false; yet how can they be, when those beliefs have persuaded us, sometimes many of us, to alter our behaviour? No, Watson—we cannot question the power of that which motivates human action, particularly that which motivates such action along the lines that we have lately witnessed. Are ghosts—indeed, are *gods*, real? We cannot know; but they are powerful facts of human intercourse. And so. . . ."

He indicated the shop across the street with his pipe. "*Did* you see that young girl playing outside the shop before you entered it? If you believe you did, your behaviour will be forever altered; if you choose not to believe it, and to think that she entered some other building, then the same effect is produced, although along different lines. Even in denying the encounter altogether, you would give it actuality. It nonetheless remains a fact; indeed, it is the *only* fact concerning the matter that will ever truly be of consequence, to you, as well as to those who are your companions and associates, whose behaviour *your* behaviour must influence. Thus, the question of whether or not the girl was there means almost nothing. Baker Street is Baker Street in part because of these tales. They may not be real; but they, like the street itself, are facts. . . ."

Suddenly, Holmes turned, waved the smoke from about his head as he deliberately changed his train of thought and conversation, and then put his pipe back in his mouth and one hand on his hip. "So, old friend! With that admittedly humble theory in mind—let us see if we cannot locate a criminal who operates solely in the realm of *material* facts. It will seem, somehow, such an easy, such a refreshing undertaking, just now. . . ."

And with that, we turned back to the papers, and set to work once more.

∞

Afterword

"DR. KREIZLER, MR. SHERLOCK HOLMES . . ."

By

Jon Lellenberg

Perhaps the most famous introduction of one literary character to another in the English language—not to mention the countless other languages into which the work has been translated—occurs in chapter one of the 1887 British novel *A Study in Scarlet* by a then-unknown British writer:

"Dr. Watson, Mr. Sherlock Holmes," said Stamford, introducing us.

"How are you?" he said cordially, gripping my hand with a strength for which I should hardly have given him credit. "You have been in Afghanistan, I perceive."

"How on earth did you know that?" I asked in astonishment.

"Never mind," said he, chuckling to himself.

The scene was a concatenation of medical men, and very deliberately took place in a scientific setting, the chemistry laboratory of London's great St. Bartholomew's Hospital. (For many years, a brass plaque has hung upon its wall commemorating the event.) John H. Watson, the narrator, was a doctor recently back from service in the British Army during the Second Afghan War. Stamford had been his "dresser," or surgeon's assistant, at Bart's before the war. The creator of these characters, Arthur Conan Doyle, was himself a doctor. The third character in this scene, as time would prove, was not one. But while Sherlock Holmes was not a doctor, Conan Doyle had based Holmes's method as a detective upon one of his former professors of medicine at Edinburgh University, Dr. Joseph Bell, whose powers of observation and deduction had made him a wizard at diagnosis.

It was, as Conan Doyle's Scotch colleagues may have murmured to themselves at the time, a very canny approach. With the exception of Edgar Allan Poe's pioneering stories about Auguste Dupin of Paris, Dr. Conan Doyle recalled many years later, most contemporary fictional detectives produced their results by chance or luck. Dissatisfied with that, he had decided, he said, to create a detective who would treat crime as Dr. Bell had treated disease. This meant, in short, the application of scientific method to crime detection. That was a novel concept in 1887, to be sure, but it worked, first in fiction and then in practice, with life imitating art as it so often does when the art in question is a work of genius.

And while Sherlock Holmes wasn't a doctor, Conan Doyle gave him a good deal of doctor's training and all the traits of modern scientific method as he knew it, from what he called the "very austere school of medical thought" in which he had himself been raised. On their way to Watson's introduction to Holmes, Stamford tells his old friend that Holmes:

> "is well up in anatomy, and he is a first-class chemist; but, as far as I know, he has never taken out any systematic medical classes. His studies are very desultory and eccentric, but he has amassed a lot of out-of-the-way knowledge which would astonish his professors. . . . Holmes is a little too scientific for my tastes—it approaches to

cold-bloodedness. I could imagine his giving a friend a little pinch of the latest vege-
table alkaloid, not out of malevolence, you
understand, but simply out of a spirit of in-
quiry in order to have an accurate idea of the
effects. To do him justice, I think that he
would take it himself with the same readi-
ness. He appears to have a passion for definite and exact knowledge."

"Very right too."

"Yes, but it may be pushed to excess.
When it comes to beating the subjects in the
dissecting-rooms with a stick, it is certainly
taking rather a bizarre shape."

"Beating the subjects!"

"Yes, to verify how far bruises may be produced after death. I saw him at it with my
own eyes."

"And yet you say he is not a medical stu-
dent?"

"No. Heaven knows what the objects of his
studies are. But here we are, and you must
form your own impressions about him."

They did take rooms together, at 221B Baker Street,
but as a proper Victorian professional and gentleman, Watson was too polite to ask his new fellow
lodger what his livelihood was; and so his im-

pressions of Holmes, after they had lived together a little while, mystified him. In a list headed "Sherlock Holmes—his limits," Watson recorded that Holmes was completely ignorant of the humanities; his botany was "variable" and his geology "practical, but limited"; his chemistry was "profound," true, but his anatomy was, at best, "accurate, but unsystematic." Holmes had a good practical knowledge of British law, was a good singlestick player, boxer, and swordsman, and played the violin well. It all left Watson at a loss; and it took Sherlock Holmes to inform him, after Watson scoffed at a magazine article about "the science of deduction and analysis" which Holmes turned out to have written himself, that he was a consulting detective, "if you can understand what that is."

Sherlock Holmes may have been the world's first detective of that sort, as he claimed, but in London in the 1880s there were, as he pointed out to Watson, "lots of government detectives and lots of private ones." Yet the curious and intrigued Watson failed to make the connection. Of course, the application of science to crime detection was something new. But what might have made the penny drop for Dr. Watson, in conjunction with the other evidence of Holmes's limits (for example, "well up in belladonna, opium, and poisons

generally"), was one more item on that list: "Knowledge of Sensational Literature—Immense. He
appears to know every detail of every horror perpetrated in the century."

"The importance of this cannot be overstated,"
writes Caleb Carr, author of *The Italian Secretary*,
in a nonfiction contribution elsewhere to an
upcoming collection of new Sherlock Holmes
stories by mystery writers: "It was in 'sensational'
literature that one was most likely to find, in British society of the late 1880s and early 1890s, many
spectacular yet semi-scholarly studies that we
would today categorize under the heading of
'forensic psychology.' "* Sherlock Holmes made
good if psychologically uncomplicated use of his
immense knowledge of sensational literature: "I
am generally able, by the help of my knowledge
of the history of crime, to set [Scotland Yard]
straight," he told Watson. "There is a strong family resemblance about misdeeds, and if you have
all the details of a thousand at your finger ends,
it is odd if you can't unravel the thousand and
first."

That was Sherlock Holmes acting within his
limits, which had to do, as Carr observes in his

Ghosts of Baker Street, edited by Martin Greenberg, Jon Lellenberg, and Daniel Stashower (New York: Carroll & Graf, 2006).

essay, with the material, physical world. As a detective in a scientific sense, Holmes always wants to know and looks for the physical evidence; he made himself a master at observing and analysing physical evidence that the police and other detectives overlook or fail to recognize at all. By his innate but also rigorously trained powers of deduction, he is able to reason backwards from this evidence to reconstruct the crime and delineate the physical attributes of the perpetrator. And this is no mean achievement. But as Carr notes, Holmes pays little attention to the psychology of crime, and neither does Watson, whose medical training and interests do not run far in the direction of psychiatry.

Suppose that legendary introduction had gone this way instead:

"*Dr. Watson, Dr. Laszlo Kreizler*," said Stamford, introducing us.

What a different experience that would have proven for the man who became Sherlock Holmes's Boswell: to have found himself lashed to the chariot wheels of Caleb Carr's protagonist in *The Alienist* and *Angel of Darkness*—a man who knew medicine quite as well as Watson did, but also vastly more about the human mind, particularly its darker side—and who used this knowledge to solve crimes differently from, but as brilliantly as, Sherlock Holmes. Holmes was not always a comfortable companion for Dr. Watson; God knows, he made no attempt to be. But Kreizler's insight into the criminal mind, and especially the mind of the serial killer—the man or woman who kills not for profit, nor from momentary rage, but instead out of deep, dark psychological wellsprings from which an eminently normal person such as John H. Watson would shrink—might have been more than Watson could have stood for long. Sherlock Holmes's role in life was to make the world safe, and Watson found that right and good. He was ready to stand beside that man, come what may. But Dr. Kreizler's role was to awaken people to the depths inside humanity, and to the madness and danger that often lurk there. In fact, his philosophy was the antithesis of liberal Victorians' conviction about progress.

Kreizler does owe certain recognizable debts to Sherlock Holmes. He has his own Watson, in a police reporter for the *New York Times,* John Schuyler Moore. The Irish surname suggests a parvenu in the social life of turn-of-the-century New York; in the eyes of polite society Moore

may have been little better than the police, even
if redeemed to some degree by the Schuyler side
of his descent, and by an education superior to his
chosen calling. (We learn that it was at Harvard
College that he, Laszlo Kreizler, and Theodore
Roosevelt, the reform-minded police commissioner in *The Alienist,* first met as students.) Like
Holmes, Kreizler has a band of Baker Street Ir-
regulars, "street arabs" on whom he may call, led
by a kid from the gutters named Stevie Taggert.
We glimpse Kreizler for the first time at Bellevue
Hospital, just as we did Sherlock Holmes at Bart's.
A distinctly Continental note about Kreizler does
set him apart from Holmes, though—a slight
accent since childhood, when he arrived in
America with his German father and Hungarian
mother, fleeing the failed European liberal revo-
lutions of 1848. (The chronology does not quite
work: surely Kreizler and Moore were not quite
as old as that would make them; but then internal contradictions are what the practice of Sher-
lockiana, the so-called "Higher Criticism" of the
four novels and 56 short stories that comprise "the
Canon," is all about.) But from Bellevue we ac-
company Kreizler and Moore to police headquarters on Mulberry Street, and then see them off to
a gourmet lunch at Delmonico's—an itinerary

that might easily have been pursued by Sherlock Holmes on any day of an adventure set down for us by Dr. Watson.

The police do not appreciate Dr. Kreizler, but the police commissioner does. In *The Alienist*, Kreizler and Moore embark upon a clandestine investigation of serial murders, the first of the studies of crime that produce what Moore, looking back years later, calls "the brilliant doctor whose studies of the human mind have disturbed so many people so profoundly over the last forty years." Here is the sharpest difference between Dr. Kreizler and Sherlock Holmes. Holmes was reassuring for people, by clearing up the mystery, identifying the guilty, and restoring order. "You need not fear," Sherlock Holmes tells his terrified client, Helen Stoner, in *The Adventure of the Speckled Band*, speaking to her "soothingly, bending forward and patting her forearm. 'We shall soon set matters right, I have no doubt.'" But even when Dr. Kreizler solves the crimes before him, he leaves people profoundly *disturbed.*

Physically, he resembles Holmes. He dresses in black, has black eyes "like a large bird's," and gives an impression "of some hungry, restless hawk determined to wring satisfaction from the worrisome world around him." Grim as this may sound, it could be the beloved sleuth of our childhood, played on the screen by Basil Rathbone or Jeremy Brett. But there are important differences too, including a physical shortcoming that suggests inner damage: Kreizler's left arm is underdeveloped because of a childhood injury. (If Sherlock Holmes had childhood injuries, they were purely psychic ones that affected his personality in ways that writers of pastiche have seized upon frequently, if not necessarily well). Kreizler's dark hair is cut unfashionably long, and he wears a neatly trimmed mustache and a small beard. This might easily be a villain in one of the Sherlock Holmes stories, and Watson would probably have cast a suspicious eye at him, though it would be interesting to know what Holmes would deduce from Kreizler's physical appearance upon meeting him for the first time.

Although a partnership between Kreizler and Watson might have taken even more adjustments for Watson than his partnership with Holmes did (though those adjustments went on continually the entire time they were partners in crime detection—nearly two decades, during much of which Watson was married and living elsewhere), Watson actually remedied some of Holmes's deficiencies, even if Holmes seldom acknowledged it or thanked him for it. The dynamic with Kreizler would have been different—a creative tension between two physicians whose approach to disease, and therefore crime, had followed different forks in the road, starting at medical school. Watson, conventional in his outlook, examined and drew conclusions from the physical evidence of the body. Kreizler was interested primarily in the mind, especially as the key to criminal motivation and behavior. But both men did realize that the mind is shaped in great part by ancestral and environmental factors, just as disease is. Watson was not insensible to the power of the mind where health was concerned, and neither doctor believed in free will beyond a certain point. Drs. Kreizler and Watson could have worked things out—though in the long run, I suspect, John Schuyler Moore, with his knowledge of sensational literature, nearly as great as Sherlock Holmes's, would have been of more value to Kreizler than another M.D. like John H. Watson. The similarities between Kreizler and Watson might have canceled out some of their differences in outlook, failing to produce enough tension to make the partnership an effective one. They could have set up a comprehensive medical practice together, but it would have belonged on Harley Street, not Baker Street, or their turn-of-the-century New York equivalents.

More differences, more tension, must be what the doctor ordered.

"Dr. Kreizler, Mr. Sherlock Holmes," said Stamford, introducing us.

Hmm. This could be going too far in rewriting literary history. Carr himself points out, in his previously quoted essay, that Holmes possessed "a positive disdain for matters of the mind generally, even down to the question of motivations for crimes—for Holmes, the magnifying glass and the microscope suffice, plus a knowledge of past crime from which to draw patterns applicable to present and future crime." Kreizler presumably would not scorn Holmes's approach, but he might grow impatient with its limitations— while Kreizler's approach might seem dangerously metaphysical to Holmes. "It is a capital mistake to theorize before you have all the evidence," he constantly warned. Kreizler's inferences from psychological data not observable by magnifying glass or microscope might seem like sheer flights of fantasy to Holmes—just as his own creator's claim that his belief in a spirit world was grounded in his scientific training and outlook would have been scornfully rejected by the detective who exclaimed, in *The Adventure of the Sussex Vampire*, that "This agency stands flat-footed upon the ground, and there it must remain. The world is big enough for us. No ghosts need apply."

Though ghosts may be "non-canonical," for the previously mentioned collection, *Ghosts of Baker Street*, I and my coeditors Daniel Stashower and Martin Greenberg invited a number of writers to give Sherlock Holmes and Dr. Watson new adventures that would be supernatural in theme and tone. I am not sure Sir Arthur Conan Doyle would approve, even if he himself was convinced of a spirit-world's reality. It was undeniably, we realized, taking a liberty with his most famous literary character. But as U.S. representative of the Conan Doyle Estate, I was able to give us permission to proceed nevertheless, with *The Hound of the Baskervilles* as excuse and inspiration. Holmes may have declared that "no ghosts need apply," but it is surely no accident that his most famous adventure of all is about an ancient family curse and a spectral hound haunting eerie fog-stricken Dartmoor.

Caleb Carr was one of the writers in question. We did not suggest to him that his story bring Sherlock Holmes and Dr. Kreizler together. For one thing, we did not want to impose a particular approach upon any of the contributors to that collection; for another, we believed that the depiction of such a collaboration would require a considerably broader canvas than a short story. Carr, an historian by education and practice, turned to a historical crime in Edinburgh that took place among the retinue of Mary, Queen of Scots. In fact, he was so much inspired by it that the short story, when it was done, had grown to the rather impractical length of a novel—so it appears separately here, as *The Italian Secretary.*

And yet we still dare hope to see Sherlock Holmes and Dr. Kreizler brought together someday by the latter's creator. Holmes was not always the brash young physical scientific type of *A Study in Scarlet,* and his knowledge of speculative sciences was greater than Watson initially surmised. We learn from the Canon, for instance, that Holmes knew Charles Darwin's work, and, quoting the father of evolutionary theory on the subject of music, he remarked that "One's ideas must be as broad as Nature if they are to interpret Nature." With that one remark, by no means a solitary example, Sherlock Holmes goes far beyond what the magnifying glass and microscope can reveal, and places himself squarely within a realm of crime detection where the imagination may be more important than a profound knowledge of chemistry, or even the misdeeds of the past hundred years.

It would take more than Dr. Watson to bring

out that side of Sherlock Holmes fully. It would
require someone whose view of criminal motivation does not turn first and last upon the traditional question *cui bono* (who benefits). It calls
for someone who realizes that some crimes,
particularly in the "self-actualizing" times that
began in the Victorian era of both Sherlock
Holmes and Laszlo Kreizler, ignore notions of
self-interest and questions of profit and express
inner lives too horrible for men like Dr. Watson—
who like so many other Victorians believed in
the inevitability of human progress—to contem-
plate easily. There is a reason why Sherlock
Holmes never investigates a series of murders resembling the Jack the Ripper case of 1888, and
that Dr. Conan Doyle, so interested in real-life
crime normally, never appears to have studied
or discussed it either. Some things are un-
speakable except in terms of a psychology that
Sherlock Holmes would have shrunk from em-
bracing of his own accord, so repulsive its philosophical implications might have seemed to him.

Still, the desire to see the two approaches—
Holmes's and Kreizler's—collide with each other
cannot be gainsaid. We must be dialecticians ourselves if we are to give both approaches their just
due. Whether a collaboration would be set in
London or New York at the end of the nineteenth

century is immaterial—both of those great metropolises offer fertile ground for a case that would challenge each of these men, and make for a partnership profoundly upsetting to both, but tremendously interesting to the reader. Sparks would fly, and it is easy to imagine Watson and Moore quietly retiring to one of their clubs every so often to get away from the scene and commiserate together. But the temptation is there. I hope Mr. Carr succumbs to it eventually.

Acknowledgments

This project was undertaken at the invitation and the urging of Jon Lellenberg, U.S. representative of the estate of Sir Arthur Conan Doyle (among a great many other things). Throughout some tough times, and with regard to undertakings including but ranging far beyond this book, Jon's friendship and advice have been steadfast and vital. He is truly "the American" in the very best sense of that sobriquet: Jefferson Smith's got nothing on him. . . .

I have dedicated the book to Hilary Hale, my editor in London. Just to clarify, at a moment of supreme importance in my life, Hilary (along with her late husband, the wise, uproarious, and much-missed James Hale) took me into her life and her home and made sure that I would always have somewhere to escape to, when the pressures of the U.S. became too great. I could not have known, when she dispatched me to Scotland once on a book tour, that a chance visit to the royal palace of Holyrood would one day become this story; but I do know that without the hard work, infinite patience, and support of Hilary (and of her brilliant coworkers at Little, Brown UK), that trip would probably never have taken place. In life as in publishing, Hilary is a perfect anomaly.

Will Balliett at Carroll & Graf Publishers has been tireless in his advocacy of this book, alternating between the roles of publisher and editor as need has required, and always with grace, good humor, and consideration. He also holds the unique distinction of being an actual editor in the American publishing world, a person willing to sweat over a manuscript rather than simply make deals all day. In crossing paths with him, I have again been most fortunate, and I would like to thank him as well as all his able staff for their hospitality.

For her continued and invaluable support, I would also like to thank my agent, Suzanne Gluck, as well as her invaluable assistant, Erin Malone. I would also like to note that without the very decent cooperation of Gina Centrello, the publication of this book would not have been possible.

Tim Haldeman once again took on the job of being my sounding board, and his comments were never more to the point or more valuable. He is as smart as he is compassionate, and he has my sincerest thanks. Also in the category of test audiences, I must once again thank Lydia, Sam, Ben, and Gabriela Carr—as well as Marion Carr, whose opinions are perhaps less gently couched than her cousins', but are every bit as valuable; as is the support of the rest of my family, and everyone else on Misery Mountain.

My deepest thanks to William von Hartz for another honest photo, and more years of honest friendship.

For their continued and unflagging efforts to make sure that I have not wandered off into the woods, never to return, I must thank Ellen Blain, Ezequiel Viñao, Oren Jacoby, Jennifer Maquire, Silvana Paternostro, Melissa and Scott Strickland, and Debbie Deuble, and Tom Pivinski.

Bruce Yaffe, Heather Canning, Douglas Heymann, and Oakley Frost have all kept after the job of refusing to see me succumb to the despair and inertia of chronic illness. Their efforts have, once again, been appreciated more than they can ever know, and have provided a standard for other American doctors that is, regrettably, too high for most to meet. Many thanks, too, to Jim Monahan and everyone at Thorpe's.

During the writing of this book, I lost the best friend and mentor a person could hope for: James Chace. That emptiness is still baffling; yet I cannot think of publishing a book without mentioning his name, because without his help I would likely never have published anything in the first place. Joan Bingham, David Fromkin, Sarah, Beka, and Zoe Chace all share in the sadness, as do James's students, and many of my own, at Bard College; I am grateful to have had them all to cushion the blow. For their continued support at Bard, I'd like to thank Leon Botstein, Jonathan Becker, Mark Lytle, William Mullen, and, again, my students; some of the latter deserve specific mention, although I dare not, for their own sakes. But they know who they are.

Finally, Mark Twain once remarked, "If a man could be crossed with a cat, it would improve the man, but degrade the cat." I hope that my own familiar and companion has not thought it too degrading to play muse, as well.